VALREN

Kelly -
You're the best!
Thank you so much for
the support!

KERRY CASTORANO

TLT Publishing
CHICAGO

THE LITTLE THINGS PUBLISHING

TLT Publishing

Chicago, Illinois

Printed in the United States of America

Cover Design by George Pastouras
Interior Design by Randi Ertz
Edited by Mariam Pera
Published by The Little Things (TLT) Publishing.

The Little Things (TLT) Publishing
Chicago, Illinois
Visit our web site at:
www.tltpublishing.com

ISBN: 978-0-9844013-8-3

First Paperback Edition: September 2011

For Grammy

VALREN

Kerry Castorano

INTRODUCTION

It was going to rain up in the Doranin Mountains, which did not bode well for the two escapees struggling across the harsh landscape.

By the time they slowed their breakneck pace the young man and woman found themselves high up on the range. The weather there rarely affected those living far below in Marrin. But for the two companions stumbling along the loose slag of the mountainside, rain was indeed a problem.

The land west of the Doranin Mountains was known for being good to farmers. The soil was rich due to the fog that would blanket and permeate the ground the day before any large rainstorm. Children loved to play in the fog. It made for great games of hide-and-seek. When particularly heavy storms were going to hit the next day, the fog would roll all the way up to a man's armpit and if he stretched his arm his fingers would disappear before his eyes. Usually though, the fog was just high enough and damp enough to soak into a person's socks and make his day unpleasant.

Tripan fell to his knees again, the fog and the setting sun making it impossible for him to see where he was placing his feet on the slippery slope. Next to him, Freyja was sucking in shallow breaths through clenched teeth. Even in the dim light of the evening Tripan could see the bruises on her face and arms, and there was a rivulet of blood moving down her neck from a cut above her eye.

He assumed the blow that caused that particular cut was also the reason his companion had passed out earlier. Either that or lack of food. He could no longer hear their former captives, trying to hunt the escaped pair down. They had managed to lose the group of mercenaries close to seven hours ago but fear kept him turning around to glance behind them.

Now they needed shelter. Tripan heard Freyja's breathing change and reached out to grab her arm just as her eyes rolled upward and she slipped into unconsciousness again. Using the small reserve of strength he had left, he hoisted the lithe redhead onto his shoulders, like he would a sack of grain, and continued on through the fog. Dire situations make for fast friendships, and though their relationship was only days old, he already owed the young woman his life.

The sun was just setting in earnest when he found shelter in the form of a small cave. Moss near the grotto entrance was heavy with dew from the fog of tomorrow's rain. The walls were slick when Tripan put his hand on the rock surface to steady himself. He lowered Freyja to the ground. Cold and damp was still better than their last residence with the Oparel soldiers. In fact, it was a marked improvement.

Tripan gently lifted Freyja's head from the rocky floor and slid a leather pouch under it to serve as a makeshift pillow. They were both in bad shape, but Freyja was worse off than he was. The cut above her eye looked awful but he could tell it wasn't the worst of their worries. Her breathing was shallow and he had seen her holding her side as she ran; broken ribs? Internal bleeding? Just because her stomach looked fine did not mean that it was. He stopped trying to guess at her other injuries when he realized there was nothing he could do to help her even if he did know what was wrong.

Fog rolled over her body and beaded on her hair and cheeks. Tripan used the drops of water on her skin to gently wash the cut above her eye and remove the trickle of blood it had left behind.

“Freyja? Come on little one, wake up…” Tripan’s voice sounded raspy in his own ears. He began to smooth back the wisps of red hair sticking to his companion’s forehead as he spoke.

He was relieved when her eyes slit open and she took in a deep breath of the damp air. The moon was almost full and gave off just enough light for his eyes to pick up details of her face.

“Gods I hurt…” The murmured complaint was the first he had heard from her lips, despite the abuse she had taken in the last few days at the hands of Sholl and his mercenaries. Freyja raised her hand to her head and gingerly touched the wound at her temple. Her deep brown eyes looked black in the dim light of the moon, their corners glistening as tears began to gather there. She shut her eyes tightly again and pushed the tears back down. She rolled onto her side so that the welts on her back were not scraping against the hard ground. Tripan sat worriedly on his heels next to her

“I know Lady, I know. Is your back the worst of it?”

Freyja took a quick mental survey of her body from the toes up. Her back was bad, but it was not the worst. The worst had come when Sholl had knelt above her, between her legs, his cronies holding her down. He may not have achieved his goal, but even the thought of it made her break out in a cold sweat. Those mental scars would never fade.

Quietly she answered, “Yes, my back…”

Tripan settled down next to her and watched her eyes as best he could. “There is nothing we can do until morning now. My feet feel as though they are on fire.” What else would you expect from running barefoot over rock and slag in the dark? Tripan thought to himself.

“Your back will not kill you even if you wish it did,” he said, “but I’m worried about your head.” He reached out to touch her face but stopped a few inches away when he saw her flinch.

"Keep talking to me, alright? I need you to stay awake for a while." His grin was halfhearted but he used it to muster some semblance of happiness for them to feed upon.

"Tell me a story why don't you?" When she stayed silent he continued. "Sholl was petrified when he first caught you, you know. He and his men were telling stories about you that made you out like some kind of bloodthirsty heathen. He said you are one of the Valren..." Tripan let the silence stretch between them in hopes she would answer.

"And if I am Valren, what would you do then, Tripan? Leave me here to fend for myself?" Anger and annoyance crept into her voice.

"No... no. I would seek your family out and tell them your story."

"My story? You make it sound like I'm already dead." A small chuckle escaped her lips, "I am not to that point yet, I don't think."

He did not respond, and she saw him lower his eyes. So maybe she was to that point. She gazed down the length of her body to take a count of the many injuries sustained over the last six days. The one good thing about having multiple wounds is that the all-over pain keeps you from focusing on one specific hurt. It is a blessing of sorts. After a while it all just becomes a dull ache.

Taking a shaky breath, she continued. "I'll tell you my story if it will help us through the night. But if you find the Valren and I am gone, you will tell them what happened, won't you?"

Tripan nodded his head and settled himself against the cave wall, his feet stretching out in front of him. He was already so wet from the rolling fog that the moisture seeping through his shirt from the wall didn't bother him.

Freyja gathered her thoughts as quickly as her throbbing head would allow and began to speak.

CHAPTER 1

Nearly three years had passed since the Marrin King Harton had been slain in battle. He had fallen in a skirmish against the Mad King, Joran of Bartorin, in the lands north of Marrin.

It was only thanks to the quick and ruthless wit of their Queen, Varonda of Calin, that the Marrin turned those northern lands into a prosperous acquisition in the months after the King's death. Though the price of her husband's life was a cost steeper than she would have been willing to pay, it was too late to grieve. There was no going back.

The old border between the two kingdoms was now like a scar just beginning to heal that blemished the land. Whole families had been slaughtered, crops were burned, and disease was only now starting to decline.

As is always the case, those families living along the border took the brunt of the war. But casualties among civilians were moderate compared to those suffered by the soldiers who had sworn their allegiance to Harton and Varonda. Now, with no heir and an army with severely diminished numbers, Varonda knew her resources were sliced too thin. And she was alone.

These thoughts were swept from Brann's mind when the city of Calin came into view over his mount's swinging mane. His horse's ears pricked forward, recognizing home, and the tired equine continued his way down the gently sloping dirt road.

Villagers outside of the city proper knuckled their foreheads as he rode by, recognizing the quality of his horse as belonging to nobility, showing the proper respect.

Brann urged Brax back into a canter and they soon found themselves inside the city walls. He kept the horse moving along the outermost streets of the city. It was a cool and clear day, which would attract people to the market in the town center. He did not wish to get bogged down by the throngs in the streets, excited by the new dyes and herbs from the lands in the north that had flooded the Calin market in the last six months.

The closer Brann got to the Queen's stronghold the narrower and less busy the streets became. The stronghold of Calin was the jewel of the kingdom. Its physical defenses mirrored many characteristics of the Queen who resided there, aesthetically pleasing and surprisingly strong.

It was a safe haven for the citizens. Queen Varonda and the city of Calin were both well loved. The seaside kingdom's naval hub was located there as well, which made the city richer than any other on the known continent.

The royal stables were located inside the stronghold itself and Brax found his way there without the help of his rider. The proud dappled grey came to a halt when a groom appeared from the barn to head the horse while its rider dismounted. Brann slid down Brax's side suppressing a grimace when his leg muscles clenched in protest at their overuse from the laborious ride.

He left Brax to follow the groom into the stables and turned to cross the pavilion heading toward the Queen's meeting room. As his eyes adjusted to the dim lighting inside the stronghold, he blinked and shifted his Damascus sword off his back, belting it to his hip. He let his fingers caress along the thin blade. He couldn't feel the patterns in the metal but he knew they were there under his skin. Dips and swirls marked the blade from tip to tang, making it look like the blade had recently been dipped in fish oil. Unlike the tight, curling patterns often found on this kind of blade, his had a rolling quality, and an almost perfect circle formed near the hilt. Every time he looked at it he thought of the sea and the moon. It calmed him.

He ran a hand through his cropped black hair and brushed offensive clumps of mud from his thighs and knees. He and Varonda had grown up together, pushing each other into mud puddles, streams, even bee hives (which only happened once; Varonda still swears it was an accident). But now they were grown and Varonda was a queen, deserving the best he could give. Brann's family had been in the service of Marrin royalty for five generations. His family had grown especially close to Varonda's while the two children were growing up. From an early age, Varonda had been chosen as a bride for the King's son, Harton. The betrothal led Brann's father to take extra care to foster a relationship between his son and the future Queen. If Brann was going to succeed in protecting her, she would need to trust him. Even as a young boy Brann took his mission seriously. His father encouraged the children to play in and around the secret passageways in the palace so they would know these places better than anyone else. By the time he was seven, Brann knew that Varonda was mildly allergic to goat cheese, where in the palace she would hide if she was fleeing an enemy, and even knew she tended to turn to her left to get away from something that was scaring her.

Brann buried his father four years ago, after making the man a promise to serve the King. He had been a shadow at Varonda's side ever since.

~

Varonda looked up from the map lying before her and her eyes lit with joy. It had been four weeks since Brann, captain of her personal guard, had left this very room to journey to the Doranin Mountains. He had been sent to verify the news coming from Della, news that made Varonda's stomach clench. Oparel soldiers were gathering on the east side of the mountains.

Brann bowed deeply from the waist when he saw her, despite the protest of his weary back and legs. The Queen used that opportunity to run her eyes over his body in search of wounds. She found none. His clear blue eyes were tired though, and the skin underneath was dark from lack of sleep. A three-day-old beard smoothed his sharp jaw line. Varonda was still staring in fascination at his newly grown whiskers when the man righted himself from his bow.

Decorum forbade her from hiking up her skirts and wrapping him in a bear hug, but it took all her effort not to do so. There were five counsel members in the chamber with her, three from Marrin, and two from the newly acquired lands in the north. Those two had already come in handy by facilitating trades across the old Bartorin border, while having two northerners on her counsel was also a show of good faith. Whether they liked it or not, the fate of the lands in the north was now firmly entrenched with that of Marrin. They were all watching Brann.

"Your Highness, the news from the east? is grim. We have little chance if the full force of the Oparel army floods over the mountains."

Varonda blinked. Brann was never one to mince words. "Your full report?"

The captain took a breath and gathered his thoughts. "Oparel troops are amassing on the eastern fringes of the Doranin Mountains. Your men in Della have kept an eye to the east as you had commanded. They report that the number of livestock around Garnal has doubled in the last two weeks, and covered supply trains are constantly moving into the fort.

"They are preparing to move more troops to the area; there is no doubt in my mind," Brann said. "I am guessing the first of the soldiers are little more than a week behind the supplies. Our ships still control the seas; no one is foolish enough to front a naval attack. The Doranin Mountains would be my choice of battlefields, if I were them."

Varonda's jaw clenched while Brann continued.

"Majesty, we cannot survive an attack from the east. Our soldiers are too spread out, and our numbers are depleted from the war in the north."

His blue eyes swept over the two counsel members from Bartorin. "The Marrin ranks are barely half full, and the lands in the north do not have the means to survive an all-out war either."

The Queen rounded on the two Bartorin advisors. "Will the Mad King's troops fight by our side?"

"My Lady, our troops fought for the Mad King but no love was lost when he was killed." Brandon's reply was to be expected, but the Queen needed to hear it for herself. "Fear of the King was what kept our soldiers fighting against you and your husband, not love."

Brandon Ruld was the younger of the two advisors hailing from Marrin's expanded lands in the north. He had proven himself on the field of battle many times but the loss of two fingers on his right hand, taken during his second charge against Marrin soldiers, was enough to keep him off the front lines. Brann ran his gaze over the man's hand. Despite the fact that two of his fingers were no more than nubs, he still wore a strange looking ring on what was left of one of them. It looked like a gypsy ring to Brann, knotted cords with a small chunk of blue metal woven into the band. It was the only piece of adornment that Brandon ever wore.

Despite the fact that Brann and Brandon had fought on opposite sides of the battle in the north, their friendship with one another solidified very quickly. They would never meet over a beer in the tavern, but they shared a mutual respect for one another.

"It will take some time to muster the soldiers together but…"

"Time we may have, but it will not be enough." Brann cut in impatiently. "The Oparel are not foolish enough to launch a winter assault. The cost, in gold and lives, of moving men and beasts in the winter is too great. Even with both of our armies fighting side-by-side we do not have enough men to hold off a full attack from the east.

"The Oparel begin to muster now at the base of the mountains and will prepare their troops through the winter," said Brann. "The first sign of spring… that is when they will march."

The Queen flexed her fingers in frustration. Her husband would have known what to do. His cunning had kept Marrin safe and prosperous for almost a decade. And now, less than three years after his death, all he had died for was going to fall.

Brann continued, but his eyes were on the Queen as he spoke. "The Oparel are nervous, My Lady. We have just gained new lands and new sources of income from the Mad King. If the Oparel gave us time to regroup, who is to say that they would not be our next target?"

Varonda nearly sputtered. "But that is ridiculous! Marrin and Bartorin have been peaceful neighbors since before Harton's grandfather reigned. If not for the Mad King's threats it would still be so. We are not warmongers constantly hounding for more land. Why would the Oparel think us so?"

"That was not meant as an insult," Brann said. "But the Oparel know we are weak. They know King Harton is dead, and there is little that we will be able to do against a full scale attack…" His large shoulders shrugged. "Were I the Oparel, I would do the same."

The Queen's annoyed gaze swung back to Brandon. "Your country was small compared to ours yet we were always on good terms until the Mad King took the throne. We can form such an alliance with the east."

Brandon shook his head slightly and ran a hand through his dark blonde hair. "I do not believe we had a formal alliance, Highness… But even if we did, the Oparel have us against the wall and they know it. They would gain nothing from such a pact and everything from a war."

Laren Haunr, the second Bartorin advisor to the Queen, cleared his throat and immediately gained the group's attention. Laren was quite possibly the oldest man Brann had ever known. He had been fair-haired and blue-eyed like most men of the north, a stark contrast to the dark-haired complexions typical in the south, but now his hair was pure white. There was no fat on his body and it seemed as though stubbornness alone was keeping the man on his feet. The children of Calin called him The Scarecrow, but only when he was without his long-reaching cane. The Queen had taken a fast liking to Laren. It had not taken him long to settle into his station as the unofficial favorite advisor of Varonda. He had been a powerful ally to the Mad King in Bartorin and Varonda was only just coming to understand the breadth of his actual power. Laren was a man who was owed many favors.

Laren didn't bother to raise his voice when he spoke and it forced everyone in the room to lean toward him so they could hear. It was those little amusements at the sake of others that kept him happy.

"Varonda, there has never been a pact between Bartorin and Marrin."

Brann's eyes darkened when he heard the old man call the Queen by her given name. The breach of conduct was noticed by everyone in the room. His fingers ached to grab the old man by his scruff and teach him some manners. Even Brann, who had known the Queen most of his life, rarely spoke her given name; even in private. He wondered if the man had been born a cocky bastard or if he had grown into the role over his significant years.

"Your husband's men came to our land only once, and they had their fill of us then and there. He had a run-in with the Valren, sure as I stand here today." The old man's chest swelled with pride. "You only make that mistake once."

Varonda and Brann both looked to Brandon, confusion on their faces. The younger Bartorin man's brows were knotted. "Laren… the Valren are a myth."

He turned to address the group as a whole, looking slightly chagrinned. "In the north we hear stories of the Valren when we are young; a glorified boogieman, Your Majesty, nothing more."

The old man drew himself up, the top of his head barely reaching Brann's shoulders. "You listen well, boy. The Valren have kept our people safe for generations. Who is it you think kept Bartorin safe all these years? King Hale? He cared more for his gardens than the strategies of war. It was not until Hale's brother usurped the throne that the Valren disappeared. And I'm glad of it, too..." Laren sniffed daintily. "If the Valren had defended Bartorin against the Marrin, the Mad King would still be on the throne. No one has stood against their full force and lived."

Brann saw the desperation in his Queen's eyes. "And where are the Valren now?" he asked.

Laren spread his hands and shrugged. "As far as I know, no one has seen them since the Mad King took his crown." He paused and his bright blue gaze fell onto Brann's face. "You're going to search for them, aren't you?"

Brann turned his gaze to Varonda, silently asking her permission.

Brandon fidgeted where he stood. His left hand clasped his right and held on tightly to the ring that rested on the stump of his missing finger.

"I don't believe this is a wise idea, my Queen." The younger advisor flicked his gaze between Laren and Brann, then back again. "We need Brann here to lead the troops. We can't afford to send him off hunting for ghosts. The men trust him, they need to see him and rally behind him if there is to be a war."

Varonda held Brann's gaze. She knew he wanted to go. If there was any chance that this person, or people, could help Marrin then Brann needed to try and find them. "Go, then, Brann. But hurry. We need you here. I need you here," she admitted. "If you fail to contact the Valren soon you will return to Calin. With haste," she added.

He nodded, bowed to her, and took his leave. He would have to pack light to travel as quickly as possible. But to where? He didn't even know where to go except vaguely north.

Brandon watched Brann exit then left the Queen's audience as soon as he was able and hurried to the docks, clutching his blue metal ring as he jogged.

~

Brann sat across a worn wooden table from Gareth and put another glass, filled to the brim with ale, in front of the aging warrior. The man ignored it, his eyes downcast as he shaved slivers from the corner of the table with a dagger he had pulled from his belt.

Gareth was a revered figure within the city. He had been a hostler in the Harton's father's service since he was a child. After saving the King's horse from a fire in the stables, the boy had been promoted to a squire. His station in life grew quickly from there, and when Prince Harton was born, Gareth became the King's trusted guard for his son. After the old King's passing, Gareth's friendship with the father transferred to the son. It had been almost three years since King Harton's death, and it was still strange to Brann to see Gareth without the King by his side. The two had been inseparable.

After leaving the Queen, Brann had sought Gareth. If Harton had fought in Bartorin, as Laren had said, than Gareth, the forty-year-old warrior would have been with him. Brann was not one to chase a fairytale, but he owed it to the Queen to weigh all the options, no matter how farfetched.

When Brann found Gareth, the man was in the stables, Brax's soft grey muzzle pressed firmly against his open hand. Brann had never seen Gareth's mood change as quickly as it did when he asked the man about his past trip to the north. Gareth's eyes darkened and his breathing quickened as if what happened that day scared him still. His unease was enough for Brax to sense and the touchy stallion began pacing his stall in agitation.

Brann coaxed Gareth from the barn and the men soon found themselves at a tavern outside the fortress walls. Gareth was into his third tankard of ale before he would speak of his sojourn to the north.

Brann told the warrior of the morning's events while Gareth stared at the foam atop the drink in front of him. Gareth took a steadying breath before he spoke.

"We crossed into Bartorin just to give the locals a scare. Our own people had been complaining about missing livestock and Harton's father believed the north was to blame.

"We took Prince Harton out with a small group of soldiers," Gareth said. "We just wanted to scare the Bartorin, was all. We crossed the border before dusk and set up camp for the night. There were only seven of us total, if you include the prince, but he was no more than a boy. He and I shared blankets to keep warm."

Picking up the ale in strong fingers, Gareth took a deep drink and wiped the foam off his upper lip before continuing. "I woke up in the morning to the sound of Harton screaming. I grabbed my sword and looked around but there was nothing to fight."

He finished his ale in one long swallow and pushed the tankard away.

"Our men had been ripped to shreds during the night. There were gashes all over their legs and chests. Severed limbs were strewn everywhere. It looked as though a pack of rabid wolves had whirled through the camp.

"Not a sound had been made though. I've always been a light sleeper… if any a man had so much as cried out, I would have heard it, and the horses were sleeping as peaceful as could be.

"Harton and I took flight to the nearest town in Marrin," said Gareth. "The locals were just as scared as we were and they started mumbling about something called the Valren. I know not what it is, but there is something protecting that land. That I *do* know. If it was this Valren that slaughtered our men, then we are better off without the monster."

"I am going to find it. Or them," said Brann.

Gareth stared at the man as if he had gone mad.

"Whatever it is, we need it to help us fight the Oparel. I'm leaving at dawn to head west. Laren believes that is where the Valren can be found. The Queen has given her blessing already."

The last was quickly added when Gareth stood up, presumably to march up to Varonda and thwart his plan. "We have little other choice, Gareth."

The old warrior ran callused fingers through his dark hair and let out a long breath. "Then tell the Queen I travel with you." He moved away from the table and out of the tavern before Brann could respond. The younger man laid payment for their drinks on the wooden table and followed his friend into the street.

~

The two companions left the next morning. Brann regretted having to take Brax after only a day's rest in the stables, but it seemed to have been enough of a homecoming for the proud stallion. The long strides of the grey and Gareth's chestnut gelding easily traversed the flat land to the north and west of Calin. On the third day of their venture the pair stopped in the city of Pique to restock their supplies before heading straight west toward the distant mountains.

On the fifth day of travel they awoke, up to their waists in thick rolling fog. Knowing that rain was not far behind, the pair traveled along the much used dirt road they had been using as a guide, heading toward the nearest town. With luck they would be indoors before the rain began.

The bloodiest battle of the war between King Harton and the Mad King of Bartorin was fought around Lake Gala, not far from the small town of Sall where Brann and Gareth soon found themselves. The people of the town gave the two men guarded looks as they passed, but there seemed to be no animosity in them. Men sent them quick smiles but almost never met Brann eye-to-eye. It amused him to think they were acting like young hounds being introduced to a new pack; not too sure about their stations in life or where they fit into the rankings.

Near Lake Gala, it was still a risk for Marrin soldiers to travel alone. Many Bartorin families had been caught between the two giant armies during the final battle and Bartorin anger and grief over their personal losses often turned to violence. Despite the fact that the two warring countries were now one, there was still a deep-rooted mistrust between the citizens.

The town's innkeeper was just placing two bowls of steaming mutton in front of Brann and Gareth when the first drops of rain began to fall. Before long the tavern was filling toward bursting with locals. Stragglers dashed in from the rain in groups of two and three, occasionally more. In a town as small as this, gossip spread like wildfire and there was no doubt in Brann's mind that he and Gareth were the cause of the inn's popularity that night. Though no single person would be brave enough to ask straight out, they all wanted to know what brought the two soldiers to their town.

A gypsy had slipped in with the rest of the crowd and began playing by the hearth. He was a far cry from the bards Brann was used to. This man wore an outrageous costume of bright mismatched colors and he had a funny little puppet sitting on his shoulder. When the gypsy moved his head left and right, the puppet, ingeniously made, would mimic the man's head movements by way of a wire attached to the back of the puppet's head and to the hair of the gypsy. The adults in the tavern generally ignored the rover, but he was apparently well-known to the children. As soon as he started playing his worn lap harp, the kids flocked around his legs in rapt attention.

Gareth took to his bed early, leaving Brann to pay their tab once again. When night began to fall in earnest the gypsy's audience of children was scooped up one by one and taken home to bed. The innkeeper lit lanterns and brought over a mug of hot soup for the gypsy as payment for his services. The gypsy took the soup and settled across the table from Brann. The man's eyes were large and friendly and he flashed a lopsided grin at the Marrinian as he sat down.

"Now you, my friend, are a long way from home." The gypsy knuckled his brow in a salute. "It was an officer's tack that I saw in the stable. Shall I be calling you Captain or General?"

"Brann will do just as well."

"The children are lucky to have you around," Brann continued. "The songs you sing teach them much about the world. History and fairytales mixed together to keep their attention."

Outside of those living in the largest and wealthiest of cities, most children had very little schooling. They learned their history, math, and letters by way of the gypsies. It had been that way since before anyone could remember, and the rovers were welcome wherever their feet would take them.

The gypsy chuckled and scooped up a chunk of carrot from his steaming soup. "They would make do without me, I'm sure." After depositing the carrot into his mouth he stabbed the spoon toward Brann. "Now, from what I hear, you're chasing a bit of a fairytale yourself." He raised an eyebrow expectantly.

It never ceased to amaze Brann how quickly gossip spread. He had told no one outside of Calin about his plans. "I pray that it is not. I am sure you are aware of the threat looming in the east?"

"Of course. Why do you think I am in the west? With all the rain we get around here, I promise you I am not here for the glorious weather. I have calluses on my hands same as you, but mine are from harp strings, not a sword. I have no reason to travel east at the moment, and we can just leave it at that."

Brann nodded. "Then you know the position we are in. This fairytale I chase seems to be the last thread of hope we have." His sharp blue eyes locked onto the gypsy's, searching for any sign of untruth. "What do you know of the Valren?"

"Ah… Well from what my father taught me, they kept Bartorin safe for generations. That is one of the oldest songs we gypsies know. How does it go?" He pulled his harp from off the floor and began fingering the strings, plucking them lightly until the song came to him. "Damn if I can remember it all. Only heard it once when I was still apprenticing under my uncle."

The gypsy's foot started to beat a rhythm on the floor. "It's about a lost child who keeps traveling west. He follows shadows that he sees around him, always heading toward the setting sun… finds himself in a town call Andora. If you ask me, whoever wrote the song was well into his cups. There's something about a blue rock, magic, and wild beasties." He drew out the word beasties as if he were saying it to scare a child. His fingers flashed in front of him, making the harp sing out dramatically. "And despite the dark topic, it's all in the tune of a lullaby. The whole thing is full of silly lyrics that make little sense."

His foot stopped tapping. "Ah yes, I remember the end, that's something at least!" His foot resumed the rhythm and he plucked a simple string of notes on his harp. "'Where the forest and mountain and sea all end, don't forget to round the bend.'" The gypsy grinned sheepishly. "Silly, I know."

Brann's eyes rolled heavenward then lowered when he felt something tug at his shirt. Beside him stood a small child with blonde hair tussled about her shoulders. She took the gypsy's shirt in her hand, letting go of Brann's, and turned toward the door. The gypsy stood and followed, looking back at Brann with an exaggerated shrug. Curiosity got the better of the captain and he, too, followed the child outside. The rain had slowed to a trickle by now and the moon was high and bright above them.

The child's eyes were luminous in the moonlight. "I heard your story about getting lost. I don't want you to get lost, gypsy." She pointed a chubby finger toward the mountains to the west. "My grandma told me once that if I got lost, I should go there."

The gypsy squatted on his heels beside her, resting his elbows on his knees. His eyes followed the line of her finger toward the western mountain range. "Why is that?"

"Because grandma is always right." Her head bobbed up and down enthusiastically. She turned to Brann and smiled up at the man who towered over her, her head tilted so far back that he was afraid she would fall over. "If you're lost, you should go there."

His eyes focused on the mountain peaks to the west where the child had pointed. "It's as good a place to start as any." Brann could have sworn that he saw the gypsy wink at the little girl before turning to go inside.

He took another step towards the tavern before he felt another tug at the back of his shirt. The blonde child had hold of his shirt. She kept tugging until he knelt before her. Once he was at her level, or as close as he could get without bending himself in two, she reached up and slipped a thick cord over his head. The cord was knotted, frayed and had no adornments that he could see.

"It is for good luck, sir. My grandma made it for me. Will you wear it?" Her blue eyes shone with excitement.

"If you wish, princess, I will wear it forever." Brann bowed his head low as if he were addressing a real princess. The girl covered her mouth with a hand and giggled. Before he could guess what she was about, she leaned forward and planted a wet kiss on his cheek, then turned and ran down the street.

The girl slowed once she turned a corner, out of sight from Brann, and reached up to slip her small hand into her father's warm one. The gypsy had been waiting for her, and gave her hand a squeeze as they began walking side-by-side to the brightly colored wagons and cheerful fires that waited for them outside the town.

"Did you give him your necklace, angel?"

The girl's blonde curls bounced around her cheeks as she nodded. "Just like you told me, Papa. I like him, Papa. He'll be safe now, right? The Valren will help him, as you said they would?"

"Yes, sweetheart, the Valren will help him now. Never doubt them."

"Yes, Papa."

~

The road that headed north from Sall soon turned into nothing more than a goat path. No more than four hours out from the town Brann began to smell the ocean.

The sun was still high when he and Gareth got their first glimpse of it. A reflection of the high noon sun glistened off the water and seagulls scuttled along the shoreline looking for a meal.

The scene reminded Brann of home and his heart gave a small lurch in trepidation. He had to find a way to protect Varonda and Calin. The people of Marrin had the sea in their blood, or so the gypsies said. And it was true that no fleet had ever been a match for the ships harbored at Calin. But on land, they no longer had the resources they needed to win a war.

Brann closed his eyes and listened to the sounds of the waves rolling slowly up the sandy beach toward him. Opening them again he looked at Gareth and saw the old warrior taking in the sound as well. The man was calmer now than Brann had seen him since they left the Queen's fort. Though pride would not allow it to be said, it was obvious to Brann that Gareth was uneasy on Bartorin land, even years after his last trip here.

Brax's ears perked forward and the stallion swung his head to the left, dark and kind eyes taking in their surroundings. His nostrils flared as he sniffed the wind, searching for something unknown.

Then Brann heard it too, a child's laughter. He urged Brax toward the sound. Over the next sand dune the soldiers found three children playing. They had built what looked like a crude castle out of sand and the largest of the children was trying valiantly to defend it while the other two took turns diving toward the structure, bent on its destruction.

The child defending the castle heard the jingle of tack right before the two soldiers crested the sand dune and he stopped to look their way. The other two children took advantage of this and merrily jumped on the fort, stomping it into nothingness and cheering their victory.

The subsequent jubilation stopped abruptly when they saw the two men on horseback. Quickly they scrambled to their feet and shuffled closer to one another. All three were boys; their blonde hair, characteristic of all Bartorin people, waving in the wind. They weren't in the least scared of the two giant men in front of them, though all three quickly put their hands in their pockets in what Brann could only assume was a nervous gesture.

Over the boy's heads Brann and Gareth could see a small town nestled into the side of the mountains. Little white specs moved across the grass that grew up the gentler slopes of the mountainside and Brann could hear the faint bleating of those sheep as they grazed. The boys were eyeing Gareth. The man's scowl could peal the bark off a tree and he was directing that look at the children.

Brann could only imagine the stories the boys would go screaming to their mothers if Gareth scared them. They would find little help in this village if the boys scattered in fright now. Brann dismounted quickly and tossed his reins to Gareth. The man caught them easily and shot his captain a questioning look.

"Go to the town and see if there is a place we can bed down tonight. There was not much available in the way of supplies at Sall. We should stock up here while we can. I will follow shortly."

"We'll meet at the inn if there is one…" Gareth nudged his bay into a trot with Brax in tow.

Brann turned his attention to the three boys then, who still stood with their hands in their pockets, watching the exchange between the two men.

"My name is Brann. I'm sorry if we scared you, it was not our intention." He held his hands loosely by his sides, palms open and in clear view of the boys so they knew he had no weapon in them.

The boys all blinked at him in confusion. "Why would we be scared of you?" The largest spoke up. "If you were bad men you would not have found us." The two other boys nodded in confirmation, their necks craned backwards so they could eye the imposing figure before them from top to bottom.

Brann looked over the children's heads again, scanning the village in the distance. There was no sign of war here. The town was so isolated he doubted many people knew about it, save for those who were born there. "You're not worried about wolves or the mountain lions that live around here?"

The smallest of the children piped up then, a giggle escaping his lips. "They can't harm us, see?" The child pulled his hand from his pocket and lifted it, holding something small between his fingers for Brann to inspect.

Brann stepped closer to the child and went down on one knee in front of him. He was a large man, even for someone of Marrin decent, and the child still had to look up to meet his eyes. Between the child's fingers was a smooth blue stone no bigger than a quail's egg. The boy kept nodding as if the proffered rock explained everything.

"It is very pretty…" Brann tried a different tactic. "Can you tell me the name of this town?"

"Andora." The oldest child spoke again, taking his hand from his pocket. "Most people only come here when they are lost… why are you here?"

Brann ignored the boy's question. Andora? This is the town that inspired the gypsy's song? There could be no more than fifty people living in such a small place. He almost growled in frustration. There were no training fields here, no soldiers that he could see. The Valren could not be here.

"Freyja!" All three children yelled in unison and ran past Brann, their little faces alight with joy. Brann stood and turned to see what had grabbed their attention and found himself looking down on a young woman no more than ten feet from where he stood.

The woman's head was bowed, her arms held out to her sides as the three boys ran to throw their arms around her waist, or leg in the case of the smallest child. The woman stroked each boy's head before looking up into Brann's eyes. When he saw her face Brann instantly felt a stab of jealousy that the boys were touching this woman and he was not. He felt like someone had just kicked him in the gut.

Freyja, as the three boys had called her, stood little more than five and a half feet tall, by Brann's calculations. Her figure was wrapped from chin to toes in a well-worn cloak, which kept out the gusty sea breeze. The three children, who were still attached to her body, were pressing the cloak tightly to her. Brann's imagination conjured a mental picture of what she looked like beneath her robe before he could stop himself.

Brann flushed hotly and covered his embarrassment by dropping into a low bow. "My Lady…" He addressed her with respect though he saw no adornment that would mark her as a noble.

She looked down to the boys who were just now detaching themselves from her. "All is well with you?" The boys all smiled and nodded. They were obviously smitten with the woman, their eyes following her every move.

Brann moved closer to the woman until they were a comfortable speaking distance apart. He was aware that his size was often intimidating so he moved slowly, hands relaxed by his sides. Unlike most women he knew, this one did not seem to be nervous of his bulk.

From this closer vantage, Brann could tell she had been walking at the water's edge. Tiny beads of spray had collected on her red hair. They shimmered in the sun and a few rebellious drops trailed down the woman's cheek. Her eyes, when they finally met his, were a rich golden brown.

"The children were alone when I found them, My Lady; I was worried for their safety. I did not realize you were nearby, else I would have greeted you sooner."

A pink tongue moistened the woman's bottom lip before she spoke. The action distracted Brann, catching all of his focus. "They have little to fear this close to the village." Her gaze flickered out to the sea then swept down to the children. "Your parents are surely looking for you."

The two older boys took the hint and started racing toward the village without a goodbye or backward glance, their feet kicking up sand behind them. The youngest child watched the others go and took hold of the woman's hand, wrapping his fingers tightly around hers. "His name is Brann."

The woman knelt and kissed the boy on the cheek. "Go find your parents, Parn." The child waved at Brann as he walked past him to where the sand castle had once stood. He gave it one last kick before racing off after the two older children.

~

Freyja shivered slightly under her cloak. An errant strand of wet hair fell across the back of her neck, dripping cold water down her skin.

The town of Andora had not seen foreigners in quite some time, but with war looming in the east, Freyja could well imagine what this man wanted. His mount was adorned in sage and gold, the royal colors of Marrin, and she had seen the ruling house's insignia etched in the leather as the horse was led away by Gareth.

The man standing before her was large and well muscled, but that was nothing new to Freyja. She had been surrounded by such men since being orphaned as a child and taken in by her stepbrothers. In her eyes there were two types of warriors; all were aware of their bodies and their surroundings, but most men who fought with a blade relied on sheer clumsy power. This worked well enough for most men, but they would never be able to compete with the other kind of fighter, a true hunter. The man before her was one of those other men.

His movements were both graceful and smooth but there was power there as well. It is men such as these that are the truly dangerous ones, she thought. Brann's sleeves had been rolled up past his elbows, revealing corded and tanned forearms. He did not have the mismatched muscling that a man usually acquired from working solely with a sword and shield. She wondered what his weapon of preference was.

She also noticed the tightly corded necklace he wore. She could make out the gypsy knots from where she stood. So, this was the man who had come through Sall.

Freyja pulled her cloak tighter about her body and bowed her head to him; a small grin was playing on her lips. "Though you are certainty dressed for the part, I doubt you have come here to single-handedly defend castle Andora."

She motioned to the now indistinguishable pile of sand behind him that the three children had been playing over. As she spoke she began walking toward the village, moving slowly until Brann fell in beside her. She cast him a sidelong glance. "You're looking for the Valren?"

Brann was beginning to wonder if the whole world knew of his plight. "You know of the Valren?" Eagerness crept into his voice.

"Know of them? Of course… they take care of this town. The Valren are no secret in Bartorin. Not this far north at least."

"What are they?"

This startled a laugh out of Freyja and she shook her head. "What are they? They are only humans, My Lord. Did you think they were beasts? Do you believe all of the fairytales you hear?"

He reached out and took her upper arm in his hand without thinking. "I need to find them, quickly. Can you help me?"

Before he could stop her Freyja yanked her arm from his grasp. "They are the kind of people who find you, sir. Not the other way around…" The anger in her voice was unmistakable as she tucked her arm back under her cloak.

His hand slowly lowered to his side. He could still feel how tense her muscles had been beneath his fingers, betraying her lilting manner. "Brann, call me Brann." He recalled what the boys had named her. "I am sorry, Freyja. I had no right to touch you."

"The people here do not crave war, Brann." His name on her tongue made his blood run hot. She did not acknowledge his apology.

"What is it you seek the Valren for?" she asked.

They were almost to the town. Launching into a story was the perfect way to keep her with him. He had bedded his share of willing partners but none had ever been as appealing as this one. There was no reason not to tell the truth, and if telling a story kept her entertained and near him, then all the better.

"My companion, Gareth, and I have been sent by the Queen of Marrin to look for the Valren. There is a threat in the east and we will not be able to stop them without help. The Queen's advisors spoke about a group called the Valren and I was sent here. It is a last ditch effort, but we had no choice but to try and find them."

They continued to walk, and as they entered the town, Brann took in his surroundings with a critical eye. As he had originally thought, the village was untouched by the war between Marrin and Bartorin. Crops and livestock were both plentiful and the two children that ran past them, much like the three he had met earlier, were unafraid of him despite the fact that he was a stranger wearing foreign clothes.

"Why should the Valren help you? Do they owe you or your Kingdom some kind of debt?" Her sculpted brows furrowed. "How will you convince them to go with you?"

"I have permission from the Queen to empty the coffers of Marrin to the Valren if I deem that they would be worth having by our side in the battle to come."

She snorted. "And if they are more interested in noble causes than money? All your Queen has done for us is brought war and destruction across our border."

Brann stopped short and barely restrained himself from reaching out and grabbing her arm once more.

"What King Harton did was for the benefit of Marrin and Bartorin," he said. "Your Mad King had little care for his people. He kept slaves, not servants, in his castle. That alone should be enough to condemn him. His people were starving while he filled his gluttonous stomach every night. He ruled through terror. No man such as he should be allowed on a throne."

He fought to keep his voice neutral. "If you had seen the condition of his servants, you would agree with me."

Freyja eyed him as they walked, making no attempt to hide her curiosity. "And is the Marrin Queen any different? Is she worth fighting for?"

"She is. I've known her since we were both young. She gives all of herself to her people. That is why she is willing to make a pauper of herself to hire these mercenaries from Bartorin."

"Mercenaries? My Lord…" She paused, considering her words. "Were I you, I would be careful how I address the members of the Valren. Some of them can have a bit of a temper. Come." Urging him forward through the small town, she continued to speak. "Your man, Gareth, must be waiting for you. He is at the inn?"

"Yes. What else can you tell me of them, Lady?" He wished to ask more about her and not the Valren. The small woman by his side was a rare beauty.

"I am not sure where to start, My Lord…"

"Brann," came the quick interruption.

She looked at him askance. "I am not sure where to start, Brann. The Valren have lived in this area for generations. They have strong ties to this town and protect all those within it. Every child who lives here is given a piece of metal."

Her left hand extended out from her cloak. Between her fingers she held what appeared to be a tiny blue rock, much like the one the boy by the ocean had shown him earlier. "These little bits of metal are chipped from a node high in the mountains, though only Valren seem to know where, for sure. They have learned to use the metal as a… conduit, of sorts. As long as your skin is in contact with it, you can convey strong emotions through metal to the Valren. Every once in a while, if someone is concentrating hard enough, the metal can relate things like direction and distance."

Her shoulders rose in a shrug. "That is why the children were not worried about being alone along the beach. If they were frightened, the Valren would feel it and come to their aid."

Freyja turned and saw Brann had stopped a few paces back, staring at her as if she were daft. "You cannot be serious."

"You asked me to tell you about the Valren, My Lord. Do you wish me to stop?"

Brann's lips pursed as he regarded the woman before him. Obviously, he was not the only one chasing fairytales around here. "Forget the metal. What else can you tell me?"

"Folklore states that long ago they made a pact with the Bartorin royal family and the two groups have supported each other ever since. When the Mad King took over, the Valren came back here to Andora to remove themselves. They had no love for the Mad King.

"If people are in dire need they always find their way here," she said, "usually through the connection that the Valren have with the gypsies. The gypsies point people in the right direction and, if the need is great enough, a person will eventually find himself in Andora.

"You are not the first to come into this town seeking them, Brann. Far from it." Freyja nodded her head in the general direction of the town's only inn. "Come, perhaps we can find what you are looking for."

~

Torne? Freyja sent a soft tendril of thought to her stepbrother through the blue metal she rolled between her fingers. *The Marrin captain has arrived from Calin as the gypsies predicted. We are heading toward the inn. Join us shortly.*

Torne's reply brushed lightly over her consciousness, making it known that he would comply, without using words. Despite the lightness of the contact between them, Freyja could feel anger underlying his thoughts. He had obviously felt her anger when Brann had grabbed her arm and was reacting to it. This meeting, Freyja thought to herself, was not going to go well for Brann.

Gareth was the only person making use of the inn when Freyja and Brann entered. He rose immediately when he spotted Brann and used his foot to nudge out a seat that was next to his own. While Brann walked toward his companion, Freyja looked over to Samal, the owner of the inn, and held up two fingers. He bowed his head and left the common room to fetch two plates of food.

Freyja ran an assessing gaze over the man named Gareth and found him not to be a threat. The man was large, and could probably handle himself well with a sword or mace, but he was bulky and Freyja saw a hint of something in his eyes – fear? He was obviously not at ease. She wanted to know what had upset him.

Brann made the proper introductions quickly before pulling out a seat for Freyja.

I am here, little one... Freyja picked up a slightly distorted image of the road in front of the inn that Torne was walking down.

Get details out of them about their quest. Also, the man Gareth is uneasy about this place. Find out what has put his tail between his legs. The whole back and forth between the two of them took but a second.

Shaking her head slightly at Brann and smiling to both he and Gareth she declined the seat. "I needed to speak with Samal earlier, and I will help him gather our plates together. Please sit and I will join you shortly."

She turned and slipped out the back, following Samal, before either man could protest.

Brann watched her hips as the redhead walked away from him, his eyes following her every move until she disappeared out the back door.

Gareth whistled low under his breath and Brann shot the man a dark look. "I leave you with three children and you come back with her? Good trade." The man grinned, immune to Brann's glare.

The door to the inn was pushed open on well-oiled hinges and a gust of fresh sea air rolled into the room. There was no doubt in Brann's mind that the man who stepped through the door was a force to be reckoned with. As tall as Brann himself, though not as thick, the man carried no visible weapons. He was dark all around; hair the color of a grackle's feathers, dark eyes, and his skin a deep golden tan. They were of even height, though Brann outweighed him by a good twenty pounds. Brann's eyes moved to the man's clothes; they were completely foreign.

The newcomer was wearing armor like nothing Brann had ever seen. The blue shine of the etched metal plates would be blinding in the sunlight, but the metal seemed to cover only strategic vulnerable places on the man's body.

Brann shot a glance to Gareth when the man moved toward their table. The blue metal looked like it was part of the man's skin, moving with him easily and making no noise. Was it the same material as the blue stone Freyja had shown him earlier?

"I hear you have been looking for me." The stranger stopped with the table between himself and the two men from Marrin. "You're a long way from your Queen, Captain."

Gareth was visibly startled but Brann forestalled his companion's questions. "As it seems you already know, I am Brann of Calin. You are the leader of the Valren?"

"I am Torne, Jroth of the Valren. The second in command." Piercing eyes moved to Gareth's face. "You smell of fear… Is there something you wish to say to me?"

Gareth's mouth ran dry and he filled it with a swallow of ale without answering.

The corner of Torne's lip curled slightly in a malicious grin. "You've met the Valren before, haven't you?" It was not a question. "Crossing the border when you were not invited? Apparently the lesson did not take well, or else you would not be here."

Brann stepped in front of Gareth, pressing the man away from the table, and away from Torne. "Gareth, go check on the horses. Torne and I will speak alone."

The two large men waited in silence until Gareth, eyes down and back stiff, left the building. "Your man is obviously not a friend of ours, Captain. It was foolish to bring him here. Usually men learn their lesson after one sitting with us. What compelled a tired soldier to our doorstep after he had been warned that he was not welcome on our lands?"

The older soldier ran into us before, little one. This is the cause of his fear... Torne felt Freyja's curiosity.

"I wish to speak to your leader, not a second in command." It took all of Brann's willpower not to try and knock the smirk off the man's face.

Torne did not even bat an eye. "The Jaryth is busy. You will speak to me or no one." He sat, legs apart and relaxed, and motioned for Brann to do the same across the table from him. "Your Queen sends you to us in response to the threat from Oparel. You are here on her authority to hire the Valren..."

"If I deem you worthy to fight beside my men."

Brann had hoped to hear anger in Torne's response, just itching for a fight, but the only undercurrent in the warrior's voice was amusement. "Men who are desperate often make comments such as that, Brann. They are trying to regain some control over a situation they are not comfortable with. I let them slide, but were I you, I would guard my tongue when speaking to other members of the Valren. What do you offer us in return for our services?"

"The Queen of Marrin is willing to pay."

"We have no need of money." Torne cut him off before he could finish. "The Valren require another form of payment."

Brann's brows furrowed. "If it is within the Queen's power to give it..."

"Two children is the price of our services to prevent this war, and keep the Oparel from spilling into your own lands."

Brann shook his head, not understanding. "Children?"

"Two children of our choosing, from Marrin stock. Once the war is averted, the children will return here with us."

"For what purpose?" Brann's thoughts were still swimming. Children?

"For reasons that will remain our own."

"I do not have the authority to… farm out someone else's child. You cannot seriously expect parents to willingly give up their own kin."

"If your Queen wishes our services she will not bother to ask the parents, she will *tell* them. Is your Queen willing to sacrifice your entire country just for the lives of two children?" Torne raised a dark brow, his shoulders lifting in a shrug. "If she is not willing to sacrifice two lives to save thousands she should not be on the throne."

Brann had never felt his hard won control slip as so far. Torne seemed to know just what to say to set him off. Brann kept his mouth shut tightly, but he could feel a muscle pulsing on the side of his jaw.

Torne… Freyja's thoughts entwined with his own. She was just outside, with the head of the gypsy troop. Torne could sense his presence through his link with Freyja. *The gypsies will back the Marrin Queen. They are made welcome in Marrin and beseech us to help. We cannot ignore their wishes. We will return with the two men to Calin and hear from the Queen herself. The far-flung gypsy bands in Oparel do not believe the people of Bartorin can survive an attack from the east. Not with the number of men they have seen massing on the east side of the Doranin Mountains. We removed ourselves from the service of the Mad King for his treatment to the laymen; we will not condemn them now.*

Amusement flowed into Freyja's mind from her stepbrother. *If they still want us. The boy looks ready to throttle me.*

This time, when Freyja reentered the inn, her cloak was pushed back over her shoulders. Brann looked her way and sucked in a hard breath when he saw the blue metal and black cloth covering her upper body. Brann stood so quickly that his chair scraped across the wooden floor and almost toppled over behind him. "You are one of them?"

Torne stood, slower than Brann had, and kissed his right hand before placing it over his heart and bowing low to the red-headed woman. "My Jaryth."

Knowing the answer to Brann's question was evident; she did not bother to answer it. "It seems your Queen and the Valren have mutual friends in the gypsies. For their sake we will travel with you and your companion. It will be up to your Queen to decide whether she can afford our services."

Brann shook his head slightly, still unbelieving. "You cannot be the leader of the Valren…"

"Because I am female?"

His silence, and rising color, were answer enough.

"I will be sure to relay your thoughts to your Queen when I see her, My Lord."

Brann flushed even hotter at that rebuke. "Myself, Torne, and another will sojourn with you to Calin. We will leave early. Torne will see that you have all the supplies you need."

She shot her stepbrother a hard look before leaving the two men. *This is not open for discussion, Torne.*

Torne bowed to her back as she moved to the exit. He watched her leave before slowly turning to the Calin soldier that stood across the table from him. He severed his connection to Freyja's thoughts. "You touched her once without her permission. Do not do so again."

Brann's hand slid down closer to his sword hilt. "How do you know she does not want me to?"

"*I* do not want you to." Torne's reply was full of malice.

As Torne left, Samal returned, leading Gareth with two plates of hot food in his hands. He placed the plates on the tabletop, waved off the payment, and disappeared back into the kitchen. Gareth was in a much better mood once he found out they would be leaving in the morning.

CHAPTER 2

Brann and Gareth fell into a soldier's routine. They had their horses cleaned, tacked and loaded with supplies just as the sun rose over the horizon.

Brann was checking his saddle girth for the last time when Freyja, Torne, and another man wearing the blue metal suit of the Valren joined them in the dirt street abutting the inn.

Brann sketched a deep bow to the Jaryth before gaining his saddle and following the Valren out of Andora. As they left the town proper, Freyja reined in her blood red bay, a massive beast that stood nearly a hand taller than Brax. She looked like a child on his back. Five Valren stood quietly in the road behind them; all kissed their hands and pressed them to their hearts in salute to their Jaryth. They would be all that Andora needed to stay safe while she and Torne traveled south.

As soon as they were out of sight of the town, Krona, the third Valren in the party, split from the group to scout the land ahead of them. Torne fell back behind the others, within earshot, but decidedly separate. Torne, apparently, had no more liking for Gareth and Brann then they had for him. Brann was quick to take advantage of this and moved his mount closer to Freyja.

When Gareth twisted in his saddle for the fifth time to look behind him, Freyja's agitation got the better of her. "I trust Torne with my life, Gareth. He will guard our backs. That is why he is behind us."

The older warrior spat. "I'm turning around *because* he's behind us."

Brann moved Brax between them. "My Lady, it means a great deal to both of us that you have agreed to an audience with our Queen."

"As I said yesterday, we have friends in common."

Gareth butted in. "I do not understand… who?"

She let her reins rest on the pommel of her saddle and took her feet from the stirrups, letting her muscles relax. "The gypsies. Apparently your Queen and kingdom both are well liked by them. They are welcome in your lands, are they not?"

"Gypsies? Of course, they sell some of the best horseflesh in the known world, and are walking history books. All children of Marrin learn to respect gypsies," Brann said.

When she simply nodded, he continued. "If we are to work together, we should know more about the Valren. We have offended Torne already and I do not wish to compound that mistake…"

"Torne's respect is a hard thing to win." She placed her hands behind her saddle, palm down on Breyog's rump, and leaned back in her seat. "We have few secrets, My Lord. Ask what you will."

"What is your relationship with the gypsies? Why are they so important to you?"

She had expected that question. "No one is quite sure when the first few men came together and branded themselves as Valren, even the gypsies don't know. Oral history states that the first Jaryth was a gypsy man, and that the fates of the two groups, Valren and gypsy, have been entwined from the beginning. The gypsies still do much for us."

She sat back up and gave her stallion a hard pat on the neck. "Our horses all come from a specific bloodline that they control, plus they keep us informed about the known world.

"News travels faster by gypsy mouth than any other," she said. "We were aware of your wish to find the Valren before you crossed the border into old Bartorin. In return for their many favors, we do what we can to keep them safe where they travel, and help them with other endeavors. It's a mutually beneficial relationship. They are like cousins to us, all of them.

"The gypsies speak very highly of your Queen, My Lord. We will make our own judgment when we meet her, but we owe the gypsies a hearing with her at least. The gypsies, like you, have a less than ideal past with the Oparel."

Brann looked to Gareth, who was listening intently, but was not going to contribute to the conversation. "Before we left for Bartorin, the Queen's advisors said that the Valren used to protect King Hale. How, then, did the Mad King gain control?"

A small frown set on her shapely lips. "King Hale was a good man. When he first came to power he sought us out to make a pact. He had enough enemies to worry about coming from outside his borders; he did not want to have to keep looking over his shoulder within his own lands.

"He kept his promise to us, making it so the gypsies were warm and well fed wherever they traveled. He fulfilled payment to the Valren as well. Part of the arrangement between our two cultures was that we would do no harm to Hale, or his immediate family. He was worried that his children would be in danger from us. When Joran killed his older brother we were still bound by that contract... We kept our word, and were unable to retaliate against Joran." She paused a moment. "Thankfully, your Queen did the job for us."

"May I ask another question?"

"You may ask all you wish. If I can answer your questions, I will."

"The blue metal that the children in Andora had, the ones that conduct feeling, are they the same material as your armor?"

Light laughter followed his question. "So you believe me now, that the metal can emit the emotions of their keepers?"

Brann looked chagrinned.

"I know you did not believe me, the look on your face said as much. And yes, our armor is made from the same material."

She pulled out a piece of small blue metal from under her cloak and flipped it to him. He caught it easily despite the rolling gate of his horse. "How does it work?"

"It is called orack metal." She watched as he pushed the blue metal round on his palm. "When it is first taken from the ground it is rough and unpolished, like the piece you have in your hand. If done properly, and over enough time, it can be manipulated into smooth metal sheets. We have found this material to be invaluable to us."

"May I hold a piece of your armor?" Brann moved his mount in closer.

"No. Our armor means more to us than just a piece of protective coating. For the Valren, our armor is our own, and it is not for others to have, even for a moment."

After a second's hesitation she lifted her hand and placed it palm down on Brann's, allowing him to feel the armor without removing it from her body. Her touch was feather light but he could still feel the calluses on her palm where it lay against his own.

Resting his reins on Brax's neck, Brann traced the metal vambrace with his fingers. The craftsmanship was amazing. It hugged Freyja's forearm perfectly and seemed to be made of one solid sheet of metal. The tiny clasps that fastened the piece together were barely noticeable, and the metal itself was paper-thin. No wonder the Valren could travel so well in their armor. It was so thin that a whole suit would weigh little more than ten pounds.

But Brann doubted it could stop even a knife thrust.

His eyes swept over her form, noting that the armor was the same thickness throughout. "My Lady, your ceremonial armor is magnificent."

"Ceremonial? This is our field armor."

Gareth nudged his mount to her opposite side, leaned over and grabbed her other arm to examine the metal for himself. He did not bother to ask. Before Brann could stop him, Gareth had pulled his small hunting knife from his waistband and gave Freyja's covered forearm a heavy tap with the intention of scratching the metal to show her how weak it really was.

As soon as Gareth moved his horse to her side, Freyja knew what he was going to do. She let him rudely pull her arm while she sent a thought to Torne. *I suppose some people need to learn the hard way.* Quickly she pulled her other hand out of Brann's grasp so he would not be caught in the powerful current.

The hot rush of anger she felt from Torne turned to amusement when Gareth's knife came into contact with the orack metal. An electric pulse shot up Gareth's arm from where the two metals touched, involuntarily constricting his muscles and making his horse rear. Before he knew what happened, the old warrior found himself flat on his back, looking up at the sky. His horse stood a few strides ahead of him, its nostrils flaring.

Brax did a little sidestep away from Freyja's stallion, but otherwise stayed quiet under Brann's firm hand.

Freyja kept moving forward as if nothing unusual had happened, and she kept talking, forcing Brann to stay by her side or miss hearing her explanation.

"Our armor is a part of us, almost a living thing. When it comes into sharp contact with most other metals it creates an amazing sensation, some sort of current." She extended her hand to him once again. "Feel free to try it if you would like. The harder you hit, the stronger the current."

Brann looked over his shoulder to Gareth, who was just now picking himself off the ground and moving toward his horse. "No, thank you."

Torne, up with me, now. As soon as she pushed her message to him through her armor, Torne cantered up from behind and moved his mount between Freyja and Brann. The Marrin man, wisely, gave no objection. The two Valren moved ahead at a brisk trot while Brann waited for his fallen companion to catch up with him.

She waited to speak until they were out of earshot. Though it was more secure to communicate silently, through the orack metal, there was no stopping the emotional tinge that went along with any thought, and she did not want Torne privy to her feelings. There were very few people that could read her well, even with the direct link of the orack metal, but Torne was one of them. The two rode so close together, their knees almost touched.

Freyja made to speak first but Torne beat her to it. "You felt his lust when he touched your armor. Freyja, stay away from him." His voice was tight and low. "It has been years since anyone has been arrogant enough to touch you without permission, yet you do nothing to this man when he grabs your arm? If your wish to keep the gypsies happy has made you loath to punish that Marrin man, then I will do it for you."

Her dark eyes met his blue ones. "Torne, leave him be for now, he does not know our rules. If he oversteps his boundaries, I will make sure he knows it."

Torne reached out and took hold of her horse's reins, slowing them both to a more sedate walk. "Freyja." She met his eyes boldly. She knew where this was going. "You have been the heart and soul of the Valren since I found you nineteen years ago. When I saw what those men had done to you…"

Her horse's ears lay back, picking up his rider's darkening mood. "This man is not like my father, Torne, or his friends, else you would have killed him before he entered Andora." She tried to lighten the mood. "For nineteen years I have resisted your pretty face. I will not start bumbling over his."

His grip on the reins tightened and hot anger surged through the bond their armor created. "As your brother, I cannot…"

"As your Jaryth," she severed the mental connection between them, creating a sharp and painful throbbing behind their eyes, "you can do nothing unless I permit it. Let go of my horse."

The man did not even flinch but she knew, from the pulsing in her own head, that the mental break had hurt him as she had meant it to. "This is not like you, Freyja. It worries me." With that, he let her horse's reins slip through his fingers.

She had no answer for him. He was right. It was not like her to be lenient. Especially when it came to her own person; and it worried her as well.

Freyja slowly rebuilt the mental bond between them before urging her horse ahead at a gallop. *Stay with Brann. I will contact Parth and Realla. They will meet us outside the Queen's city. They have already found the children we want.*

When Brann asked why Freyja was moving ahead, Torne's only reply was a tightening of his fists.

~

Freyja let Breyog have his head for a few minutes before reining the stallion back to a trot. She was glad he wanted to run, partly because she needed to gain distance between herself and Torne, and partly because the blood red bay needed to release some energy. He had felt his rider's agitation and his muscles were tense, ready for trouble. The short run Freyja allowed him helped the animal relax.

Breyog slowed to an alert walk, head held high and ears pricked forward. Freyja took a calming breath and sent two tendrils of thought south and east, picturing the slim face of Parth and scarred face of Realla as she did so.

My Jaryth and *I am here*, came the two responses within seconds of her opening her mind to them. Her connection was intentionally light, not wanting the two to pick up her underlying emotions. If they noticed the lack of intimacy that the Valren usually shared through mind touch, which she was sure they did, they were smart enough not to comment on it.

Torne has informed you of our current situation?

Yes, My Lady and *We are aware* came back to her at the same time, both thoughts wrapping around her consciousness and emitting an aura of calmness and stability. Freyja wondered if they were inadvertently picking up on Torne's anger and trying to placate her, knowing she was the most likely cause.

You will ride with us into the Queen's palace. Will there be a problem with the children?

This time their answers did not congeal. *The child has no guardian to oppose us.* But from Realla came a less reassuring response. *The boy's father will be difficult. He is a member of the Queen's court and a drunk. If he gives us too much trouble I will dispose of him, but I doubt he has enough lucidity in him to raise a fuss. We shall see.*

Brief the children, get their acquiescence; the wishes of the parents are of no consequence to us. If the Queen is as desperate as she seems she will overrule the parent's any way she has to.

Yes, Lady and, *As you say,* were the replies.

Freyja gently loosened their link, letting the men retreat back to the privacy of their own minds. She then turned her thoughts inward.

Torne had been right, she had felt Brann's physical reaction when he had touched her, and it bothered her. The last man to touch her without her permission had his arm taken off by her own blade. She assumed he had bled out, though she had not bothered to wait and see. What was wrong with her now?

She had stopped Torne before he could dredge up the memories of her childhood, with her father and his friends. She had learned, years later, that they had all died the day Torne found her with them. Torne and his brothers had made sure they would never touch a child again.

It had been nearly three years later when Freyja finally became comfortable with the Valren. They had been careful with her all that time; brushing their fingers over hers when they passed her a cup or dish, gently moving her arm to the correct position when teaching her to fight.

She would never forget the first time since she joined the Valren in Andora that she felt comfortable with being touched. It was when Torne had carefully wrapped his fingers around hers to close it into a fist, showing her how to tuck her thumb out of harm's way when her knuckles connected to a target.

Freyja tried to forget what it had been like living with her father. Torne had enough hatred for the man stored for the two of them. Aside from her initial instinctive reaction when Brann had grabbed hold of her arm on the beach, Freyja had not felt revulsion from the contact. Why was that? It had taken her a long time to bear the touch of even the brotherhood. Her grip turned white knuckled as she realized that she did not want to hurt Brann.

She did not want to hurt Brann. That thought played itself over and over in her mind. What would happen if he acted upon his body's lust for her? Freyja, despite her size, had been trained from childhood by the Valren and she had no doubt that she could easily drop most men who crossed her.

But what about Brann? She knew he was a superb fighter; she could see it in the way he moved and watched his surroundings. What would happen to her if he moved to pin her and she hesitated to react? She knew what would happen. She would be helpless. She fought to kill. All of the Valren did. That was all she knew. What other options were there to deter someone if you did not want to hurt them?

A chill ran down her spine and Breyog picked back up into a trot, eyes wide as he looked about to identify the source of his rider's distress.

She did not want to hurt Brann. Her own safety relied on the fact that she had few scruples about killing men. This weakness was something new, something she did not know how to deal with.

Freyja consciously slowed her heartbeat, which had risen dramatically since she left the company of Torne and the two men from Marrin. She carefully rebuilt the mental wall she had put between herself and her brothers. When she felt suitably under control, she turned Breyog's head around and rejoined the group, which was moving steadily southward a mile behind her.

When Freyja came close, both Torne and Krona moved their horses up beside her, an impenetrable wall to her left and her right. Torne understood all too well what was bothering his Jaryth. Krona knew only that Freyja was disconcerted, but that was enough to keep him close to her side.

~

The group drew to a halt an hour before sundown on the third day of travel back to Calin. Freyja, Torne, and Krona had led the others unerringly across the Bartorin border. It seemed to Brann that the Valren knew the landscape of Marrin better even than he did.

Brann knew they would make it to the capital city by the afternoon of the next day. By now, Torne had managed to fray Gareth's very last nerve. While Torne was more cheerful than Brann had ever seen him, Gareth was not. The captain learned quickly that he should keep himself between his man and the Valren. Apparently, if it came to blows, Torne had little trouble keeping himself on his horse and the older warrior on the ground.

They followed a side path that took them from the main road and set up a makeshift camp abutting the edge of the Euma forest. Brann took his turn at hunting and left the group to see what could be found. After seeing to the horses,

Freyja walked deeper into the woods. A quick five-minute walk and she reached the Kymel river. She was out of earshot from the camp and used that moment of privacy to clean the travel dust from her face.

She was gently splashing water onto her cheeks when the hairs on the back of her neck stood on end. She got to her feet slowly, knowing someone was coming up behind her, and used her body to shield the view of her hand. Her fingers slid down to her waist and gripped the hilt of a hidden dagger.

The man was moving stealthy behind her, barely twenty feet away. How had he gotten that close to her without her noticing? Whoever it was, he was good. She waited until she knew he was within arm's reach then spun to her right, leading with the blade in her hand at neck level.

Brann. The thought registered a split second before her blade would have bit into his neck. Her fingers released the metal, letting it drop. She caught the dagger in her left hand before it fell below her waist.

"What in the Gods' names do you think you're doing?" Freyja gave the large man a stiff shove to move him away from her.

"Me?" Surprise colored his deep voice. Quick as a flash he caught her left wrist in his hand and pulled her arm up to eye level, her blade sparkled in the light. "I knew Torne and Gareth were having differences, but I was not aware that I had offended you."

The man grinned at her. He was taking this extremely well considering she had just had a blade to his neck. "You move so quietly, I thought someone was trying to sneak up on me."

Large shoulders rolled in a shrug. "Years of training have taught me to be cautious, and quiet."

He let go of her left arm before she had a chance to remind him to do so. He lay down the spoils of his hunt, three fat pheasant.

Freyja sheathed her dagger and looked up just as Brann began pulling his shirt over his head, exposing a tanned and muscled chest. Heat radiated off his body in waves.

She instinctively backed up, stepping into the water behind her, and would have kept moving away from the man if he hadn't grabbed her shoulder and forcefully pulled her towards him.

"The air isn't hot enough to dry your clothes tonight if you get them wet." He made sure she was not going to retreat into the water again before letting her go and continuing to talk. "Freyja, you have no need to fear me."

He saw her mentally prepare an excuse for having backed up – her chin kicked up a little and her mouth tightened. He forestalled her having to lie by changing the subject.

"You are not wearing your armor." He knelt by the river's edge and splashed water over his face and neck, using the back of his shirt to dry his skin and slough off the dirt.

"Torne is keeping watch over it."

"Do you feel lonely?" He looked over his shoulder at her, still kneeling.

"Lonely? Why would I feel lonely?"

"Without the connection of the armor. You use the metal to reach out to the other Valren, right? Is it strange to you, not having them in your mind?"

She was having trouble following his line of thought. Her bothers knew where she had come from, and the situation Torne had found her in, so they were always careful to stay modestly clothed when she was around them, unless they were treating each other's wounds. Brann's broad bare back was distracting her more than she would have thought possible.

"They are with me. They are always with me." She pulled a necklace from under her collar and showed him the blue metal that was affixed to the loop.

"Aren't there times you wish to be alone?" There are, he thought to himself, plenty of situations where he would like to be alone with her.

"No."

He stood up and slid his shirt back over his head. She did not fear him, so she said before, but he had seen the flash of panic in her eyes when he had removed his shirt. Why did she fear him so much? "That little piece of metal, is that truly strong enough for you to convey your thoughts?"

"You would be amazed at what a little necklace can do. For instance, that one around your own neck." Now that he was clothed again she could feel her pulse beginning to slow. "A gypsy gave that to you. That is how they marked you as being in their favor, and why the children you met on the beach were not afraid of you. They are all trained to recognize the marks of the gypsies."

He fingered the cord about his neck. "A little girl gave me this…"

"Lorna," she nodded. "I know. Beautiful blonde curls; she cannot be more than five yet. Her father often frequents Lake Gala. So I am assuming that is where you met them."

The look on his face told her she was correct. "Being nomads can leave gypsies in precarious situations; they need a strong communication network to pass information quickly to their far-flung relatives. Physical tokens are just one way to do that."

He nodded his understanding. "If only Marrin had a resource like your orack metal." He lifted his hand slowly, giving her time to back away, and reached out to hold the necklace away from her skin, letting it dangle between his fingers. "So right now, you cannot call to your brothers?"

It was amazing to him how fast she could hide her emotions. If he had not been staring into her dark eyes he would have missed the surprise and anger that shone under her calm exterior.

"It is possible for me to take care of myself without their help, Brann." She may be able to physically hide her emotions well, but her voice was baleful, bordering on hostile.

"Peace. Please." He let go of the necklace, letting the metal drop back onto her skin. Her hand immediately moved up to cover it in what Brann considered to be a very telling gesture – she didn't like the loss of contact with her brothers.

"If you and your men are to help us, then I would like to be able to understand how your group functions as a whole. We can better serve each other if we understand each other, true?"

He continued, "I would like to understand you better, Freyja, not just your men. You are a queen of sorts, yet you have calluses on your hands. As a queen, you should be protected, yet," he raised his hand to his neck, touching the spot where her blade had almost cut him just a minute before. "You are apparently used to taking matters into your own hands. Do you sometimes train with your brothers?"

"I always train with my brothers, and fight by their sides. My life is no more important than any one of theirs."

"They obviously trained you well, not many men can get a blade that close to my skin. You're very quick." He opened his hand, palm up, between them. "May I see your dagger?"

She handed it to him without a trace of trepidation.

How strange, he thought, that he had seen such fear before, when he had moved the orack metal away from her skin, yet she seemed completely fine with handing him her only—that he could see—weapon. What was she so afraid of, then, if not a physical attack? He had seen that haunted look from someone else, but he could not remember when or where.

He fingered the edge of the blade. It would have sliced through his jugular with little physical persuasion. He held the blade and offered it back to its owner. She took it gently from his palm and slid it back up her sleeve where it disappeared from view.

Brann chuckled, his teeth flashing from a good-humored grin. "What else are you hiding under your belt?"

Freyja immediately stilled, her eyes moving over his face to try and read his intentions.

Then he remembered. He knew where he had seen that look before. It was one he had tried hard to forget.

During the recent war with Bartorin he and his men came too late to a small village south of Lake Gala. He had been moving quietly, hunting for any raiders still in the area. When he rounded the corner of a house, he came face-to-face with a shivering female form, bloodied and beaten. Her skirt was still pushed up above her waist and he could already see bruises in the shape of gripping fingers around her waist. He had reached down to help her.

That was when he had seen the look. It was fear, but also helplessness. It was something that Brann never wanted to see on the face of another human being.

Brann's grin faltered as the realization hit him. A fierce protectiveness washed over him as he reached toward her. "Freyja, who…"

He didn't have time to finish his sentence because a hand clamped around his throat like a vise.

Torne, let him go. As soon as Torne heard her voice in his head he looked over his shoulder at her, but he did not release Brann.

Brann slammed his fist into the other man's elbow, forcing Torne's grip to loosen. He pressed his advantage and started to lunge at the Valren but Freyja was suddenly between them.

"Stop." Freyja did not raise her voice above a whisper, but the sound brought him to a dead stop. He saw her reach behind herself, her palm resting on Torne's chest. "Both of you."

I could not hear you, Freyja. When you came back to us I could feel your panic, what conclusion would YOU have me come to?

Torne pressed his chest against her back, letting his arm slide across the front of her shoulders in a protective embrace. He watched Brann from over Freyja's head, daring the other man to protest his closeness to her.

Torne's dark eyes locked with Brann's as he leaned forward and pressed his cheek to Freyja's before kissing her lightly on the temple. The challenge was unmistakable.

Brann was seething. "Your brother and I need to talk."

"You don't seriously think I'm leaving the two of you alone?" She sounded incredulous.

Let us settle this, Freyja. If we are to work together in the future we need to come to an understanding now. Torne tightened his arm around her before letting her go.

She looked from one man to the other then back again, her jaw clenching. "Fine. But I expect you both to come back in one piece."

I mean it, Torne. He has done nothing wrong.

Both men watched her leave in silence. They waited until she was gone from view before turning back to each other.

~

Torne clasped his hands behind his back to fight off the temptation to once again wrap his fingers around the other man's neck. "If you ever deliberately separate our Jaryth from us again I will kill you whether she protests it or not."

"Are you worried that she will spill your little secret without you around to stop her?"

That made him pause. "Secret? What are you talking about?"

Brann's eyes flashed. "You keep her close to you so that she cannot tell anyone how you have abused her…"

Torne's head jerked up as if he had been punched. If Brann had not been seeing through a haze of red, he would have noticed the shock and revulsion on the other man's face.

When Torne did not immediately reply, Brann continued on. "How old was she when you first took her, you bastard?"

Torne's control snapped. His fist connected squarely with the left side of Brann's jaw. Even though he saw it coming, Brann had not counted on Torne's anger and was not quick enough to deflect the blow. His head jerked to the side under the full weight of the large man's punch.

Torne's voice sent a chill down Brann's spine. It was murderous. "How dare you?"

Brann realized that he had just made a life-threatening mistake.

Torne and Brann were well matched in height and weight. There was no way a fight would end quickly or cleanly. Fortunately, Torne still remembered his promise to Freyja and would not kill his opponent. But there were some insults that could not be left unpunished.

Near the end of their struggle, both men were dripping with sweat and blood was showing through their clothes in patches where their skin had been dragged across the rocky ground or slammed against a nearby tree. Brann had a dislocated finger and Torne could feel that at least one of his ribs had been cracked.

The two men were both sucking in air, faces mere inches away from one another. Torne was at a disadvantage, flat on his back, with all of Brann's weight pressed against his chest. He was not above playing dirty and was about to bring his knee up into Brann's groin when the man spoke.

"Torne, I made a mistake… listen to me." He was leveraging all of his weight down as hard as he could through his knees, which were pressed over Torne's lungs.

"You're damn right you made a mistake." Up came the knee, and Brann was not ready for it. He doubled over in pain and Torne easily slid out from under his opponent.

Torne was practically yelling now, and was back on his feet standing over the man. "I love her! We all love her. You think any one of us would lay a hand on her?" His rage, which had been momentarily used up during the fight, was resurfacing now.

Brann was just starting to stand. "Torne, she has been with you since she was young, she told me that herself. When I learned that she had been raped…"

"She told you that?" He was stunned.

Brann shook his head slowly. "She didn't need to. She acts bravely, but you can see it in her eyes. Tell me I am wrong."

Torne remained silent.

"Tell me who."

"They have already been taken care of."

"They? There was more than one?

Again Torne was silent.

Brann would not be deterred. "When did this happen?"

"She was seven when I found her. And I found her with them. Trust me when I say they have been taken care of."

"Damn it, Torne, I care about her. Tell me what I want to know."

Torne barked out a harsh laugh. "What, you think love her now?"

"Love her?" Brann was taken aback. It took him a second to realize that, though he may not love her, his feelings for her were growing stronger with each moment they shared. "Don't be ridiculous, Torne. But that does not mean I can't care about her. Tell me what happened to her."

"Her story is not mine to tell. If she wishes you to know she will speak of it herself." Torne reached out a hand to the man in a sign of peace. "You know now why she acts as she does around you. She's not going to fall all over herself like most women do to get your attention.

"If you truly care for her, you'll give her time to adjust. She has feelings for you that she does not understand. *She* may not wish to harm you, Brann. But if you hurt her in any way there will not be a place on this world where you will be able to hide from the Valren."

"It would be your right to hunt me down." Brann took the man's arm in his, grasping it tightly. "Now we understand each other."

They walked back to camp in silence. An uneasy alliance may have been agreed upon, but that did not make them friends.

~

Freyja lay on her back, eyes wide open. Tree branches, tightly packed with leaves, allowed her to see only a few of the stars in the otherwise dark sky above her. She turned her head toward where Torne lay across the fire from her. It had been allowed to burn down to embers, making her companions look like nothing more than dark mounds against the forest backdrop.

Krona had the first watch. Light snoring was a testimony to Gareth's sleep. Brann, who had placed his bed between Torne and Gareth, feigned sleep. His breathing was deep and even, but Freyja could feel his eyes on her.

Torne could feel Freyja's wakefulness through his orack metal and sent his thoughts to her. *He believes that he cares for you.*

He does not know me. She knew whom he meant. Freyja rolled her head to the side, letting her cheek rest on the smooth leather of her saddle. It was doing double-duty as a pillow. *I was surprised to see you both return in one piece. Did something prompt that childish outburst, or did you both just feel the need to prove your testicular fortitude?*

Torne ignored the barb. *He thought that I had taken you.*

Taken?

Raped... She could feel the distaste radiate from him when he said the word. *He was trying to defend your honor. The fool.*

Brann, from where he lay, saw Freyja shiver under her woolen blanket. His gaze moved between the woman and her adopted brother, but he could only wonder at her thoughts.

Brann does not understand our relationship, Torne, that is all, came the quiet reply.

He understands a great deal, Freyja. The accusation of rape against me was not a lucky guess. He said he had seen the pain in your face, and knew where it came from. I had hoped never to see that look in your eyes again, little one.

He could see her roll onto her side in the darkness, but she did not respond to his words. *He is not a threat to you. You are quicker than he, and have had better training. It would not be the first time that you took down someone far larger than yourself. I do not understand your worry.*

I do not want *to fight him.* She said. *That is my worry.*

Then it was Torne's turn to be silent.

She sat up, her back pressed against her saddle, knees pulled to her chest so she could rest her head on them. Torne watched her every move from where he lay, wishing he could see her face clearly.

Krona. She widened her link, allowing both of the Valren to hear her. *I'll take over the watch. Take your rest.*

A moment later Krona appeared and wrapped his cloak tightly about him. He used a thick tree trunk as a backrest while he slept. Freyja stood and left the clearing to take her place as sentry. Torne and Krona watched her go and exchanged meaningful glances, but kept their thoughts to themselves.

CHAPTER 3

The next day, slightly after noon, the group crested a hill and had their first sight of Calin. Brann was uneasy. His feeling of happiness at arriving home was overshadowed by worry. They were putting all of their hopes into the hands of a few individuals. And what did any of them know of the Valren? Very little. Too little.

"Wait, please." Freyja's voice interrupted his musings and, as always, warmed his blood.

"What for? We're almost there." Gareth was obviously impatient to rejoin with the comforts of his own home.

"Two of my brothers will join us before we enter the city. We wait for them." She stood up in her stirrups and shielded her eyes from the sun. The terrain around Calin was hilly, but it took her only a second to find two men on horseback coming towards them. "There they are."

Moments later two Valren pulled up facing Freyja and Torne. Both rode stocky, shaggy beasts that Brann would swear were the ugliest horses he had ever seen. Freyja's horse huffed to the newcomers and stretched out his neck to greet them.

The two men bowed low to Freyja from their saddles. The stockier of the two spoke with a deep voice. "My Jaryth. Torne."

Freyja opened her thoughts to them, letting her happiness at seeing them be felt. Both Parth and Realla had stayed close to the city of Calin during the last year and it had been months since Freyja had seen them.

As they began to move toward the capital city, the Valren each pulled a thin sheet of worked metal from their saddlebags and slid it over their faces.

Brann watched them. He had never seen anything quite like the helmets. In fact, they were more like masks than actual helmets, with open backs and no neck protection. The metal seemed to adhere to the skin it touched so the mask was free of buckles, ties or straps. Each one was delicately etched in a myriad of patterned swirls. The design on the mask that Realla wore was asymmetrical and mirrored the scars on his face. Each mask was a single sheet of metal, worked to look like an actual face. There were no eye, nose, or mouth holes that Brann could see; yet their vision was obviously not impaired.

Freyja held her mask in front of her, admiring the metal but not placing it over her face. "We have found it beneficial if our faces are not well known in places where we will be working," she said by way of explanation.

Brann looked down to her hands where she held the mask. Hers was perhaps the simplest of the five. The few patterns that adorned the metal were small and delicate. But the detail in the face was astonishing. It looked like that of an angel. Its eyes were large and hair was etched into the mask that flowed across parts of the face. It looked as if a woman with long hair was caught in a storm and had not bothered to move the errant locks when they blew across her features. Light caught the edges of the etching. The glint in the eyes of the mask made it look like the angel was crying. A decorative tear was caught half way down one cheek. The effect was stunning.

Freyja slid the mask over her face before turning to see that the others were ready as well. She was oblivious to Brann's scrutiny. Four other blue-hued masks looked back at her.

Brann took the lead on his grey and the others moved their horses in behind his.

Unlike the last time he rode through the streets of Calin, the people gave Brann and his group a wide birth. The citizens took one look at the masked figures riding behind Brann and hastily moved out of the way.

~

As soon as Brann and the others neared the city of Calin, the Queen's soldiers sent her word of their arrival. When the group was led into the throne room the Queen was already seated and waiting for them, her Marrin and Bartorin advisors standing on either side of the throne.

Varonda meant to impress her company in a low cut dress of blue silk, which complimented her complexion. She was practically dripping with jewels. It was too bad, thought Freyja, that the Queen's display was wasted on her. If Freyja were a lustful and money hungry male, as the Queen obviously expected her to be, she would be falling over herself to work for the people of Marrin. Too bad.

The Queen watched the group enter. Brann and Gareth immediately crossed the floor and sketched a low bow to her, but it was the five other individuals who drew her attention. They were all dressed the same – blue-tinted armor was padded by black cloth, and masks covered their faces. Only their height and build discerned them as individuals.

The smallest of the five stood slightly in front of the rest who were showing deference to the leader. Varonda knew the other reason for their positioning - to guard the leader's back while his attention was elsewhere.

They carried no weapons that she could see, but she knew by the way they walked that they did not need weapons to be dangerous. Brann moved like that sometimes. But whereas she felt safe in Brann's presence, the Valren were making her nervous.

Brann straightened from his bow. “Your Majesty, may I present to you five members of the Valren. They have heard our initial plea for help and have refused the payment offered. It is my hope that you and Jaryth Freyja will come to an understanding.”

It was disconcerting to speak to a mask, and not be able to see the foreigner’s expressions. “Jaryth Freyja.” Varonda spoke to the individual who stood at the front of the other four, believing that person to be the leader, and praying that her guess would be correct.

“Your Majesty.” Freyja inclined her head slightly before sliding her mask from her face. The other four Valren kept their masks in place, and would continue to do so until they were out of the public eye. Freyja, the liaison between the two groups, would be making herself less aloof by necessity.

Freyja could see the confusion in the other woman’s eyes at seeing a woman address her, but the Queen recovered quickly. “Please forgive my lack of immediate hospitality, but I hope we can speak at some length before letting you rest from your trip.”

“Of course. Time does seem to be against you.”

“You have been informed of our situation with the Oparel?”

“The massing Oparel troops have been known to us for quite a while. It is good to see Bartorin men in your attendance.”

Varonda paused at the change of topic. Her two advisors stepped forward and bowed to the Valren. They showed more deference to these strangers than they did to their own Queen.

“Marrin and Bartorin are both my responsibility now. I am sure Brann told you that I will offer you all I can from the treasury and…”

“Your Majesty,” Freyja cut her off. “As we told Brann, the Valren are not interested in money. We have our own conditions on which we will not capitulate."

Again the Queen paused before replying, "And what are your conditions?"

"There are two children currently living in Calin that we want. They will return with one of us to Andora before we agree to help you."

The Queen could not hide her shock. "Children? I cannot just... *give* you someone else's child."

"Before you say no, and the Valren leave you on your own, may I suggest the children be brought to you? They may be more willing to cooperate than you imagine."

Varonda looked to her two Bartorin advisors; both bobbed their heads in agreement with the other woman. Of course, Varonda thought to herself, they were falling over this woman the second she stepped into the throne room. Did no one else see the absurdity in this situation?

The effort Varonda made to appear serene was visible but commendable. "Tell me the names of the children and my men will find them and their parents. I hope that, when the caretakers say no to you, we can come to some other kind of agreement."

"It is my hope that you will look past the discomfort of two families in order to save the thousands of lives that a war with the Oparel will take from you. The children in question are familiar with the Valren. We will find them and bring them to you. There is no need to inconvenience your own men."

Parth. Realla. Find the children and bring them here. Bring the drunk as well. Torne...

Yes, Jaryth?

You and Krona will meet with the gypsy heads. Let them know what is going on.

As you wish.

The Valren turned and left the room without a by your leave to the Queen.

They were out of sight before anyone thought to stop them.

Freyja clipped her mask onto her left shoulder where it would rest, staring at both Brann and Gareth. "While they find the children, we can discuss what else we need of Marrin to support you in the upcoming war."

It took very little time to come to an agreement. In the end, Marrin would supply the Valren with lodging, food, and other contingencies wherever they traveled during their service. The Valren were, for the most part, self-sufficient.

Freyja knew that the child Parth was looking for might be hard to find. When Freyja announced that the Valren would not return with the children for a few hours, the Queen's skills as a hostess manifested themselves in full force. Within moments, Freyja had a private chamber with food, a fireplace, and a bath, which was being drawn as she entered.

The Queen had offered Brann as her host for the afternoon, a job Brann was more than happy with. He led Freyja to her room and held the door open for her so that she could precede him inside. As soon as the last bucket of hot water was poured into the bath, the servants scurried out of the room, bowing quickly before shutting the door behind them.

Brann knew he may never get a chance to be alone with her again and he planned on using this opportunity to the fullest. Freyja was taking a mental survey of her new surroundings when Brann lightly placed his hand at the small of her back, moving her toward the table holding the food.

It was sheer willpower that kept her from shivering when he touched her. Skin to skin contact with a stranger was completely foreign to her.

"You have not eaten since early this morning. You must be hungry." Brann spoke quietly, knowing she was on edge.

"Your Queen is very gracious." She slid around the table and picked up a thin slice of cheese and piece of bread. Now that he mentioned it, she was famished.

Brann let her put the table between them. "May I join you?"

He grinned in amusement at her suppressed sigh. She could not refuse him without seeming callous. "Of course." She did not go so far as to lie and say she was glad of the company.

"I am glad you met the Queen. What do you think of her?"

"I think she is a fool if she does not accept our offer," came the frank reply. Freyja slid another piece of warm bread past her lips.

A deep laugh rumbled in his broad chest. "Do you realize how refreshing you are?"

The slow blink she gave him in reply told him that, no, she did not.

"Most people guard what they say about the Queen. At least when I am around," he clarified.

Her eyes finally lifted from the table and met his. In this light, Brann could see a ring of green on the outer edge of her irises. Gods, she was beautiful.

"I doubt you are one to go running to your Queen because of a moment of slander. It seems like it would take more than that to throw you off guard. At least it should, if you have truly earned your rank as captain."

The barb was made to keep him at bay, but he ignored it completely. "True. I have a penchant for taking care of my own problems."

Brann reached out to take her hand from where it rested on the table. She snatched it away before he got close, her eyes darkening, showing her wariness.

He realized his mistake immediately. Still holding her eyes with his he held his hand out to her, palm up, asking her to come to him. When she did not move he murmured softly. "Freyja, I'm not going to hurt you."

He left his hand extended and watched her face. It was curiously blank, but he could see in her eyes that she was struggling with herself. Her gaze left his, but she lightly placed her hand in his across the table. He could feel her pulse speed up with every beat where his fingertips rested against her wrist.

He gently turned her hand over, letting it rest palm up in his own. Her hand was finely carved, but had calluses and even a few scars, which looked like knife cuts. "You must also like to take care of your own problems. You wouldn't have these marks if you were not familiar with fighting."

"I told you before, I train often with my brothers, and have done so for years."

"But these cuts are defensive wounds… not something your loving brothers would do to you."

Her hand curled into a fist so the scars were no longer visible.

He remained still, watching, as her hand grew colder in his own. She was genuinely scared. Moving very slowly he covered her hand with his, uncurling her fingers and keeping her hand pressed between his palms to share his warmth.

When she did not protest, Brann leaned forward, bringing her hand to his lips to breathe warm air onto it. As soon as his lips touched her skin she tried to jerk her hand away. Brann gripped her wrist tighter, but lowered her hand away from his mouth.

He did not want to let her go.

Wanting her to respond to him with something other than fear, he tried to distract her with innocent questions. "Freyja, your mask. I have never seen anything so beautiful. Where did the image come from?"

She shivered visibly before answering. Obviously, it would take more than a single question to make her forget about him touching her. But she did answer.

"When someone joins the Valren his foster brother creates the mask that he will wear. It is designed to remind him of where he came from, and why he became one of us."

"You say 'he,' but obviously it works the same for the women."

"I am the only female member of the Valren," she replied.

That did not surprise him. There were very few females with the stamina to train with men like Torne. "Your mask is haunting… Who created it for you?"

"Torne."

Brann could have guessed that. "Whose image is on the mask?"

"My own."

"The mask is crying."

She just looked at him, not volunteering a response.

He tried again. "What is the image supposed to remind you of?"

Unbidden, her mind began to replay the minutes of her life before Torne had found her. Her arms being held down by her own father while one of his friends pushed himself between her legs.

Freyja's whole body flushed in reaction to the memory, first with a chill, then with an awful heat. This time she did pull her hand from Brann's. Her breathing came shallow and uneven.

"Freyja? Are you alright?"

Freyja? Torne's mental presence pushed through her memories, wrapping her in a familiar shield that blocked the images from her mind.

I'm sorry, Torne; I did not mean to draw you in. I must be tired, she finished lamely.

His response did not come in words, only pure feelings; love, forgiveness, friendship, support.

Freyja let out the breath she did not realize she had been holding. *The Queen had a bath drawn for me; I will be without the orack metal for a few minutes. Contact me when you return from the gypsies. My armor will be back on by then.*

As you wish.

Looking up at Brann she tried to remember the last thing he had said. "I'm sorry, Brann, I am only weary from our travel." The lie sounded awkward to both of them.

She looked over her shoulder to the tub behind her. "I wish to bathe, and the water will soon be cold. Please…"

"May I help you?"

She stared at him. "Help me bathe?"

He laughed and one eyebrow rose. "I meant may I help you out of your armor. But your suggestion does seem more appealing."

Her skin flushed again, but this time it was from embarrassment.

Before she could protest, Brann stepped behind her and ran his fingers through her hair along the base of her scalp, something he had wanted to do since the moment he had seen her on the beach. "Your armor is so well made I can barely see how it comes together."

Freyja stood still, the pulse in her neck beating strongly against her smooth skin.

He found the clasps at her shoulder and began to remove the ornate plates of metal. Under the armor she wore a close-fitted shirt made of material dyed a pitch black. The fabric moved and stretched when she did, something Brann had never seen before.

His eyes slid over the shirt where it covered her breasts and flat stomach while his nimble fingers removed the breastplate from her body.

Brann could imagine pressing her tight stomach against his. She was so small that he could pick her up and slide her down the length of him. As soon as that thought entered his mind, Freyja shot him a look that could melt bark. "You do not know me well enough to think of me in such a way."

He was taken aback. "For all you know I was thinking about my dead grandmother."

She rolled her eyes heavenward in exasperation. "When you touch my armor I can feel what you are thinking. I *hope* that you do not think of your grandmother in that way."

Brann stilled, his eyes growing serious. "Do you fully understand what I am feeling, then?"

He was touching her armor with one hand while the other crept up to cup her face. He then slid the same hand around to the back of her neck, caressing the sensitive skin at the top of her spine. He stared deep into her eyes; catching them and not letting them look away. "If you did, then you would know I would not hurt you. You would stop trembling every time I touch you." He paused. "And if you did tremble, it would not be from fear."

He continued, "Can you feel how much I care for you?"

She could. His thoughts pressed in on hers. It was like the love she could feel from Torne, only hotter, more primal. She did not trust it.

Brann took pity on her and dropped his hand from the back of her neck. He took one step back and let his gaze roam over her lithe body. She was covered from head to toe in the tight-fitting black cloth. The only adornments she carried were her necklace and her bright auburn hair.

"Let me help you with your necklace, then I will leave you in peace to bathe."

"No," she replied. "I will tend to it when you leave."

He could not help but wonder if she would ever trust him enough to be in his presence without a piece of the orack metal. "As you wish."

He tried to catch her gaze but she would not meet his eyes. After a moment of silence, he bowed his head to her and stepped out the door, closing it behind him to give her the privacy she wished for.

~

Parth and Realla met together outside the palace gates with two young boys in tow. They sent word to Freyja of their arrival through the orack metal, then entered the palace to join their Jaryth and the Marrin Queen in the throne room.

When Freyja entered, both Brann and Varonda were in attendance. Though she had her armor on, the only noise she made was the soft tread of her feet on the marble floor. Parth and Realla entered only a moment after her, each with a child at his side, silent as death.

The young boy who stood near Parth was filthy. Curly blonde hair fell across his eyes. It made him either toss his head back or puff the hair away with a breath of air every few minutes. His clothes were worn and too large for his spindly frame. There was no doubt in Varonda's mind that he was a street-boy, an orphan.

The child shifted nervously from foot to foot until Parth moved directly behind him and placed both his hands on the boy's shoulders. As soon as he felt the contact of Parth's hands, he relaxed. The look on his face was one of hero worship. The child obviously had a history with the Valren, and trusted the man behind him.

The Queen looked over to the second boy and drew in a sharp breath when she recognized him. "Lian?"

The boy stepped forward and bowed deeply. "Your Majesty."

Varonda immediately shook her head at Freyja. "Lian is the only son of one of the richest earls in Marrin. His father will never let him leave with you."

Realla sent to Freyja: *The child left his father a letter. The man should be here shortly if he can drag himself away from the bottle he was in.*

"Lian's father will be here soon. We will see what happens then," Freyja spoke back to the Queen. Lian, being raised in the same social circles as the Queen, knew he should not address her without being spoken to first.

Brann, Realla, and Parth were also silent during the exchange. The two masked Valren stood like sentinels next to their young charges.

Freyja continued to speak for the Valren, "In the meantime…"

Parth gave the blonde-haired boy a push on his shoulders. The child stepped forward so that he stood directly to the right of Freyja and bowed as best as he could to the Queen. It was obviously not an action he was used to performing.

"Your name, child?" The Queen smiled to the boy, not wanting to intimidate him.

The boy glanced over his shoulder to Parth. At the older man's nod he looked back to the Queen and cleared his throat. "I'm Zaven, Majesty." The boy curled his toes while he spoke, trying to pull them under the hem of his pant leg.

"And do you know why you are here?"

"Yes ma'am. I was told I could go home with Parth, but I have to talk to you first."

The Queen flicked her gaze to Parth's masked face then back to the boy's. "Do you know who he is, Zaven?"

The child looked confused. "Course I do, he's right there. You can ask him yourself."

Varonda smiled. "But do you know what he does?"

"He does lots of things, ma'am. He gets food for me and the other kids at the orphanage, for one. He makes sure that the dock-kids don't harass us when we have to go down to the water to run papers… He does lots of stuff."

"Do you know where he lives, and who the members of the Valren are?"

Zaven rubbed the back of his neck, sending little flakes of dust and mud falling to the floor behind him. "The Valren is his family, ma'am… I don't know if I would call them members. I mean… 'cause we are both Marrin, right? But you're not my family, it's different."

The child flamed red from the tips of his ears to the tips of his toes, which Varonda could see peeking out from the bottom of his loose pant legs. "Meaning no disrespect, of course…"

I bet that tongue of his got him in a bit of trouble on the streets, Freyja sent to Parth.

You have no idea…

"Your Highness. The boy has no home here, nor family. Why would you condemn him to this fate if he could leave with one of my brothers?"

"Because I do not know what awaits him if he goes with you. For all I know he will be worse off." Behind Varonda, Brann cleared his throat, trying to stop her.

The Queen did not realize on what thin ice she was walking until Freyja replied rather smartly, "You think we would abuse helpless children?"

Brann spoke up before the Queen could answer. "We just wish to know why you want the children, Jaryth. We do not mean to question your integrity."

"You will make your decision in ignorance because you have no other choice," Freyja bit out angrily. "If you cared for your people as a queen should, you would be pushing these children up onto a saddle with your own manicured hands."

Zaven, knowing he owed Parth his life five times over already, tried to help. "Majesty, I don't honestly care why they want me to go with them, I am just glad they do. If you tell me I can't go with them when they leave, I'll just take off on my own until I can find them again." He crossed his arms and puffed out his chest, making a stand for the older man behind him. "I've got nothing here."

At that moment Lian's father entered the room and was announced by his personal herald.

The man who walked in was nothing like the composed aristocrat that the Queen usually dealt with. As soon as he neared the group she could smell the alcohol on his clothes and breath.

"Your Majesty, may I introduce you to the real Sir Lancard. It occurs to me that you are used to seeing him a bit tidier, but I am afraid he did not have time to sober up before his trip to the palace today." Freyja's disgust was obvious.

Varonda's sense of smell was offended by the man and she took a step back. "Sir Lancard, are you quite alright?"

He bowed, staggering slightly as he did so. "Your Highness, I am simply distraught that I came home to find my son missing, with nothing but a letter to explain his disappearance." Lian's father shot his son a look filled with hate. To Lian it meant, "Just wait until I get you alone..."

Freyja moved up to stand beside Lancard in order to address the Queen. Brann instinctively moved forward, wanting to place himself between Freyja and the drunk next to her in case he lashed out. He saw Parth crouch slightly, ready to intervene as well.

"It is fortunate for Lian, Your Highness, that Realla has managed to divert his father's drunken attention more than once when things got a bit out of hand. I doubt he can ever remember how many bones he has broken in his son's body."

"You?" Lian's father spat. "You're the ones who keep taking my boy."

"It became necessary after you nearly beat the child to death in a drunken rage."

Varonda's eyes widened. "He what?"

Sir Lancard did not hear the Queen. "Who are you to tell me what I can and cannot do in my own home? Huh?" He snapped his fingers and pointed to the ground in front of him, calling his son to him like a dog. "Lian, here, now."

The boy flinched, but did not move from his spot in front of Realla.

His father's face turned a blotchy mix of red and white. He moved toward the boy and raised a hand to punch Lian, not caring that he was in public.

Realla reached over Lian, grabbed the man's fist mid swing and yanked him off balance. The Valren helped him fall by planting a blow to the man's kidney.

Lancard fell hard and curled up into a ball on the floor, holding his side.

Lian stepped back, pressing himself against Realla's front. "You will never hit me again, father. I have a new family now."

"Brann, take him out of my sight..." At the Queen's orders, Brann and two other guards dragged Lancard from the throne room. A small nod from Brann once away from the others was all the encouragement his soldiers needed. They would not kill the Earl, but he was going to have a very long night. Lancard's drinking may not have been known to the Queen, but the soldiers had seen it first hand in the past.

By the time Brann returned to the throne room both Lian and Zaven were in the care of the Valren. Krona had come and gone from the palace and was leading the children to Andora.

~

"That went better than expected." Freyja ignored the hint of sarcasm in his voice. The two were shoulder to shoulder, watching the sun set over the ocean while they leaned out of a wide window. The Queen had put them up in a lavish suite on the second story of the palace. They had separate suites but Torne and Freyja met together in the larger of the two as soon as they were settled.

Everything in the room was polished to a high shine. The floor, walls and small sculptures all caught light from candles placed around their rooms, making the space seem brighter than it should have been as the sun settled beneath the horizon. Freyja found the room more than a little ostentatious.

Torne chuckled next to her. "Well, Lancard could not have had better timing. Trying to hit his boy right in front of us, not to mention the Queen. What was he thinking?"

He popped a grape into his mouth and eyed the other food on the tray that was left for them. "He deals in metals mostly. The gypsies will make sure that his business fails in the upcoming years, as payback for the boy's suffering."

Freyja nodded and lifted her gaze to the sky. The first stars of the night were beginning to shine. "I do not like the Queen."

He shrugged, "She is easy on the eyes, at least."

Torne winked at Freyja when she snorted. He pushed his shoulder against hers good-naturedly. "Neither boy is timorous, that is for sure. And the Queen let them go. That is all we needed from her."

"It is good to be back on a side, isn't it? After a few years of lying back. I did not like watching the Mad King on the Bartorin throne." Torne was never one to sit back. It was one of the qualities that made him such a powerful leader among the Valren. His energy was infectious.

Freyja's eyes were drawn downward to the rocky beach below them. Brann was there with Gareth. Freyja could easily pick out Brann by his size, and the stocky Gareth always favored his right leg, which give him a distinctive rolling gate. They were deep in a discussion that Gareth obviously did not like, if his wild arm movements were anything by which to judge.

Freyja could feel Torne tensing next to her as they watched the two men by the water. Torne's hands were flexing very slowly, giving Freyja the impression he was dreaming Brann's neck was between them. She reached out to him, seeking to understand what was upsetting him. *Torne?*

He cares about you, Freyja. He let out a small sigh, his eyes glancing toward her before moving out to sea once more. *He has only known you a few days. But he cares about you deeply. I could feel it when he touched your orack necklace.*

And because of that you want to strangle him? Speaking mind to mind with her brothers was always intimate. It was very difficult to block emotions from one another and still communicate. For the Valren, who were usually men of few words, it was often easier for them to open their minds to one another than try to explain their emotions verbally. Torne and Freyja's bond was deep, but she could not understand Torne's unrest, even when she touched her mind to his.

He felt her confusion. *You do not understand because I am uncertain as well, little one.* His mental voice sounded strong, but she could feel and hear the edge of uncertainty in it. *Brann means you no harm. It became very clear when he touched your piece of orack, and when he became your champion against me.*

But he makes you uneasy. I am not sure if he is a threat or not.

They stood together in silence, lost in their own thoughts.

Torne snapped out of it first and moved away from the window. Freyja slid up onto the windowsill, her back to the ocean, her eyes tracking his movements. "You were coordinating our brothers while I spoke to the Queen. Where do we stand?"

He settled into a low chair by a candle and moved his fingers slowly through the flame. "Krona and the two boys have met no resistance. He will stay with them in Andora and begin their training. Parth and Realla have tested them both over the last year and a half, they show great potential." His fingers left the candle flame and he leaned forward in the chair. "They will most likely survive the training."

"And the others?"

"Parth and Realla will travel with the boys today then break off to the Oparel border for some reconnaissance work. The Horani gypsy troop will meet them there and relay all the information they know. Ten of us are moving back to join those already in Andora. That will be enough to ensure the town's safety no matter the scale of the upcoming war. The rest are gathering into their conas and will wait for more instructions." Each cona consisted of between eight and fifteen Valren. Freyja would only have to reach out to the cona leaders for her information to be spread throughout the whole group.

She nodded then closed her eyes while Torne sat in silence beside her. Speaking with one or two of her brothers at a time was child's play to her. She had picked up the skill of mind-to-mind communication faster than any of the Valren before her. But finding all eleven of the cona leaders, scattered across the continent, took more than a little concentration, even for her.

Freyja raked a hand through her hair and opened her mind to them. Her thoughts ran like lightning over the lakes, forests and fields to find the eleven she was looking for. They all knew she would be reaching out to them, and they were all prepared to latch onto her thoughts as they flowed by.

When Freyja felt those she sought she opened her mind to Torne as well before projecting to the twelve leaders. *My brothers, by now you are aware of our pact with the Queen of Marrin. You are all men who enjoy the hunt, else you would not be one of us, so you will be happy to know we have a new patron and will be moving on the Oparel soon.*

She felt their responses, all eager to hunt with each other again. None of the Valren had a death wish, but they would never purposefully avoid a confrontation either. They were men of action.

The two closest conas will take up in Calin. Out of those twenty, at least two of you will be in the palace at all times. Make sure nothing happens to the Queen. One cona is to stay near Lake Gala. The rest of us will gather at the Doranin Mountains and will move across the border together. She felt their agreement and their happiness at the thought of working together once more, after years of relative inactivity. *Torne and I leave the capital in three days time. Happy hunting, my brothers.*

She broke off the connection and fixed her dark eyes on Torne. "It has been too long since you and I fought side by side in a real battle. I miss the challenge of having to watch your back."

Torne's chuckle was deep. He was about to reply when they both heard a rap on the door. Torne stood up and moved to the door, palming a small knife in his right hand. He opened it wide and stepped back to allow Brann to enter.

Brann's large frame filled the doorway, blocking the candlelight from the hallway. He moved into the room and allowed Torne to close the door quietly behind him.

Brann stepped across the room toward Freyja. He stopped a good distance away from her when the hairs on the back of his neck began to stand on end.

Torne, who was positioned behind him, was radiating aggression that multiplied with every step he made toward Freyja. They were now fighting on the same side against the Oparel, but it was clear Torne did not consider them to be the best of friends. Brann did not like having the Valren behind him.

"Jaryth, I have arranged for a large suite for you to stay in while the Valren move on the Oparel. You will be residing on the same floor as the Queen, providing you with the best guards in the palace." Brann wanted to ensure her safety even though Gareth had objected feverishly to the arrangement, not wanting the two women anywhere near each other.

Freyja leaned against the side of the window frame, the ocean breeze curling her red hair around her face and neck. One delicate brow lifted in response to his message. "You expect me to stay here, Brann?"

Now it was his turn to quirk a brow. "You wish to travel back to Andora instead?"

She shook her head slowly. "Of course not. Torne and I are traveling to the Doranin Mountains together. We leave in three days"

"You're what?" His eyes flashed angrily and he turned to face Torne. "You are going to drag her right into the middle of a battle?"

Torne folded his arms across his broad chest. His eyes were ice cold. "If you raise your voice to her again, you are going to regret it."

Brann ignored the threat. "You cannot be serious, Torne. None of us can ensure her protection in the middle of a war. I don't care how good of a fighter you think you are."

"Protect her?" Torne's smile did not reach his eyes. "Apparently you have never seen Freyja fight. She is the last person who would need protection."

"I cannot allow this…" Brann's voice was low.

Freyja pushed herself off the windowsill, her feet making hardly any noise on the marble floor. "Brann, I don't believe you have a choice in the matter. You may be able to order your men around, but you have no say about what I do."

"To hell I don't. Torne, leave us. Give me just a few minutes to talk some sense into her alone."

"No." Torne shook his head. "Brann, you do not understand. She belongs with us. She is one of us. If she wishes to fight then she will fight. We do not own her. *You* do not own her."

"I'm only asking for a few minutes, nothing more."

"No," Torne repeated.

Their gazes locked together. "If you think she can defend herself on a battlefield she sure as hell should not be scared to be alone in a room with me. I am only one man."

Torne. He could feel her annoyance at that remark. *Give him the time he wishes. If he has to try and dissuade me to clear his conscience, then so be it.*

Torne did not reply right away. After a few heartbeats, he extended his armored arm to Brann. "Take my forearm."

Without hesitating, Brann grasped the darker man's forearm where it was encased in blue-tinted armor.

Through the orack metal, Torne could feel Brann's anger. It was not anger at Freyja, or even Torne, but anger born out of fear. Fear that Freyja would be in danger. Torne's cold gaze swept over the man holding his arm. This man would hurt himself before he ever intentionally hurt Freyja. The Valren was surprised at the depth of emotion radiating from Brann. The man may not even know it yet, but there was more than lust binging him to Freyja.

"I will not be far away." The threat was clear in his voice. Torne gave Freyja an assessing glance before leaving the suite. She could see the warning in his eyes before he reached out to her with the orack. *Be careful, little one, he wishes to play a game that you have no experience with.*

What game would that be?

One of the heart.

Freyja stared at her brother while he closed the door behind him. She suddenly felt very awkward. Her dark eyes traveled up the length of Brann's body, trying to assess his mood. He seemed slightly more relaxed now that Torne was out of the room, but he was far from happy.

"Please sit, Freyja." Brann motioned to a high-backed chair with its back to the window. She slid into the chair, her body almost disappearing into the shadows that were thrown about the room from the moon and the candles. Her armor and Torne's were laid out on the bed in the other room. The tight-fitting black mesh she wore left very little to Brann's imagination and she was glad of the shadowy protection the chair offered.

Brann picked up another chair from across the room and placed it directly in front of hers. When Brann sat, his muscled legs trapped her smaller ones between them. Freyja could feel her body temperature rising. She did not like being trapped.

Brann leaned forward, resting his elbows on his knees and Freyja immediately leaned back in her own chair. She saw his lips quirk into a small grin at her reaction. "Freyja, will you listen to me?"

"I am listening, Captain."

His eyes caught hers. "Have you forgotten my name?"

"Of course not."

"Then use it, please."

Her lips pursed together in a frown. Brann's gaze moved down from her eyes to rest on her lips. They were perfection. He would do almost anything to feel those lips pressed against his skin.

"I am listening, Brann." Why was he staring at her mouth? Freyja licked her lips nervously, pink tongue sweeping out before disappearing behind white teeth.

"Give me your hand." He opened his hand, palm upward, and rested it on her thigh. Freyja took his hand quickly to remove it from her leg, just as he knew she would, and his fingers curled gently but firmly around her own.

Well, Freyja thought to herself, that was a sneaky trick. The laughter in Brann's eyes told her that he agreed. "Sometimes when we talk it seems like you are far away from me. Maybe you're speaking to your brothers. I just wish to keep your attention, that is all." The pad of his thumb brushed lightly over her knuckles, sending a jolt up her arm.

"We are very much alone, Brann. Trust me, you have my attention…" And she did not sound happy about it.

"Not alone." His free hand reached out to touch the orack metal at her throat. "But I will take what you are willing to give." He leaned back in his chair, his hold on her hand making her lean forward to accommodate him. Her face was now illuminated by the candlelight so that he could see any changes in her expression.

He steeled himself for the argument he knew would come. "Freyja, you cannot go to the Doranin Mountains."

"Why not?"

"Why not? Have you ever been in a battle? Do you know how dangerous it can be for a woman?"

She tilted her head slightly to the side. "Brann, I believe that you are confused as to my role as a member of the Valren." She paused, and when he did not interrupt her, she continued. "I realize that the Marrin Queen is a figurehead. She stands for the country as a whole and will sacrifice her wealth and her men for the good of her people. The position of Jaryth is slightly different…"

He stayed silent, his eyes still locked with hers, but his thumb began its subtle caress against her skin once more. "I train with my brothers so that I can join them in battle, not watch from a distance while they have all the fun."

"Fun? War is not fun, Freyja. If you had ever killed a man you would know that."

She licked her lips again, a nervous reaction. She was not sure how much she wished to tell him, or how much he would believe. Should she tell him that she killed her first man before she was fifteen years old? That she was one of the best assassins in the brotherhood?

"What if you were captured?"

She let out a long breath, trying to hold onto her patience. "You do not mind if Torne lays his life down for your country, or any of the other Valren. I am part of them, Brann. You are just separating me because I have breasts."

Brann's bright blue eyes dropped to her chest. It had been the wrong thing to say, and she knew it the moment it was out of her mouth. All of a sudden her black clothing felt too tight. She fought the urge to yank her hand out of his and cross her arms over her chest.

"Freyja, I don't care for the others like I do you." He tried to hold her gaze but she kept looking nervously at his hand where it held her own. Her tension was palpable.

"You barely know me. And I have enough brothers to look after me. I do not need another man thinking I should stay tucked away safe and sound while my family goes off to fight." She tried to loosen his grip on her hand by pulling back but he was impossible to budge. "Please let go of my hand."

To her surprise, he did, but only to slide his hand up her arm, leaning forward, so that his palm cupped her elbow. "I know you don't trust me, but even Torne can see that I mean you no harm. He would not have left us alone if he thought I would do anything to hurt you. He believed what he felt through the orack metal. Let me show you the same thing. I don't know how you have become so much a part of me but you have. It makes me sick to think of you in danger."

"It is not my fault if your ego cannot handle me going in…"

He cut her off, his eyes darkening. "This has nothing to do with my ego and everything to do with your safety." His grip on her elbow closed like a vise. "Let me show you what I want."

"I know what you want. You want what every other man wants. It's not yours to take, it is mine to give, and I do not know you well enough to give it. I have no desire to enter a fleeting relationship."

Her voice was strained; she was out of her element. She may be able to break his arm to keep him away from her, but how do you stop someone that you do not want to hurt? She had never been taught how to do that. "Brann, please let me go."

"I will let you go if you take off your necklace. I had asked to speak to you alone, and that is not what we are doing."

Red hair tumbled over her shoulders when she shook her head. "Just because I am wearing a piece of orack metal does not mean that the rest of Valren can hear what you are saying."

"But they can feel what you feel, can they not?" His left hand reached out to snake around her neck, his fingers burying in her hair. His other hand held her forward, not letting her out of his grasp.

"If my emotions are strong enough, yes, but we can block each other out if the need arises." It was frightening to have a man as strong as Brann have his hand so close to her neck. His fingers were remarkably gentle, and actually felt good as they massaged the base of her scalp. But she knew what he could do if he wished, his hand could easily span her throat, stopping airflow. Freyja trembled and he felt it all the way to his toes.

"I suggest you block them." Brann's bicep flexed as he pulled her forward, toward him. His lips met hers before she could even register what he was about. The kiss was undemanding. He kept it light because he knew that if she felt the true extent of his need she would bolt. Though he tried to keep himself in check, he could not help but run his tongue lightly over her lower lip. Gods she tasted good.

His left hand tightened around the base of her neck, a possessive move that shot panic and, to her chagrin, excitement through her mind.

Little one. Torne sounded strained, something that did not happen often. *Unless you want him disposed of, you need to stop projecting to me.*

Freyja gasped against Brann's mouth. She hadn't realized she had let her guard down enough for Torne to feel her thoughts. She quickly reached up and pulled the orack metal away from her skin, holding it by the chain to effectively cut herself off from the other Valren.

The feel of her breath against his lips and the small sound of distress she made when she gasped were too much for Brann. Her lips opened and his tongue ran along them, gently, inviting her to do the same back to him, urging her to explore.

Heat rolled over her skin, beginning at the juncture of her legs and spreading rapidly through her body. Confusion temporarily paralyzed her. Her mind was screaming at her to get away, to not let him force her, but her body was craving his touch, wanting more and more. The need to get away was normal for her, but the need to touch and be touched was something entirely new. It was more than she could handle.

When Brann felt her body freeze against him he bit back a curse and loosened his hold on her neck. Reluctantly he leaned back away from her, giving her space. When he looked down into her eyes he could see the naked panic there. Her breath was coming in short, shallow gasps. His right hand was back to her elbow, not letting her retreat from him fully.

"Freyja? Lovely, it's all right. You can relax. I will always be careful with you." His left hand moved from her neck to her cheek. He ran his knuckles along her soft skin.

She jerked back as if she had been burned, then tried to stand. Brann stood with her. Their two chairs were so close together that when they stood Freyja's chest pressed tightly against his. Her hand, still clutching the orack metal, was trapped under her chin.

Brann took her hand and opened it, letting the stone drop to her chest. He brought the empty hand to his lips and pressed a chaste kiss to her knuckles before pushing his own chair backward to give her more room. He watched her and waited.

"I should go…" She spoke so softly he had to lean forward to catch her words.

"You shouldn't. But you may if you wish." He paused, and then continued, "I hope you do not."

Her eyes finally raised to meet his and her face flushed a rosy pink. "Torne will return soon. I doubt it is a good idea to have you both in the same room right now. Give him some time to cool off."

"Give *you* some time, you mean?"

Freyja could feel herself blushing. Hell, she was surprised she wasn't glowing in the dark. Who needs candlelight when an embarrassed redhead is nearby? It irritated her. Who was he to make her feel like this? If he wanted to play dirty then so be it.

"I propose a bet, Captain. I challenge you, or one of your men, to a fight. First to tap out loses. If I lose, I will stay here while the rest of the Valren head north. If I win, I go with them, and you stop your arguments about keeping me here." Though it sounded like a legitimate reason to wager, in truth she was just itching to knock the man down a peg or two. If she had to publicly humiliate him in front of his men to do so, then that was fine with her.

He stared at her, then very slowly his lips tilted up into a cocky grin.

"You're challenging one of my men to a fight?" She was priceless. What other woman would do such a reckless thing?

She raised a finely shaped brow. "Or yourself. But I understand if you are afraid." She pressed her hand to her heart in a show of empathy.

"You're serious?" This was insane, but if it kept her at the palace then it would be worth the effort.

"Of course."

"A private fight then. Between you and I."

Freyja frowned slightly. "Why a private fight? Why not let your men in on the fun?"

He shook his head and rolled his shoulders in a shrug. "Private or not at all."

"Fine."

His voice turned husky and ran like silk over her skin. "Give me one hour. I'll meet you at the salle next to the stables."

Brann left the suite and Freyja began to stretch out her muscles. This was going to be fun.

~

The hour passed quickly but Freyja had spent her time wisely. Unlike Brann, who would likely underestimate her, Freyja took the time to actually prepare for a fight. She worked up a light sweat before leaving the suite and her muscles were loose and warm.

The door to the salle was unlocked. When she opened it she was welcomed by warmth and light from many candles placed around the large open arena. The dirt floor was packed hard, but would provide more give than an actual wood or stone floor. The arena was lined on two sides with mirrors which reflected the light from each candle, making the room seem reasonably bright after coming in from the dark night.

Brann was near the center of the room. He turned when he heard her enter and flashed her a warm smile. Freyja felt that slow heat begin to seep over her skin again. She took a deep breath and let it back out, shaking her legs to make sure they were still warm.

"We're really going through with this then?" There was humor in his voice.

"You didn't expect me to come?"

He shrugged and waited for her to join him in the middle of the floor. "I thought Torne would have a thing or two to say about your crazy challenge."

She found herself grinning up at him, her uneasiness fading slowly. "He does not have to know everything."

He was right though, she thought to herself. Torne would be furious if she lost concentration on the orack metal and he caught a glimpse of them fighting in her mind. He would not know it was only practice. She had not thought of that before. Always in the past, she had absolute control over the stone. Something about Brann flustered her though, caused her to slip – which made Brann a threat. Torne knew it, too.

Freyja removed her cloak and placed it in the corner of the room where it would be out of the way. Brann watched her hesitate before she reached up and unclasped the stone from around her neck as well. She rested it gently on top of her cloak.

Brann's stomach muscles tightened. She trusted him then, even if only minutely. He doubted that the metal left her skin often, lucky metal.

"Rules?" he prompted her.

"No weapons." He watched her hands slide over her scalp while she pulled her hair into a tight ponytail and tied it off with a bit of twine. "Pretty simple."

"Fair enough." Though in reality it was not fair at all. It was far from fair, in his eyes. He outweighed her by at least hundred pounds. How did she expect to fight him hand to hand?

He soon had his answer. Brann wasted little time before shooting in low, thinking to get the spar over and done with. He was trying to be gentle, but before he got anywhere near her legs she darted back and to the side, easily dancing out of reach. They both laughed, then Brann spoke. "Come on, Freyja, you know you cannot keep that up all night."

"I don't intend to, I'm just letting you know you may actually have to *try* in order to beat me. Are you going to take me seriously or not?"

Thinking to placate her, he moved in again. This time he was quicker, though not at full speed, and went for a headlock. He had no intention of throwing her anywhere, but it would be easy to get her to admit defeat from that position.

Freyja saw the attack coming and became frustrated. Did he really think she was such a beginner? So she did the only thing her mind, and temper, could think of to get him to actually fight. She waited until he committed to the headlock and easily stepped aside, throwing a not-so-light kick to his kidney as she did so.

She was on her toes, weight balanced, ready for him to retaliate. Brann turned to face her and just blinked down at her. "You actually do know how to fight?" He ran a hand over his side to rub away the sting of her kick. She could hear the admiration in his voice. Brann heard it too, and it surprised him because what he heard in his own voice went deeper than admiration. He was slowly falling in love with her.

Freyja rolled her eyes. "You thought I was lying to you all this time?"

Then he started to advance on her seriously. Freyja could see the difference in his stance and her body reacted automatically, crouching lower to prep for an attack.

Instead of letting him come to her, Freyja took control, determined to make him spar in earnest. She moved forward with small feints, pretending she was going to grapple, but faded out again before he could return with a solid grip.

Slowly Brann began to speed up his actions, realizing that the woman in front of him did in fact know how to spar. And she was fast. The kick to his side had hurt more than he would have liked to admit, and she had meant it to.

Minutes later and the two of them were both exerting themselves. Brann had the obvious height and weight advantages, but Freyja was using her speed to control the distance. Every time he went to get a hold on her to pin her, she blocked him with a swift cut of her arm. Weight did not mean a victory if your opponent knew how to use leverage against you. Both of them were going to be covered in bruises by the morning. It was the most fun and challenging spar he had had in years.

Five minutes went by, then ten; both of them were breathing hard and covered in a sheen of sweat. It had been a while since Brann had been truly challenged in the sparring ring. He taught most of the younger Marrin soldiers to fight and they could almost never surprise him in the ring. Fighting Freyja was a rare treat. If this was what the smallest member of the Valren could do in a fight, he would hate to face Torne in a real battle.

Her style was like nothing he had ever encountered. She danced about on the balls of her feet, drawing him into striking distance before launching an attack. She was wonderful.

He called a halt to their play to allow both of them to have a brief reprieve. He backed away from her with his hands up. "Hold." He laughed when she shot in, thinking he was trying to fool her. "I need a drink, and so do you." He continued to back up until she stopped.

Freyja relaxed her stance, arching her back to stretch tired muscles. Her eyes were sparkling. "Agreed." She followed him to the corner of the room where he had thoughtfully hung two water skins.

"You're really good, but you already knew that," she said. She took the offered water skin and uncorked it, taking a long swallow of the cold liquid.

Brann did the same, and then wiped his mouth with the back of his hand.

He grinned. "I do know that, and yet you are giving me trouble. I've never met anyone who fights like you. Whom did you learn from?"

She chuckled and poured some water in her cupped palm so she could splash it on her face. "The Valren all practice together, but I suppose Torne taught me the basics." She ran her wet hand over her face then wiped it with the bottom of her shirt, exposing a tight and tan stomach. "I cannot fight like you do, or like Torne. I do not have the reach or the weight to be effective. It took us a while to find a style that would work for me. We made things up as we went, and it seems to have worked out well."

"It has worked very well." His eyes ran over her body appreciatively. "If only my men could be so light on their feet." He took another drink from the skin before hanging it back up. "Alright, enough fun. Are you ready for round two?"

She nodded and winked up at him, thrilled at the chance to expel some energy after days in the saddle. She replaced the cork in the water skin and hung it back up in the corner next to his. "I'm always ready."

It was warm in the salle and Brann, as he always did when sparing seriously with his men, stripped off his shirt then tossed it to the side. It was such a common thing for him to do in the ring that he didn't even think about what Freyja's reaction would be.

She was walking toward him to meet him in the middle of the ring when his shirt came off. Her eyes took in the sight of his broad chest, at the muscles rippling under tight skin, and she fumbled to an awkward halt.

Brann saw her falter and cursed himself for not thinking. They had found a common bond and she had finally begun to relax around him. It was too late now.

His gaze collided with hers in a challenge. "Come on, little one. We were doing just fine. Don't back down on me now. If you forfeit, you lose the challenge," he prodded.

It was strange for her to hear him call her 'little one.' It was the same endearment Torne always used. Strangely, it gave her a measure of comfort. Freyja reluctantly met him in the middle of the salle.

Brann, who had been thinking of nothing but the spar ahead, suddenly found his mind wandering to other things. Knowing that Freyja was so acutely aware of his body sent blood rushing through his system.

They began circling each other once more and after a few feints, it became obvious that Freyja was more bothered than she let on. She still moved with a fluid grace but she was reluctant to engage him, she was on the defensive, not wanting skin-to-skin contact. He used that to his advantage and slowly began to push her to a corner of the ring where her foot speed would not give her such an edge.

Freyja realized she was being herded; it was something her brothers always tried to do to her to get her to slow down. She waited for an opening in his guard then closed the distance. She wrapped her leg around his and threw her hip into the back of his thigh, trying to push him down.

He went down hard but took her with him by grabbing her back arm by the wrist and yanking it behind her, forcing her to follow him down to the dirt floor. He landed on his back with Freyja on top of him, her elbow pressed hard against his windpipe while her other arm was pulled up tightly behind her back at an awkward angle, one that could easily cause a broken arm if he was not careful.

They both froze immediately, knowing they were at a standstill. Freyja could push her weight forward and cut off his air supply, but there was no way she could do so without causing serious damage to her arm. But neither one of them was going to tap out.

Freyja's stomach was pressed tightly against his. When he let out a soft laugh she could feel the vibrations along her entire body. His blue eyes were full of mischief. "So, what do we do now?"

She laughed nervously. "I can stay here all night. You're big; you're bound to get hungry before I do. I'll take my chances and try to starve you out."

Her energy was infectious; he could not help but grin up at her. "That's playing dirty."

She shrugged, keeping a good portion of her weight against his neck to keep him in place. "I play to win."

"Apparently. Speaking of 'dirty'…" His free hand moved from between them up to her cheek to rub off a smudge of dirt. Freyja let him; her mind was still on the fight and not on anything sexual, despite the fact that his bare chest was tight against her.

His touch on her face lightened when she did not protest, turning into a caress. His eyes bore into hers.

He flexed his grip on her arm, reminding her that it would hurt if she tried to pull away. "Are we calling a truce then?"

"Truce." She replied quickly, expecting that she would be let up if she agreed.

"I still don't want you to travel with your brothers." He let her see the worry in his eyes. His hand still held her arm firmly, effectively trapping her against him.

"I'm going with them."

The pad of his finger trailed over her cheek then traced the line of her jaw. "I do not wish to fight you right now, Freyja. Let us talk of something else."

"About what exactly?" His finger running along her skin was distracting, but the warmth seeping into her muscles from his chest felt wonderful. Despite her better judgment she found herself starting to relax against him.

He shifted his bulk so that more of her body was resting on top of him. Brann let go of her arm, sliding his palm up to her shoulder so that he could lightly massage the muscles there. The position he had had her arm in was uncomfortable at best and he wanted to soothe her.

In response, she shifted her weight from off his neck. She pushed herself down his chest, trying to give herself more breathing room, until she felt his hands reach for and tighten around her waist. Her nipples hardened against her shirt when they slid across his skin. Her eyes were level with his shoulders.

"Talk to me about you. I want to hear about you." His thumbs began a slow glide up and down her waist, so light that she could barely feel it. It was amazing to her how something so minute could affect her so deeply.

"About me?"

"If you rest your arms on my chest they will make a very comfortable pillow for you." His hands moved up her waist to her arms, holding her wrists and crossing them under his chin. Freyja shifted against him before resting her cheek on her arms. He had to look down his nose now to see her, so he stared straight up at the ceiling instead. "Where are you from?"

"Torne found me outside a small town called Tauber. It's out on Bear Paw Point."

"Yes, but where are you from originally? Bear Paw Point is Marrin land, and I have never seen someone from Marrin with your color hair." He looked down at her then. "It is beautiful."

He thought he saw her blush, but the candles were burning low and it was hard to tell for sure.

"I don't really know… I am Valren. That is all that matters, I suppose. Where I came from is of little consequence as long as I know where I truly belong."

"You really love them, don't you?" It was not a question. "How did Torne find you?"

"It's really not something you want to hear about," she protested.

"But I do. On our way here from Andora, when I found you by the stream, I accused Torne of something. I was wrong about him and your relationship with him and I want to know more about the two of you. I am trying to understand you better, that's all."

Freyja released the breath she was holding. The air tickled the short stubble on his chin. Her voice, when she replied, was very soft.

"Orack metal is attracted to individuals who can use its power easily. Since it is such a large part of the way we communicate, we use the stone to find people who may be able to join the brotherhood."

"Is that how Zaven and Lian were found?" he asked.

He felt her nod. "They were identified a little over a year ago, but were too young to make a conscious decision whether to join us."

"Zaven was found in the streets, and Lian was heir to an earldom," he said. "What was your life like before they found you?"

She stiffened against him, drawing into herself. "What did Torne tell you?"

"He told me he found you with your father. And that if I wanted more details I should ask you myself."

"There is nothing else you need to know."

Brann's fingers ran through her hair, burying them in her thick ponytail. "It's not enough, Freyja. You said that your mask was etched to remind you of the time before the Valren came to you. I have never seen anything so haunting as the face you wear. What was happening when he found you?"

She put her elbows on either side of his chest and pushed up, trying to stand. "You know what was happening. Torne all but admitted it to you that night by the stream."

He did not let her go, his hand tightened around her hair, gentle but firm, keeping her body against his where he lay. "I want to hear it from you."

She looked utterly defeated. All the fight left her body and it was replaced by a feeling of total loss. "Why? Do you get off on making people feel helpless?"

Brann felt her tense above him, prepping to do some serious damage to get him to let her go. His voice was patient. "So you know that it is alright… and not your fault."

He could see tears begin to build in her eyes. The candlelight caught the pooled liquid and made it shimmer. With her hair all tussled from their earlier spar, the view was exactly like that of her mask, come to life.

He cursed under his breath and caught her face between both of his hands, thumbs running gently under her eyes to wipe away tears that had not yet fallen. "Who could ever want to hurt you?"

Her whispered response was so low he barely caught her answer. "My father."

As gently as he could, Brann guided her back up his chest so her face was close to his. He wanted desperately to roll her under him and show her that she could share pleasure with a man, not just pain. But he knew the moment she felt trapped she would fight him.

"Let me show you that it can be different." He let out a deep breath. "I should have been more careful with you up in the suite."

He felt her swallow, saw her pulse beating a quick tattoo under her smooth skin. He lifted his head from the ground and let his lips trail over her pulse. A small distressed sound escaped her lips.

He backed off enough so his lips were not touching her skin but she could feel every breath he took. "I should have asked last time, before I kissed you." Her scent was intoxicating. "But I feared you would say no."

She still didn't respond to him. Resting his head back on the ground allowed him to see her face. This woman, who had no qualms talking back to the Queen of Marrin, or walking into a battlefield, was frightened of him.

"Little one, you have nothing to fear from me. The only thing you should be feeling when I am this close to you is pleasure."

Freyja would not meet his gaze. Her eyes fixed on his mouth instead; reminding her of the last kiss he had given her and the strength she had felt in him. A shiver ran down her body.

Brann felt her tremble, causing her body to rub over his chest and thighs. His stomach tightened in response, as did the fit of his pants. It would have been obvious to anyone that he enjoyed having Freyja so close to him. He let out a small groan and her eyes instantly found his, not sure what had caused it. He saw the sadness in her eyes, and she saw the determination in his.

His heart began to squeeze painfully in his chest.

"As soon as you tell me to, I swear I will stop." He whispered those words then raised his head slowly, giving her time to pull away if she wanted to. To his surprise, and pleasure, she did not.

His mouth brushed over hers, barely touching, letting her become accustomed to the feel of his skin against hers. He laid a gentle kiss on the corner of her mouth then the line of her jaw. His lips skimmed over her ear then stayed there as he whispered to her, "I have wanted for so long to touch you."

Brann's scent reminded her of home. He smelled of horses and leather, of the outdoors. Things she knew and loved. Things she was comfortable with. It gave her mind something to latch onto, and kept her thoughts from retreating back to when she was younger, back before Torne has rescued her. She was trying desperately to push those memories away.

He could see the fight in her eyes. She was forcing herself to allow him access to her. "That's it, little one." The pad of his thumb ran across her bottom lip and it parted for him. His tongue followed after, asking her to respond in kind.

As Freyja felt his tongue move across her lip, her breath left her lungs in a rush. She did not know how to react until his finger found her lip again and lightly pulled it down, allowing his tongue to sweep in and find hers.

Brann's gentle assault on her senses was something completely foreign to her. She had never been kissed like this before. When her father had held her down for his friends, the only thing they had done to her face was slap it when she began to cry. She had no experience, but deep down she knew what Brann wanted. He wanted her to respond to him.

Tentatively she ran her tongue along his. A jolt ran down her body and made her stomach clench. She heard a low growl from Brann's throat and his fingers flexed against her skin, he had felt it too. His mouth slanted across hers, deepening the kiss, demanding more from her.

Brann's arm slid around her back like an iron band, holding her body tightly against his. It was an instinctual move for him. He wanted her closer, so he pulled her closer. It forced her hips to come in contact with his arousal. The sensation, to him, was pure pleasure. For Freyja it was something else entirely.

She could feel Brann's body tighten and grow where he was pressed against her. Even fully clothed she could tell he was large, just like the rest of him. Brann bent one knee so that it separated her legs. The pressure of her hips against him was doing things to his body that he could not control and bending his knee gave him at least some reprieve from the torture.

Freyja felt his knee slip between her legs, pushing them apart without her consent. That was something she recognized, something she feared, something she hated. The change in her demeanor was instantaneous.

She put her hands on the ground on either side of his body and shoved herself up as much as she could when his arm was still locked tightly around her waist. "Let me go."

Brann closed his eyes tightly, wishing he had a bucket of freezing water he could pour over himself. He managed to release her without saying a word. He had promised he would stop if she asked, and he did. No matter how much his body was screaming at him to continue.

She quickly rolled off him. Her lips were swollen from his kiss and sensitive where his facial hair had rubbed against her skin. She touched her lips with the back of her hand to try and stop the tingling. "Brann, I…"

"Don't," he cut her off. "You're fine." He finally opened his eyes and looked up at her from where he lay. "I understand." Slowly he rolled to his knees. It looked like it hurt. She wondered if they had overdone their sparing earlier.

"Are you sore? Maybe you should stretch."

Brann blinked slowly. It took him a moment to realize she just did not understand how his body was affected by her. "I'm alright." At her dubious look he could not help but chuckle. "I'll stretch later, I promise."

He stood up and she took a small step away from him. He tried to meet her gaze but she refused to look up at his face. In the dim light it was hard to tell if she was blushing, but Brann would have put money on it.

"Please don't back away from me like I am some sort of monster. What went on between us should have been pleasurable for you. I didn't mean to make you nervous."

"I know… it's just…" she never talked about what happened with her father and his friends. Even to Torne, despite the fact that he had seen everything first hand.

She tried desperately to explain how she felt but could not find the right words so she just let her sentence trail off.

He waited for her to continue, keeping his distance from her, knowing she needed her space. After a long minute he heard her let out a deep breath and she finally lifted her gaze to his face. His heart constricted when he saw the confusion in her eyes. She had no idea how to handle him.

He scooped up both of the water skins from the corner of the room and tossed one to her, knowing she would catch it. He had not realized until tonight just how keen her reflexes were.

"Go rest, we have been traveling for days. The Queen will want you to breakfast in her chambers in the morning. May I escort you?" It was the most tactful way he could think of to ask her if she was afraid of him now.

She nodded and took a long drink from the water skin. She picked up her cloak and necklace on her way to the exit, slipping both around her neck, then paused at the door, half way into the night, and looked back at him. "Thank you, for understanding."

She was gone before he could reply, but Brann did not mind. He had two more days to convince her that she did not belong on the battlefield with the rest of the Valren.

~

Brann spent a restless few hours in his quarters but found it impossible to sleep. His mind kept straying to Freyja. As soon as the sun began to rise he went to the stable and saddled Brax. The powerful stallion greeted him by pressing a warm muzzle into his hand. Soon they were outside the city gates.

He stood in the saddle, surveying Calin and the surrounding villages. The wind off the ocean made the air taste salty. He could hear the joyful banter of fishermen and soldiers who were working in the port.

Brann's eyes moved back toward the city gate where he saw two horses galloping at breakneck speed along the cobblestones and out onto the dirt road. They cut north off the road.

His eyes narrowed. Those were the Valren horses – one was Breyog. The faces of the two riders glittered in the sun. They were wearing their masks, but it had to be Freyja and Torne.

The Queen would be up for her morning meal within one hour's time. If Freyja was going to break her meeting with the Queen then something had gone wrong.

He bent over Brax's neck and urged the stallion in the direction of the Valren. Even though Brax was warmed up and the Valren horses were not, the stallion could not keep pace with the two horses running ahead of him. Thankfully, they had left the road, so their horses' wide hooves made a clear trail for him to follow. When they raced out of sight, he could still follow.

The trail led Brann to a goat path that wound through the woods, forcing him to duck low over his horse's neck. The further he went from the city the more he wished he had traveled armed.

A sense of foreboding passed over him. Brann reached to his waist to feel the long knife that rested there. He had that at least, but his sword hung in his bedchamber where he had left it last night.

Brann heard voices ahead of him and reined Brax to a walk. Dismounting, he looped the horse's reins over a branch, not tying him. Slowly and quietly he moved toward the voices.

The goat path opened up to a small field. A worn road headed to the west and east. Freyja and Torne were still on their mounts, the animals pawing the ground, working themselves into a lather. The two Valren looked calm, but the mounts were feeling their riders' agitation.

On the other side of the road, Brann saw a small gypsy train of three carts surrounded by heavily armed men. He counted eleven, but knew there would be more scouting the road for other travelers.

The gypsy family was tied and bound at the feet of the armed men. There were five gypsy adults. Three children were being held at knifepoint in front of them.

The armed men were shouting to the Valren from across the road, making sure to keep a good distance between them. "You have one minute to make your decision! These gypsies are part of your family, Valren! Eight lives for one hostage. The trade is more than fair."

The man who spoke was barrel-chested and short, apparently the leader of the band. Brann growled low in his throat. They were Oparel. How did they get so far into Marrin without being noticed?

The two Valren were sorely outnumbered. Having sparred with Freyja, and knowing Torne was her teacher, Brann had no doubt that the two Valren could do severe damage to the group on their own.

But with children being held hostage he doubted they would take that chance. They could not get to the children in time to stop the slice of a knife. And the Oparel knew it.

Brann moved out of the woods to stand next to the Valren. Freyja's eyes never left the children, but Torne's masked face turned toward Brann, acknowledging his presence. The Oparel guards tensed but did not move.

Torne knew Freyja had already made up her mind, but he tried to dissuade her. *With three of us, little one, we could take out most of the men in front of us. The others will most likely scatter once the leader falls.*

Not before they kill the children. Her mind was detached, barely perceptible. She was keeping a distance between his and hers. She did not want him to know what she was feeling.

Torne whipped his head around to look at her. *Freyja, I have played in your mind, as you have in mine. Do you honestly believe you can block me out that easily? I know what you are thinking. Your life is worth three of theirs, family or not.*

Freyja continued to watch the children. Torne saw her take a deep breath and exhale slowly. He could not see her expression through her mask but he knew her. Her eyes were closed, and she had made up her mind. *It will take at least five days to reach the border, Torne. You had better find me before that happens.*

Torne let out a string of curses under his breath. Freyja dismounted and began walking across the road to the armed Oparel troops.

Brann stepped forward to stop her but Torne leaned down and caught him by the shoulder. He pressed his orack armor against the exposed skin along Brann's neck so they could speak mind to mind. *She does not want to risk the children's lives. Let her go for now. We will track her through the armor and catch up with her before she gets more than a mile away. Once the children are free, we will have more options.*

The voice in Brann's head was obviously Torne's, but it was still a shock to communicate mind to mind. He did not know how to respond with words, but he knew Torne could feel his seething rage through the mental bridge.

Freyja stopped half way across the road. "Let them go, my life for theirs."

The leader leered at her and tightened his grip on one of the children. "Leave your weapons where you are. And your armor, too."

She did so without hesitating, shedding her weapons and piling her armor neatly on the road. She stood in her black clothing, her necklace still tied tightly about her throat.

The Oparel leader tossed a bag at her feet, staying well away from her. "Your necklace and bracelet, too." His eyes flashed triumphantly. "That bracelet is a garrote if I have ever seen one, and the necklace is probably the same." Put them in the bag.

The bracelet was indeed a garrote, but the necklace was for something else entirely.

Shit. Torne and Freyja both cursed at the same time. Torne's voice came to her again. *Freyja, you cannot do this. We can track you without the metal but we will need more time. This man must know us. He will not let his guard down just because you are a female. You will have little chance of escaping.*

I am not letting these children die. She looked over her shoulder at him and gave him a wan smile. *It's not like they can do anything to me that has not already been done.*

Is that some kind of jest? Torne's anger rolled off him in waves. It was so hot on her mind she was amazed that the other men could not feel it as well.

Torne's hand tightened painfully on Brann's shoulder. Brann knew they were communicating but he was unable to hear.

Just find me quickly, Torne. Her gaze ran over his face then slid away. She would not look at Brann. *He will leave people with the children so that you do not follow right away. Kill them, and then find me.*

She reached up and took off her necklace and bracelet, putting them in the bag before tossing it back to the Oparel leader.

The leader pushed the child he was holding to one of the other men. Three men and the three children separated themselves from the group.

"In five hours my men will let the children go," he said. "You two will stay here and wait. If you try and follow us before then, or try and take the children, my men will kill them and this whole trade will be for naught."

Freyja let herself be tied. She was not going to risk the lives of the children.

It was strange, not being able to feel Torne in her mind. She forced her heartbeat to slow while they tied her hands tightly behind her back. They tied her again near her elbows, making it impossible for her to get her arms in front of her.

One of the Oparel hoisted her onto a horse and sat behind her, not trusting her to have her own horse. The gypsy adults were left tied on the ground as the Oparel troops departed to the north.

As soon as the troops were out of earshot, Torne turned his masked face to the three men and the children they were holding. The smug looks on the foreign men's faces disappeared instantly. They had just realized that their leader had left them to die.

Torne dismounted and stood silently next to Brann, as he would for the next five hours. The odds were three to two in the favor of the Oparel. But Brann looked at the faces of the children, all had knives pressed to their throats, and they were smiling up at Torne. They knew what the Valren could do in a fight. All they had to do was wait. In the eyes of the children, the Valren were unbeatable.

Five hours later, the first three of many Oparel men died on Marrin land.

CHAPTER 4

Freyja had to grudgingly admit to herself that the Oparel knew what they were doing. With her arms double bound behind her, and a man's body pressing them tightly against her back, there was little hope of getting free.

She had been blindfolded while they rode, though it seemed almost silly to do so. She knew where they were going, and so did Torne. They would head to the Doranin Mountains and try to slip through the pass.

The water in the gulf between Marrin and Oparel was too violent for passage by a small boat at this time of year. A larger vessel would be impossible to hide from Marrin soldiers. That left only one option to get back onto Oparel land.

It was going to be a race to get to the pass.

They had a five-hour start on Torne and Brann. But the rest of the Valren would have mobilized as soon as word got out that one of the gypsy families was in trouble.

By now, Torne would have spread the news about her capture and the Valren would be closing in on them. If the nearest cona could not find them on the way to the mountain pass, the Valren already en route to Della would be there. There was no way for the Oparel to slip past them.

Despite Torne's obvious dislike for her plan, it was a sound one. There was no way the Oparel could get her across the border without fighting the Valren at some point along the way. And the Oparel would lose that fight.

What Freyja was worried about was the time between then and now.

It was a five- or six-day ride to the Doranin Mountains if they maintained their current pace. That gave the Oparel troops more time alone with her.

After four hours of hard riding, Freyja found herself being pushed off her horse by the man riding behind her. She twisted in midair so that she would not land on her trapped arms. Her shoulder took a solid hit to the ground instead.

She was dragged to her feet by a sweaty, meaty hand and her blindfold was removed. She squinted while her eyes adjusted to the light. The Oparel leader, Sholl, was standing in front of her.

She quickly took in her surroundings. They had met up with another group of soldiers. There were close to forty of them now. She also noticed another captive, tied face down over the rump of a horse. He had the stark blonde hair that was the trademark of Bartorin men.

She snickered up into Sholl's face. "What's the matter, can't find…"

Sholl's fist connected with her cheek before she could finish her sentence, the force of the blow snapping her head to the side violently. Apparently she didn't need to finish her insult to goad him into violence. She worked her jaw to try and get the sting out of her temple but she could already feel her eye swelling shut.

"You will stay silent." When he spoke the fat rolls around his neck rippled; it was fascinating to watch. Freyja instantly felt bad for the horse that had to carry the man.

Sholl left her under guard while his men watered their horses. Freyja had a grasp of their language but they spoke carefully around her, making sure to pitch the conversations low so she could not hear. As soon as the horses were rested the men remounted.

Just as she feared they would, the Oparel troops split off into four groups, each heading north on different paths. If Torne and Brann followed behind with soldiers they would be forced to split the troops and follow all of the trails if they wanted to find her. And for the sake of speed, they would be traveling with a small number of men to begin with.

Freyja cursed under her breath. Her arms were beginning to ache and there was no doubt that her eye was swelling shut from the punch Sholl had given her. She would pay him back for that.

The other Bartorin prisoner was in the group with her, as was Sholl. A blindfold was reapplied, pressing painfully on her injured eye, and she was tossed back onto a horse. A man settled in behind her and the group was off, heading to the mountain pass.

~

Sholl and his men were forced to stop that night, or else risk harm to their horses. The path they followed was riddled with roots and holes and could easily cause a horse to turn up lame. It was small consolation for Freyja. She knew if the Oparel could not travel safely, neither could Torne and Brann.

Again she was shoved unceremoniously from the horse she was riding. She heard the Bartorin prisoner fall next to her. His breath left his lungs in a loud rush when his body hit the ground.

She tried to sound cheerful and nonchalant, neither of which she was actually feeling.

"You from around these parts?" She heard the whistling of the air right before a booted foot connected with her midsection, causing her to double over as much as her tied arms would allow. A glutton for punishment just does not cover it, she thought to herself.

Again her blindfold was removed. She was lying in the direction of the Bartorin man. He, too, had bruises on his face and, she assumed, the rest of his body as well. But they were both in good enough condition to run if given the chance. That had to count for something. The man's blue eyes locked with hers. He didn't speak, but he mouthed his name. Tripan.

Freyja mouthed her own name back. He nodded. Instant friend. There is nothing like danger to bond two strangers together.

The Oparel set up a crude camp no more than one hundred yards from the path they were traveling. They lit no fire and rarely spoke. They were being cautious.

Freyja and Tripan were tied to steaks driven deeply into the ground on opposite sides of the small camp. They were tied so tightly, it was impossible to pull the offending stakes from the ground.

Freyja tested hers a few times anyway. Tripan, who had apparently spent more than one night with the Oparel already, did not bother. He knew they would not budge.

A man came to Freyja with water in a small flask. She drank when he tipped it up against her lips. Why not? There would be no poison. If they wanted her dead they would just slit her throat. She drank as much as he would allow, grateful for the small reprieve.

Freyja watched the Oparel man walk over to Tripan and she stiffened. Tripan was going to do something stupid. His muscles were bunched, ready to attack. No, no, no. Freyja thought to herself.

As soon as the Oparel was within kicking distance, Tripan struck him in the shin. There was just enough slack in the ties binding him to give the soldier a light bruise at best. All it was going to do was anger the man.

And it did. The heavy fist of the Oparel soldier slammed down on the man's chest in retaliation before he rubbed his shin.

Freyja felt another soldier come up behind her and she closed her eyes. Tripan was probably no older then she, but he was obviously more naive. When

Freyja had insulted Sholl earlier that day, it was when she knew the soldiers were in a hurry and he would do little to retaliate. Now they were bedded down for the night. They had plenty of time to take out some aggression and burn the nervous energy that had been bottled up all day.

She opened her eyes and watched as a man roughly gagged Tripan. The Oparel that had come up behind her did the same, shoving a sweaty rag between her lips and tying the ends behind her head. It smelled disgusting. She had to fight the urge to gag.

She watched the small group of soldiers circle Tripan. His eyes were wide. He was just beginning to realize the mistake he had made. Freyja could do nothing but watch as Tripan was beaten. The gag stifled most of the noise he made, which was good, because the other men were getting more and more excited by his sounds of pain. They only halted the beating when the man on the ground ceased to move. He was unconscious. Or dead. It was hard to tell with such little light.

The men waited a minute, nudging Tripan with their toes, trying to get him to wake up so that they could start again, but he did not.

Then one of the men turned and looked at her. A slow grin spread across his face and the others followed the line of his gaze. They all smiled and began to move toward her. Freyja took a deep breath. The last good breath she would get for a while, she knew. All she could do was try and protect her head when the soldiers continued their fun on her.

They circled her first, grinning down at her like a group of cats that had found a mouse. Freyja knew she would survive this; she had been beaten before. She was not so sure about Tripan, but she was worth a great deal alive, and the Oparel knew it. Sholl would not let them kill her.

Freyja quickly closed her eyes and slowed her breathing. She tried to shut her mind away from her body by building a wall between her physical form and her consciousness. She had been hurt before, and this mental exercise would lessen the pain.

The first blow landed on her bruised shoulder, the second on her stomach. The pain was bad, but her body would go into shock soon, she hoped, and then she would hardly feel it at all.

This was nothing new. With luck she would pass out quickly and remain unconscious through the worst of the beating. Freyja tucked her head, protecting her face as much as she could, and tried her best to curl into a ball. There was nothing else she could do.

The men became discouraged after a few minutes when they did not hear her screaming behind the gag. In truth she wanted to. But she knew better. Instead, she bit down on the gag. Her lips became so dry they began to bleed. She couldn't taste it yet, but she could smell the copper odor always associated with blood.

The men left soon after. Amateurs. She lay where she was, letting her mind slowly reconnect with her body, and took mental note of the more severe injuries; a cracked rib, a large gash above her eye that was weeping blood, and what was either a broken or dislocated pinky finger. Nothing she could not get over.

One eye was still swollen shut from the punch Sholl had given her earlier that day, but she fixed her other eye on Tripan. It took her a moment to locate him in the darkness, but she did. She watched him. She saw him breathe. Good. Not dead.

Slowly she uncurled her sore body and lay flat on her back to keep pressure off her cracked rib. They would leave her alone for the rest of the night. Freyja closed her eyes and willed herself to sleep.

~

The next five days followed in the same basic pattern as the first. Both prisoners were watered, fed, unceremoniously dumped onto horses, blindfolded, and well tied. The only difference was at night.

The last section of their journey would be the most risky for the Oparel troops and they knew it. Freyja could smell it on them, the nervousness. If anyone was going to stop them from crossing into Oparel, it was going to happen here, near the Doranin Mountains.

After the first beating, the Oparel soldiers left the prisoners alone. Most likely due to Sholl's reprimand about their condition. How could they travel as quickly as they would like if the prisoners had to be carried around like sacks of potatoes?

But each night, as they drew closer to the mountains, the soldiers were getting more nervous, and more aggressive. To keep the prisoners weak the guards would take turns nudging them awake during the night to keep them from getting rest. In all the nights that followed the first, Freyja doubted she had more than seven hours of sleep. If, by some miracle, they had broken free they would not be running far or fast.

Freyja understood the soldiers. They were good at their jobs and determined to return home. For all she knew they had children and families of their own. Each one of them had a mean streak to be sure, but it was only Sholl who truly worried her. He was a man of calculation.

Her injured rib was now nothing more than a dull throb in her side. Her body was becoming accustomed to it, much like one's eyes become adjusted to the dark.

She kept a worried eye on Tripan. The other prisoner was not getting the sleep he needed to heal his body, and neither was she. Every night, Freyja was able to close her eyes and consciously slow her breathing until she drifted off. It was one of the first things the Valren taught her. After all, if you are stuck in a battle for days on end, you will need your sleep, no matter what pain you feel, or the noises around you. There was nothing she could do when one of the guards nudged her awake moments later but try and rest again.

She lay, watching the stars much like she had every night during her trip from Andora to Calin. The camp was quiet. Because they were so close to the mountains all of the men but three, Sholl and two others, were pulling guard duty and had hidden themselves outside the perimeter of the small camp. Freyja guessed they were up to a half-mile away.

Freyja could feel Sholl's eyes on her.

She willed herself to stay calm. Her breathing was even and deep. Maybe he would think she was sleeping. Her gaze flicked over his face and she saw the lecherous look there. It reminded her of her father's.

Sweat broke out all over her body. Please, no.

She heard Sholl move toward her. She watched him approach. The other two men followed behind him. She could see the bulges in the men's pants and knew what they were thinking. They could die in the morning, might as well make the best of this night.

Without a word the two men grabbed her hard and knelt on her shoulders, holding her down with their weight while keeping away from her kicking feet. Deep down she knew it was pointless to struggle. Though her legs were loose, her arms were too well tied to escape, but she tried anyway. She knew how to take a beating and live. What they had planned was something different. It was unbearable.

She felt Sholl shove himself between her thighs and she immediately locked her legs around him, trying to squeeze the air out of his lungs. The men struggled but soon had one of her legs bent and held up against her chest. Sholl was snickering down at her, his incredible weight pressing against her bent leg.

She tried desperately to retreat into her mind, like she had done during the beating, like she had always been taught. Ignore the pain, ignore the thirst. But her mind was beyond that point. Feeling Sholl's hand between her legs, fumbling with his pants, was too much for her to run from.

She jerked her bent leg down and planted a kick square to the fat man's chest. It was satisfying to hear the thump of impact. The two men holding her down grabbed for the leg and dug their knees into her stomach, not letting her breathe. One of the men slapped her hard across the face and for a blinding moment she saw stars. The lack of breath was causing her eyes to become unfocused. She knew she was losing consciousness.

She could not see past her stomach; both men were leaning across her body to hold her down. She could feel the cold touch of steel when Sholl used a knife to cut her pants away from her body, and the trickle of blood that followed when he slit too deeply.

She promised herself she would not make a sound other than her shallow breathing. She would not. She would not… She felt Sholl's clammy skin against the inside of her thighs and she renewed her struggles despite the fact that she knew it was no use. She felt him pushing, pushing. The pressure was unbearable as he tried to invade her body.

A small sob escaped her before she could stop it. A heave from Sholl jerked her whole body upward and her tied hands pressed against one of the soldier's thighs. Freyja was silently begging unconsciousness to claim her when her hand felt the cool touch of metal. It was a blade. The guards on top of her were too busy playing the voyeurs to be careful. She only had one shot at this.

Her fingers closed over the hilt of the blade and she pulled it smoothly out of its sheath with a practiced flick of her wrist before burying it up to the hilt in the soldier's thigh. The man screamed and went up on his knees, exposing the back of his legs. Freyja used the small amount of slack she had to pull the knife out of the man's leg and slice the back of his knee, severing the tendons there. She felt hot liquid pour over her stomach from the wound. It was satisfying.

She took advantage of the other two men's surprise and landed a kick square to Sholl's jaw, knocking him backward. She heard a lovely crunch when her heel connected. Even better.

The third man was sliding away from her, panic on his face. She started sawing her arms free before the man realized he still had the advantage over her. One arm came loose, and then the other and she quickly took care of the injured soldier next to her, slitting his throat to stop his screams of pain.

Sholl was unconscious so she turned her attention to the second soldier. He took one look at her, at the hatred in her eyes, how she had so easily dispatched his comrade, and he ran. He made it three steps before his friend's knife buried itself into the base of his neck. She could hear the gurgle as blood began to enter the man's lungs, then he fell.

Freyja limped to Tripan and cut his bonds as quickly as she could. He had awoken as soon as the first soldier had started screaming. She knew it would bring the other troops as well. They did not have much time.

She kept getting dizzy. The soldier had hit her hard, and now that the adrenaline was wearing off, she could feel it. Her ribcage was on fire.

Freyja bent over just as she finished cutting through Tripan's bonds and vomited violently beside him, her stomach emptying itself into the dirt. At least, she thought to herself, all she had in her stomach was water. Her body started to shake. She knew she was going into shock.

Tripan rolled stiffly to his feet, ignoring her heaving, and grabbed her arm. "Let's go," his voice was raspy from lack of use. "We don't have much time before the patrols come back."

She was having a hard time concentrating. She waved a hand at him, shoeing him away from her. "You go, I can't go fast enough… Too dizzy."

Tripan had been looking away from her, out into the darkness, but he turned to her then. His eyes ran over her battered body, ripped clothes, bloody hands and he swore.

He quickly knelt next to Sholl and pulled off the man's cloak and the bag he always carried. He wrapped the cloak around Freyja's small waist and tied it there like a tartan.

He took her arm and they began to run as fast as their abused bodies would allow, towards the mountains. It was the only place that would provide any kind of cover. Their bare feet slapped hard against the ground. Soon there was a thick fog rolling around their knees. It was going to rain.

~

Tripan watched as Freyja's eyes began to close, her voice getting softer and more slurred as sleep finally caught up with her. Sleep or unconsciousness, Tripan did not know which. But the pain lines on the woman's face were easing and that was all that mattered to him at the moment. She deserved to rest. Her head, which was cradled on a small knapsack he had managed to steal from Sholl, had stopped bleeding an hour before.

Though he could not hear her breathing, Tripan could see the swirls that the woman's breath made in the fog that was settling around her. It was not long before he too let sleep claim him.

When Tripan woke, the moon was still high above him, the rain had stopped and the fog had dissipated. He had not slept long. Freyja was curled up tightly, her knees pulled against her chest and her hands tucked between her thighs for warmth. She had rolled over so that her back was to her companion, her head resting on the hard ground.

Tripan reached out and lifted the discarded knapsack that had been Freyja's pillow. He scooted closer to the cave entrance to glean more light from the moon before dumping the sack's contents on the ground between his outstretched legs.

There was a thin garrote with three knots along its length, a small vial of clear liquid, some silver coins, strips of used leather tack, bits of brass, and a rock. No food. Tripan was sure he could travel another day without food. His injuries were minimal. But Freyja? He doubted she could make it another day, not with her injuries.

In despair he looked out of the mouth of the cave, focusing on the grey and black shadows the moon had flung across the landscape. The ground was steep enough here that he could throw a rock straight out from where he sat and hit the top of a tree further down the mountain.

No wonder he and the woman were able to outrun their captives; horses were useless on this slag. Going faster than a sedate walk would have been dangerous. He barely remembered their headlong run up the mountainside. His eyes had been on the rocks directly in front of him, or on the shadows chasing behind him.

In terrain like this there was little food to come by. There were mountain goats, but he had no way of bringing one down on his own and he did not have enough time to wait for one to fall into a snare.

With a snarl of desperation Tripan picked up the rock from Sholl's pack and threw it violently against the wall of the cave. It hit with a resounding crack and blue flashes radiated from the place of impact, jumping along the flows of water that dripped down the surface of the rock.

Tripan swore and pushed himself away from the tiny bolts. They were so bright they had burned residual images into his eyes. He rubbed them with the back of his hand until the images dissipated, then moved to where the rock had fallen. He scooped it up, ready to drop it if it was hot. But it was cool to the touch and felt smooth in his palm.

He stepped out of the cave and turned the stone between his fingers to catch the light of the moon. It was completely smooth, and reminded him of one of the river rocks he and his brother used to skip along the glassy waters of Lake Gala when they were young.

Tripan raised the stone above his head and held it up toward the moon. The edges of the stone had a metallic gleam that cast a tint of blue onto the fingers that held it.

Blue? There are no natural stones of that color in this part of the kingdom. His mind raced with the possibility. Could this be the Valren metal he had heard about?

Clasping the stone tightly in his fist, Tripan hurried to cross the span between him and his younger companion. He went to his knees beside her and gently rolled her onto her back, sliding a hand between her head and the cold slag floor.

"Freyja? Look what I have." Tripan pressed his ear to the hollow of her chest, listening to the slow but steady beating within. He ran his free hand through her auburn hair, pushing it away from her face. Still she did not wake.

So, he had been right earlier. It was unconsciousness that had taken her, not sleep. Reaching out, Tripan clasped his hand against her limp one, catching the blue metal in between their two palms. The metal rested coolly on their skin.

Then, for the first time in his life, Tripan prayed.

Please... Please, if anyone can hear me, if this is Valren metal, we need your help. Freyja is here, and she is injured. I cannot move her and we have no food. Hello? Anybody... please... Freyja needs you.

If Tripan expected an obvious and reassuring response he was sorely disappointed. The stone stayed cool in his hand. He clutched it harder between their two palms.

Later, Tripan could not remember how long he stayed in that position — one hand firmly gripping his friend's, his mind calling out in desperation to anyone who would listen.

~

When Tripan awoke again, the sun was beginning to rise above the peaks of the Doranin Mountains. He could hear Freyja's shallow breathing next to him. She stirred when he moved. Sleeping then, he thought to himself, not unconscious. That was an improvement.

Outside of the cave he could see the sightless rodents that usually live under the slag of the mountainside. They were moving slowly over the slippery rock. The creatures surfaced after heavy rains when the ground was too wet for comfort.

The former captive got up as fast as his sore muscles would allow and left the cave. The native rodents made no move to run from him. Most likely they assumed the vibrations of his steps were the same as the beating of the rain against the earth.

He made quick work of catching a handful of the fat rodents and snapping their backs. Tripan dropped his bounty by the cave entrance and pulled the blue metal from his pant pocket, a grin forming on his lips.

"Well, if you can't help me find the Valren, you can at least cook our dinner."

He gathered an armful of fallen branches and built a tiny pyre with dried leaves in the center. Placing a small stone amid the leaves he stood back and threw the blue metal at it. His aim was true and the metal collided with the stone in a shower of blue sparks, which instantly set the leaves on fire. Within minutes a small fire was burning and skewered rodents were dripping grease onto the embers below them.

Freyja woke with little prompting. Her head was spinning and the edges of her vision kept fading to black. She felt like she was looking through a pipe, but she was awake and aware.

She was quiet while the two of them ate. Tripan stayed silent as well, letting her conserve her strength. The woman had to concentrate on her breathing between mouthfuls of food else she would end up gasping. Tripan added broken ribs to the long list of injuries he knew she had suffered. Freyja was sweating by the end of the paltry meal.

Tripan stirred the embers of their small fire and looked over at her. She had propped herself up against a rock, her eyes shut. He thought she was sleeping until he heard her take a deep breath and lean her head back. Her eyes opened, unfocused, staring up at the clear sky.

She did not ask if he wanted to hear more of her story. She just began, quietly and haltingly, to fill the dark void of silence.

"We left from Andora the next morning. The man Gareth and I never seemed to see eye to eye and, I suppose, none of the Valren made it any easier on him as we traveled. We are not used to the company of the weak or fearful, so my brothers and I did tend to ostracize him…"

~

Tripan and Freyja spent the night recovering as best they could in a small cave high up in the mountains. Freyja had finished her story about the events leading up to her capture.

The two companions found themselves shoulder to shoulder, staring out across the land that spread below them from the base of the mountain range. Freyja had talked through the morning and the sun had risen overhead.

The rodent she had the night before was more food then she had eaten in the past six days. Having full stomachs was lolling both of them to sleep. The altitude was not helping either.

Freyja used the silence to weigh their options. They had been running blindly the night before, only knowing that the higher they got, the harder it would be for Oparel horses to follow them.

Now, looking around, Freyja realized it would be risky to move. They were below alpine level, but still there was little cover from trees. They needed to move back down the mountain but would be easily spotted by scouts on the way.

Moving at night was another option. It meant slower travel and a greater possibility of injury, but she would rather risk a broken ankle than another run-in with Sholl and his men.

The sound of metal hitting stone caught Freyja's attention first. Tripan felt her stiffen next to him. Then he heard it too. Horses. At least five of them.

Tripan immediately crouched and moved back into the shelter behind them. Freyja lay down on her stomach; her cracked rib protesting wildly, and began a painful slide to the nearest drop. She heard Tripan hiss behind her when he realized she did not follow him, and the next thing she knew he was on his stomach beside her with a bag in his hand.

"If it's Sholl and his men we need to know where they are. We'll have to travel at night if we are going to get off this blasted mountain without getting caught." Her eyes scanned the side of the mountain below them, searching for movement.

"Maybe it's your family." Tripan began rifling through the bag he held, looking for the blue metal he had found the night before. "I couldn't show you this last night because you had passed out, but I held it as long as I could. Is it a piece of your metal?" He drew his hand out of the bag so that Freyja saw her garrote and, thank the Gods, the metal from her necklace shinning bright in the sun.

The look of joy that crossed her face made Tripan smile despite his aching muscles and protesting joints. She cupped the metal in both her hands and pressed it to her chest. She closed her eyes and forced her tired mind to reach out through the stone. *Brothers?*

The flood of warmth, reassurance and strength that hit her through the metal was astonishing. Every Valren within reach had his mind open, waiting for contact from her. Since Torne had found her years before, and given her the orack metal, she had never gone more than a few hours without it touching her skin. After being alone for over five days, the emotions pushing into her mind were overwhelming. She pulled back her reach, targeting the Valren closest to her to give her mind time to adjust. *Torne?*

The other Valren felt her confusion and dampened their connection to her, helping her sift through them to find Torne. In a matter of seconds he found her, their minds winding together like old friends.

Freyja, thank the Gods you're all right. We felt another's call and followed its trail as well as we could.

She felt him dig deeper into her mind, pulling information about what she could see in order to find her. He noted how high on the mountain she was and which peaks she could see from her current position.

Then he pushed even harder so that he could feel the status of her physical condition. His anger was immediate and she could feel it spread as the rest of the Valren picked up on the pain Torne was pulling from her. For a moment, when his control slipped, Freyja could see through Torne's eyes. She knew the second he locked onto her physical position and swung his horse's head toward the mountainside on which she waited.

We cannot come to you, Torne. There are troops searching for us still and we don't want to risk being out in the open. Neither of us is in any condition to fight. In the back of her mind she was still listening for the sound of hooves coming from below. She heard them, but they were getting softer as the soldiers drew away from their hideout.

Who is with you?

She looked over to Tripan, who was watching her face intently from where he lay on the rocks next to her. *Tripan. He is a Bartorin man, another hostage. You saw where we are?*

I will find you. There are eight brothers with me, and Brann. I am not worried about running into the Oparel troops. In fact, Freyja could tell he very much wanted to run into them.

Torne could feel the fatigue in her and retreated from her mind as much as he could without letting her go completely. He wanted to be able to feel any changes in case she ran into trouble. But he kept his touch as light as possible, using it as a guide as his horse galloped unerringly toward the base of the mountain.

"They are coming," she looked over to Tripan and let out a deep breath.

He was silent a moment before nodding his head. "You saved my life, you know."

"And you returned the favor last night. There are no debts between us." She ripped a length of cloth from the bottom of Sholl's cape, which she was using as a makeshift skirt, and ran the cloth through a hole in the orack metal. She tied it around her neck so that the metal rested on her skin.

Tripan clenched and unclenched his fists slowly. "They killed my family."

Freyja paused, studying the man next to her, then spoke. "If you want retaliation, stay with me. The Oparel will pay for what they have done these past days."

When he did not immediately reply, she continued on. "Tripan, why were they holding you hostage?" She knew Sholl would not waste his time on someone who wasn't important.

She did not think he would answer, but he did. "Tripan is my middle name. My real name is Leland Clonas."

"Clonas? Mad King Joran had a son?" She was shocked.

He shook his head slowly. "No, Hale was my father, not Joran."

She blinked at him, clearly startled. Hale was the Mad King's brother.

Tripan shifted nervously. "Freyja, please tell me what you are thinking."

"You need to stay with me…"

~

The two escapees moved back into their shelter, knowing it would take the Valren time to reach them. They sat side by side, listening for approaching horses in case the Oparel came back. Despite valiant efforts by the two companions to stay awake, they were both asleep hours later when the Valren found them.

It was a measure of their exhaustion that neither of them woke at the sound of heavy hooves striking slag on the slope below the cave. Freyja only stirred when Torne knelt in front of her, blocking out the light that had been resting on her face.

"Can you stand, little one?" His voice was soft, though rough with concern, and Tripan did not wake. Torne knew better than to touch her before she was fully awake and aware, so he kept his hands at his sides. He watched her nod and struggle to stand by pushing her back up along the wall.

She managed to get to her feet but sweat was beginning to bead on her forehead from the effort. Her ribs were screaming.

Torne did not ask if she could walk, knowing she would say yes regardless of her injuries. Instead he scooped her up gently with his hands behind her knees and around her back. She had always been light, but after six days with little food she seemed to weigh less than his saddle.

His sharp whistle brought two other Valren into the cave, and woke Tripan, who struggled to his feet and grabbed a loose rock, ready to fight. Torne looked the man over and deemed him harmless, too damaged and tired to fight even if he wanted to.

"Be easy, we are her brothers."

Tripan visibly relaxed, dropping the stone. The Valren came up on both sides of him, supporting him between their larger frames to help him outside. Torne followed behind with Freyja in his arms.

The other Valren had crowded Brann to keep him outside the cave. Torne had wanted to get to her first and assess her condition. When Torne stepped outside, Freyja had already fallen back to sleep, her head pillowed on his chest. Brann felt a deep stab of jealousy mingled with the relief of seeing her.

Torne handed Freyja over to another brother before gaining his mount. She was passed back to him without waking. He motioned for Tripan to mount behind Brann before he spoke to his brothers. "Find the Oparel. We will meet up in Della."

Torne and Brann turned their mounts, the largest in the group, and began a slow journey down the mountain. The eight other Valren, all mounted on the same kind of shaggy ponies Brann had seen Parth and Realla ride, began moving toward the pass. Their ponies picked their way along the loose rock like mountain goats, never stumbling. They may have been ugly, but they were perfect for this terrain.

When they reached level footing, Torne nudged his mount into a rocking canter and Brann did the same behind him.

Marrin troops had been amassing in the town of Della for weeks. The town was no longer contained within its walls, but sprawled into the surrounding fields. When they neared the town, to Brann's surprise, Torne did not head for the inn, or even for the Marrin soldier's temporary barracks. Instead he veered towards a small circle of wagons on the outer edge of the crowd. When Torne and

Brann drew up to the caravan, the gypsies were already outside waiting for them with water, food, and warm blankets.

~

Freyja woke slowly. She tried to open her eyes but found them heavy and reluctant to do her bidding. She kept them closed.

What she did know was that she was warm for the first time in days. Someone close to her was breathing the deep breaths of sleep. She recognized it as coming from Tripan. The man made a small snorting sound she had heard during their capture.

Her ribs were bound tightly, it felt like thick cloth had been wrapped around her feet, and what she assumed was a cool cloth dripped water down the side of her face from where it rested above her swollen eye.

As soon as she opened her mind to the orack metal around her neck she felt Torne with her, and knew he was beside the bed even though she could not hear him breathe. His thoughts met with hers.

It would have been just as easy to speak verbally, but there was a security in touching mind to mind. Her hand went to her necklace and she realized that the cloth from Sholl's cloak had been replaced by supple leather.

She heard Torne snort and felt the back of his hand rest against her cheek. *If there was ever a worry that our brothers would not wish to fight the Oparel it is now gone. The men who took you did not die well.*

Good. Even Torne, who knew her so well, was surprised at the malice he felt in her. She forced her eyes open and looked over to Tripan where he rested. *He is well?*

His wounds were not as extensive as your own, but you are stronger and more... accustomed to such things. Knowing her next question before she could ask he shook his head. *You have been here a day only. The last cona will arrive tomorrow night. On the next day we will be ready to hunt.*

He is Hale's son.

Surprise colored his thoughts. *One can only hope he has more of his father's qualities, and less of the brother's. His father was a good man.*

She felt her thoughts straying to Brann. Torne picked up on it immediately and gave her the information she wanted. *Brann is here. He is with his men. He wishes to see you. Your captain has a hot head in many situations, little one, but his restraint has been admirable these past few days. He travels well, not like most city men.*

He is not my captain, Torne.

He wants to be. Stubbornness is a trait we all have in some small doses, but you... How do you not see what he wants?

Torne saw heat creep into her face and did not tease her further. *Your armor is beside the bed, and your arms are here as well. Breyog has been put out with the rest of our horses. Everything has been made ready.*

Thank you, Torne. Is there food? She would have to regain her strength quickly if she was to leave with her brothers in two days.

I will have Brann bring it to you if that is your wish. He leaned over the bed a moment to remove the cool cloth from her forehead. She flinched. Torne's eyes rested on hers, his hand on the cloth. She had not flinched from him in years. He knew then that her scars were not only the physical kind. *Or I can keep him away.*

Brann had apparently won Torne's respect over the last few days.

Let him come.

~

Brann had seen the bloody remains of the Oparel men that the Valren had snared in the mountains. He had ridden in his first skirmish when he was only thirteen and had, by now, killed more men than he could count. News of the captain's exploits during the war with Bartorin had been turned into stories that parents told their children at night.

He was not one to be squeamish over blood and violence. But even so, Brann had been taken aback when the Valren rode into the gypsy camp, dragging sacks of dead bodies behind them.

It had taken Brann a moment before he even recognized the bloody masses as having been human. He silently thanked the Gods that his own men did not see the bodies being dragged through the mud and stone. He wanted his men working side-by-side with the Valren and they would not do so if they believed the Valren were so unremitting and uncaring of the dead. Even if the bodies were of the enemy.

From the moment their Jaryth had been taken, the Valren had not spoken a word to each other that Brann had heard. They must have been communicating through the metal that was hammered into their armor.

He and Torne had met up with eight others only two days after Freyja had been taken. Brann now understood how the stories had begun about the Valren being in league with demons. There were very few men in the world foolish enough not to be afraid of the brothers. They moved together like a pack of wolves. With the powers of the orack metal, they would always be a step ahead of their enemies.

Brann was thankful for them as he walked from his soldier's camp to the ring of gypsy wagons resting further out in the field. This morning ten more brothers had appeared in the camp. They sat among the wagons, three of them in front of the wagon that housed Freyja and Tripan. Brann knew, without doubt, that these men would form an almost impenetrable wall to protect their Jaryth. The safest place was inside that wagon.

The brothers were silent as he passed them, but their masked faces followed his every movement. Their masks stood out in grotesque forms, each one unique.

He climbed the three small steps to the wagon's door and ducked his large frame through the portal. When he stood, the canvas roof nearly brushed his head. He reached back and shut the door.

Freyja was in a deep sleep, calm in the comfort of knowing her brothers were nearby. But the smell of warm bread and broth woke her.

She pressed a finger to her lips, nodding toward Tripan, who was sleeping on a makeshift bed against the opposite side of the wagon.

Brann padded to the side of her bed and rested the food on his legs while he watched her push herself into a sitting position. He heard her breath hitch once and he knew she was still in pain. But she managed to sit, her back pressed against the wood and cloth wall. Brann gently placed the food in her lap.

She was starving, but knew she would just make herself sick if she tried to eat too quickly. With methodical care she ripped into the bread and used it to soak up broth before bringing it to her lips.

Brann shifted next to her, wanting to communicate without waking Tripan. Freyja held out a hand, motioning for him to wait, and took her necklace off. She handed it to him before reaching to the floor near the head of the bed to pick up what Brann recognized as a gorget. The curved metal would slide around her throat to protect her neck in a fight. It glittered blue even in the low light that fought its way into the wagon through the cloth roof. He realized it was a piece of her armor.

Her dark eyes studied his face, looking for a sign of recognition. Then Brann felt it. It was an odd sensation, having someone else dancing in your own mind. But it was not intrusive, it was thrilling. At first he heard a voice that seemed far away, and the more he concentrated on it the closer it came to him, until her voice was ringing clearly in his mind. *Brann?*

His answering grin made her stomach clench, she had almost forgotten how much he affected her. She realized she was glad to see him.

You can speak to me as well. She paused, trying to remember how Torne had taught her this trick. *Think at me, not to yourself. Find your mind's voice and push it toward me.*

At first his thoughts were jumbled. She caught them in snapshots of color and emotions, but slowly words began to form.

She helped him coax the words and suppress the rest. It would take him a long time to master the art of speaking mind to mind, but with her help he was able to latch onto his ideas and focus them. When the thoughts came together she almost shivered at the way his mind moved along hers. It was like a caress. It was no surprise to her that his first thoughts were of her own comfort.

Eat while we... talk. Is this called talking?

She grinned down at the food in front of her. *Talking is fine.*

He ran a callused hand over his face and through his dark hair. *I don't think I have ever been as scared as I was watching you ride out of sight with the Oparel.* Red and yellow colors followed this declaration.

She concentrated on chewing her food slowly, savoring the feeling of it sliding down her throat. It was a feast after being starved for the past five days. *I am certainly used to better company then the Oparel. But I've dealt with worse.*

She felt his gaze roam over her body. She did not know if he was with the Valren when they had wrapped and stitched her wounds, but she doubted that they had let him near her. He wanted desperately to know the extent of her injuries. *How did you escape?*

He felt her thoughts swirl for a moment before she spoke. It was obvious even to him that what she said was not the whole truth. *One of the soldiers became lazy. I managed to take his knife from him before he could react. After killing him I was able to cut my hands free and kill the other soldier in the camp. Tripan and I ran and could only hope that we would find a place to hide before the others found us.*

I am sorry you had to do that. He took her hand in his without thinking.

She watched his hand as it folded over her own but she did not pull back. *Do what?*

Kill a man.

I'm not. I have killed better men than they were, and I do not regret it. That time he could feel no dishonesty in her voice.

Brann reluctantly released her hand to allow her to eat. As he watched her he felt the thread of another conversation in his mind. He recognized Freyja's mind voice but he was picking up another as well. When Brann focused his attention on the new individual he came up against an invisible wall, which seemed to muffle his senses.

He reached out and touched Freyja's arm to get her attention and she visibly jumped at the contact. Her face blushed hotly when she met his gaze. He pretended not to notice and pitched his voice low so as not to wake Tripan. "Who are you speaking with?"

"Torne," she replied softly. "Can you hear him?"

"I can feel him, but not understand him."

She nodded. "Gather your men to you tonight. We will meet in the barracks and review the next plan of action two cries after the dinner hour. That was what he and I were discussing." She used the thick bread to soak up the last of the broth in her bowl.

Brann took it from her immediately and set it on the floor with a soft *tick*. He glanced over his shoulder to where Tripan lay, then he focused his thoughts toward Freyja once more. *How badly is he injured?*

Many bruises and cuts. Nothing that will not heal given time. He also broke two toes, but I believe that happened during our run in the night, and not at the hands of the Oparel.

And your wounds?

She placed a barrier between her thoughts and his immediately, frustrating him, and responded verbally. “I will be fine as well. Nothing is overly serious.”

Brann reached out and caught her chin in his hand. He turned her head so that he could examine the stitched wound above her eye. His hand was warm and rough against her skin. “I would appreciate it if you never lied to me so egregiously again.”

Her mouth twitched into a frown, but she nodded as much as his hand would allow. “I do not want you to be upset about what happened.”

“You think I should not be upset?” He was straining to keep his voice low.

“Yes, I do.” Even with the wall she put up between their mental connections he could feel a tinge of her confusion. “I understand why Torne is upset. I understand why all of my brothers are upset. But I do not understand your feelings at all. I would think you would be happy that this happened. After all, now this war is personal for us. You have assurance that the Valren will seek revenge against the Oparel. Doesn’t that help Marrin in the long run?”

He could not believe her words. His hand left her chin and moved to cup around the back of her neck. She remembered what happened the last time his hand strayed there and could not help but think about how wonderful his lips had felt on hers. “Despite what you think, this is not about Marrin and the Valren, Freyja. It is about me and you.”

She could not look away from the weight of his gaze. “I am not ready for it to be about you and me, Brann. Not yet.”

“Then you will have more time.” He picked up the empty bowl from the floor and stood, then quietly ducked out the door.

~

Freyja left the wagon while Tripan ate bread and broth. It was not the best of meals, but there are precious few things a stomach can handle after not eating for as long as he had.

The sun was low in the sky and cast long shadows across the fields of soldiers and horses. She watched her own shadow as she walked away from the town, noting with distaste how stiffly she was moving.

The Valren she passed bowed their heads to her. While they were close to the Marrin troops, in the public eye the Valren were a fighting unit, not a family. Appearances and formalities must be kept.

It did not take her long to find an unoccupied section of field. Due to the number of people moving in and out of Della every day the wheat had been trampled, creating a soft bed to walk on.

Freyja sat down, tucking her feet under her, and began to stretch out her aching muscles. She started with her fingertips and worked her way to her neck, rolling it slowly.

Feeling her muscles loosen was always relaxing to her. After having her hands bound for so long it seemed like a great freedom to expand them above her head.

Unlike the muscles that could stretch and would soon forget about being sore, her ribs were a source of constant throbbing. The Valren had bound them, which had helped, but the lack of mobility made her gait stiff and uneven. She would have to remember to remove the wraps before she did any real work.

She carefully stretched her legs out in front of her and pulled her body down until her head rested against her knees. Her ribs protested but she ignored them.

She stayed in that position, bent in half, while the sun set in the west. When she heard the first cry of the scout she slowly unwrapped herself. She stood. She didn't want to admit it, even to herself, but she was glad she would be seeing Brann again so soon.

~

Freyja entered the Marrin barracks with two Valren. Her brothers had both donned their masks before leaving the gypsy caravan.

The garrison was filled with soldiers, most were veterans but there was a sprinkling of new blood in the crowd as well. Their unscarred skin was unmistakable. When the Valren entered, the men, young and old alike, fell into silence. They'd had no contact with the brothers before this, and the masks the Valren wore did their intended job of intimidation. Freyja was certain that the Marrin men had been warned about the Valren's strange attire, but apparently it had not been enough of a warning. Half of the men in the room dropped their gazes to the tabletops, pretending the grain patterns in the wood had suddenly become fascinating. Others shifted in their chairs as if they were trying to figure out if they could leave quietly without being noticed. A few of the youngest looking soldiers even leaned back on their stools as if trying to put as much distance between themselves and the Valren as possible. Freyja was very pleased.

Torne's voice pressed into her mind. *My dear, you always draw so much attention to yourself.* She felt him grin.

I do believe it is Haron's mask that is drawing everyone's eye.

Freyja looked over her shoulder and up at the man's face. The mask staring back at her was etched to resemble a grinning man. There were laugh lines next to the eyes and Freyja always swore she could pick out the beginning of a jester's hat near the crown of the mask. When asked about it, Haron always replied that people deserved service with a smile. Even if that service was the slitting of a throat. She had to admit, seeing that mask come out of the dark was chilling.

They moved through the soldiers and into a small room partitioned off from the rest of the barracks by a thick canvas. The material was dropped into place behind them. Brann rose from where he sat and bowed formally to the Valren before nodding to Tripan. "You are all welcome here. Allow me to introduce my second in command, Ghent."

Ghent also sketched a bow to the Valren. Freyja looked him over, and she knew both Torne and Haron were doing the same. The man was built like a bulldog. He was barrel-chested, compact, with upper arms that looked like they were the same circumference as his thighs. He stood a good four inches shorter than Brann or Torne, but he was just as wide.

She spoke for the group. "It is a pleasure. My name is Freyja," she motioned to the Valren behind her. "Torne and Haron." As the Jaryth, and the only Valren in the small group not wearing her mask, she would do all of the talking for her brothers.

The men took their seats once more, except for Torne and Haron who remained standing behind Freyja, guarding her back as she spoke. "Our scouts have confirmed that the Oparel troops number little more than seven thousand men, only five hundred of which are cavalry. How many Marrin troops will we have by the end of the month?"

"No more than five thousand, though at least a fifth of that will be on horses." Ghent's voice was low and reverberated through his wide chest.

We will have to weaken the Oparel troops before they cross into Marrin lands. Nothing that a cona or two cannot handle. Haron was always more than happy to show off his skills.

Torne's thoughts came next. *The gypsies who have managed to slip through the mountain pass took note of the camp. The Oparel leaders have segregated themselves in more flamboyant tents than the other soldiers; they will be easy to pick out. We should have no trouble finding our targets.*

She addressed Brann and Ghent. "A small contingency of my brothers will be leaving tomorrow to cross the mountain pass. We will do our best to disrupt the Oparel while they are still on their own land. It will lessen the loss of Marrin civilians. We will be in communication throughout. Have your troops ready to march in three weeks time. We will stall the Oparel as much as possible until then."

A small contingency of my brothers? Torne quoted her. *You are not mentioning to Brann that you will be joining that small contingency?*

She shot him an exasperated look. *I am not in the mood for this, Torne.*

He took the hint and retreated from her mind.

"Your liaison will be Lintha. He has been ordered to relay any communication from the east side of the mountains directly to Brann. Ghent, you will also be informed if that is your wish."

"It is," Brann answered for him. "Ghent will be the primary contact. I would like to travel with the Valren to scout across the mountains. He will be in charge in my absence."

She could not see Torne's face behind his mask, but she knew he was grinning. *If he is traveling with us to Garnal I think he may figure out that you are there as well... But I may be wrong.*

If I didn't know better I would think you were baiting me.

Of course not, My Jaryth.

She pursed her lips. "My brothers will be faster to cross the mountains without the addition of any Marrin soldiers."

"I will not slow them down."

If he used one of our horses he would be able to keep up with us, but he would have to leave that hulking beast of his here in the camp.

Or he could just stay here, was her curt reply.

Ghent was in agreement with Brann. "A large group of your own people will be here with the Marrin troops. Sending our captain out with only Valren at his side will show the trust that we have built with each other. Quite frankly, My Lady, our men are uneasy with the Valren."

"And that needs to change?"

Brann cut in before Ghent could even venture a reply. "I will travel with the group across the mountains, and in return I promise not to interfere in any way. If I begin to slow you down," which he knew he would not, "you can move on ahead and I will catch up when I can. You would have no obligation toward my personal protection."

Yet again, Torne's thoughts came to her unwanted. *It may help your situation in the long run if he was to see you work, little one. Then he may finally believe that you are capable of taking care of yourself.*

And what, exactly, is my situation, Torne? She felt Haron graciously exclude himself from their conversation. She caught the mental image of him stuffing his hands in his pockets and whistling while he walked away, which was exactly what he wanted to do.

Do you still deny that he cares about you? Torne countered.

To you? Yes.

Then I would say the situation you are in is one of denial.

"Do we have your word that you will in no way interfere with the Valren?"

The reply was instantaneous. "Of course."

She nodded. "You will leave your horse here and use one of our own stock to traverse the mountain range. We will be leaving early so that it is dark by the time we reach the east slopes."

"How many of us are traveling?"

"There will be twelve of us, including you, Torne and myself."

Brann's eyes darkened and he stood. "You? You are completely malnourished, and I guarantee that you have at least one broken rib. You are in no shape to travel."

Freyja stood as well, though slower than he had. "Only a minute ago you swore you would not interfere with any of the Valren plans. Does your word mean so little? Your argument does nothing but waste time, as it will certainly not change our minds."

She bowed her head slightly in respect, turned, and left with her two brothers at her back. Even Torne's large shoulders could not buffer the swarm of curses that followed them out of the room.

~

Brann found the trip across the Doranin Mountains to be an enlightening experience in a few regards. First and foremost was the realization that the little mean-spirited beasts the Valren used for transport were not only rebellious, strong-willed, stubborn and ugly, but also highly intelligent.

He had been dubious that the pony the Valren led him to would be able to carry his weight under any strenuous conditions. But when he mounted the shaggy beast for the first time and settled himself into the saddle, the animal simply turned its head to watch him with one dark eye.

He learned that the Valren do not rely on leg signals like his own soldiers do when communicating with their horses. They assured him that the pony would respond to leg commands if need be. But they recommended either using the time it took to travel over the mountains to learn the voice signals the beast's are accustomed to, or just leave the pony to its own devices.

On closer examination of his pony's tack, Brann realized that his saddle was lined with pieces of orack metal beaten into the leather. Freyja had laughed when he asked if the pony could understand his words through the metal, but she admitted that they were taught to pick up feelings of need, direction and speed.

Brann put his pony to a test once the twelve individuals began to trot east toward the base of the mountains. The group had moved out at a steady pace for some time when Brann silently willed his pony to stop, putting some urgency into his thoughts.

The pony immediately came to a jarring halt. Its ears turned back, listening for further cues from its rider.

Brann had to admit that communication like this would be invaluable during a battle. Brax seemed to be able to read his rider's intentions during battle, but with the pony it was actually happening.

He silently urged the pony to catch up with the group, which it did without any qualms. As promised, the Valren did not bother to slow down and wait for him when he strayed, but he did see Freyja look back.

The group soon found itself in the shadows of the mountain. The air temperature immediately dropped when the ponies began their surefooted climb up the rocks. There was one easily traversable path through the Doranin Mountains, but they were not taking it.

By the time the group reached above alpine level Brann could see his own breath. The Valren never spoke during the trip. Not out loud at least. The sound of the horses' hooves striking the rocks as they scrambled their way up the mountainside was cathartic to him.

In the end he was content to stay in the rear of the group and keep an eye on Freyja. She was obviously comfortable in a saddle, never once losing her seat, even on the rare occasion when her pony did slip on the rocks. But she sat stiffly. Brann did not know the true extent of her injuries, but he could see she was hurting.

The Valren were indeed talkative during the travel across the mountain range, but they did not see fit to allow Brann in on their conversations. Freyja was quiet even through the metal, and did not join in on her brothers' conversations unless specifically prompted to do so.

She had known she would be unable to bring Breyog on this trip; he was simply not suited for mountain terrain. The ponies most of the Valren favored were bred by gypsy families and spent the first three years of their lives on the side of the steep mountains near Andora. The rocky terrain the riders now found themselves climbing was just like home for the ponies and they had little trouble. Freyja had purposely found a mare with a smooth gate for the journey, but even with that precaution her ribs were pounding.

She was so deep in thought she did not realize when Haron asked her a question until he nudged his mount next to hers and lightly tapped her on the knee. When she looked over at him he repeated his question. *We will stay with the original plan, then?*

Yes. She looked around her, taking in the entire group. *We will base directly west of Garnal, part way up the mountain. The gypsies marked a spot with adequate cover for us where we will be able to view most of the camp below.*

Haron, you and I will move in, the rest of you will provide visual cover. With my ribs being in the state they are in, I will take the kill and Haron will extract the officer to be interrogated. She knew it would take more physical strength to force a living person out of the camp quietly than it would to kill someone. Her blades were light as air.

She felt no resistance from them, so she continued. *Once we have a prisoner in hand, I will keep Brann away. He does not need to see the interrogation, only the end results.*

How do you plan on distracting him? It would be Torne who would ask such a question.

I think you have more important things to worry about, was her reply.

The group stopped early and spent the beginning of the night on the west side of the mountain ridge. They awoke well before dawn so that they could finish their travel down the east slope under the cover of darkness.

As they broke camp on the morning of the third night, Brann noticed two of the Valren moving among the ponies. The men were placing a roughly textured cloth around the animals' hooves. When the group began to move down the mountain, the cloth muffled the clicking of hooves against the rock ground. Sound, at least, would not give away the location of the travelers to any Oparel soldier.

They reached the viewpoint the gypsies had staked out and took a moment to break down the cairn marker. The Valren, with Brann among them, split into two teams and took turns scouting the area and keeping watch on the camp below them.

By the time the sun began to set, the Valren had their targets picked out and they were prepping for the night's work.

CHAPTER 5

Freyja took one more look at the camp below her before sliding the cool metal of her mask into place. Haron did the same beside her. The orack mask felt wonderful against her skin. It had been far too long since she last wore it. None of the Valren masks had eye holes, which unnerved even the most seasoned soldiers. The metal resting in front of Freyja's eyes had been hammered so thin that it was actually translucent to the wearer. The thin coat of metal tinted her vision slightly, but nothing more. Her eyes adjusted to the change in seconds. Because there was never any light coming from behind the Valren masks while they were being worn, it seemed to anyone looking at them that there had to be some magical way the brothers were seeing through the metal. In truth, there was no magic, just hours upon hours of painstakingly worked metal. There was a river of sweat pounded into each mask.

The two Valren moved from their rock perch and began their long crawl into the Oparel camp.

Everyone is in place. Brann, Torne and the rest of the cona were spread along the mountainside, giving them enough of a vantage point to see a good portion of the sprawling camp below. As long as Freyja and Haron stayed on the west side of the camp they would have visual cues from the others sent to them via the orack metal.

The edge of the camp abutted the mountainside, and though there was little cover to hide the two Valren, they did not have far to travel before they could slide between the enemy's tents.

Freyja had been watching the higher-ranking officers' movements earlier in the day and she knew where her target slept. She slowly crawled toward the lavish tent in front of her. To her left she could sense Haron veer away, making for the larger meeting tent where the officers had gathered hours before.

All clear in front of you, little one. There are two soldiers walking the main perimeter path between the outermost tent rows. Torne and half of the cona were spotting for her while the other half was following Haron's movements.

Torne's thoughts reached her again. *Freeze in three... two...* Freyja stopped her slow crawl as the two soldiers passed the tent in front of her and then were hidden again as they passed behind the next tent over. Though the moon was full, it would be hard to spot her in the high grass. *You're clear.*

She began moving once more. Her ribs were hurting, but most of the pain was covered by the adrenaline pulsing through her body. She stopped within fifteen feet of the nearest tent and settled herself into the ground, resting her head on her arms. Torne and his men would not take long to complete their part of this mission, but she may as well be comfortable while they did. *Haron?*

In place.

Torne, you are all set. We will wait for your return.

Though Freyja could get in and out of the camp quickly, Haron was going to have the task of dragging another body out with him. No matter how strong he was, it would not be easy to hide. The border guards needed to be disposed of before they entered the camp to ensure a safe exit.

Torne motioned for Brann to follow him and they both moved north to their targets. The patrol group they came upon contained three men. None of them seemed too concerned. After all, they expected no one to attack so close to the bulk of the Oparel army. Brann and Torne crouched low, out of sight from the group of men, and spoke quietly.

"The rest of the cona are taking care of the other patrols. This needs to be done quietly. I'll circle around. Get as close as you can. When my knife takes the first one you will have to act quickly on one of the others. I will take the last one as well."

Brann nodded, waited for Torne to leave, and then began moving forward to get into place for the attack.

It took Torne only moments to circle the men. They were standing in a loose circle, cutting at low branches with their swords in lazy arching swings. Torne hefted his knife by its six-inch blade and waited until all three men were looking away from him. As soon as they did, he struck.

His knife buried deep into the first soldier's neck, blocking any chance he had to call out and raise an alarm. As soon as the blade left his hand he followed in its wake, closing the distance between him and the two remaining soldiers.

The one furthest from him turned to face Torne and was hit hard from behind when Brann slammed his full weight into the man. They both hit the ground with a muffled thud.

The third man raised his sword in a halfhearted defense, taken so off guard by the attack that his mind was still processing the fact that he was being attacked.

Torne used his armored forearm to smash the soldier's nose, forcing the nasal bone up into the man's brain for a quick death. He turned and saw Brann had dispatched his target. His was a slower death, a knife in the side, but Brann's hand around the man's throat made it impossible to yell for help.

When the soldier under him ceased his struggle, Brann rose to his feet and took a quick look around. The whole attack had taken less than one minute. He pitched his voice low in case there were more guards nearby. "That was nicely done."

"We do try to be efficient. Freyja and Haron are probably getting bored and Haron has the attention span of a gnat." Torne placed his booted foot on his first target's back and gave a hard yank on his knife, pulling it from the man's flesh before cleaning it on his jacket. "We would not want to keep them hiding in the grass too long."

~

By the time Torne and Brann returned to their original post the rest of the Valren were already there. They were spread almost a fourth of a mile across the side of the mountain in order to retain all possible views of the camp below.

Torne clasped hands with a thin man of average height. The man's mask was a plain sheet of the orack metal with no etching or decoration. It was expertly fitted to his face, but there were no distinguishing marks. His name was Hyana. "The other four patrol groups to the north have been taken care of."

"Good, then Freyja and Haron should have no problems."

Brann cast his gaze to the north along the mountainside, spotting many of the Valren crouched in discrete rocks. They were wrapped head to toe in their cloaks to stop any light reflection from their armor, which would give away their positions.

He was just beginning to understand the havoc the Valren could bring down on a mass like the one resting unaware below them. Assassins were deadly hunters who usually worked alone. A group as large as the Valren with the skill, familial ties and orack metal working together could deal serious devastation on any group that foolishly stood in its way.

In a span of no more than twenty minutes this small group of Valren had killed twelve guards with not a soul in the Oparel camp being the wiser for it.

Torne moved to stand with Brann. The two men, with cloaks wrapped around them, would look like nothing more than another jutting rock face from the camp below.

They both stared down to where they knew Freyja was lying in the high grass. She must have been staying perfectly still because neither of them could distinguish her from the uneven shadows cast over the earth.

Torne opened his hand to Brann, showing him a small piece of orack metal. Brann picked it off the dark man's palm and rolled it between his fingers.

Worry about Freyja overrode any sense of caution and he automatically pushed his mind down to where she was laying. He felt her there, calm and relaxed. She actually seemed comfortable, exposed and alone near the enemy troops. There was no sense of fear in her.

He pulled his mind back from her and put the stone in his pocket. There was a look in Torne's eyes that Brann could not read. "You had better make your intentions clear to her, whatever they may be."

~

Freyja felt Brann's consciousness try to find hers, reassuring himself of her safety, then she heard Torne's thoughts in her head.

Clear ahead of you. Torne had moved back to his perch and now had an unobstructed view of Freyja's target — the flamboyantly decorated tent on the outskirts of the Oparel camp.

Once she heard him she quickly rolled to her feet and sprinted the few yards to the tent. The moon was bright, casting shadows in the camp, and she made sure to keep the tent between her and the moon so her shadow would not fall on the canvas walls.

She had always felt calm when she worked. Despite the adrenaline coursing through her body she was collected and her mind was at ease. This is how it is with all of her brothers, and why they are so effective. Emotions rarely get in the way.

Freyja kept her gaze ahead of her, watching the walking paths. She let her fingertips slide lightly along the fabric of the tent until she felt the opening. Her hand immediately moved to pull a small throwing knife from a sheath at her back and she slid into the tent without making a sound.

She heard two separate breathing cadences aside from her own. One was the deep even breath of a restful sleep, but the other was not. She quickly spotted the woman who was just beginning to sit up in her cot and crossed the distance between them, firmly pressing her hand over the woman's mouth and pushing her back onto the blankets.

Freyja removed her mask so as not to frighten the other woman, then lifted a finger to her own lips, signaling for silence. The wide-eyed woman below her nodded and stayed still. Freyja could see the slave mark branded on the woman's shoulder. It was no wonder the Valren had not seen this woman enter or exit the tent; she had been stuck in there. She would stay quiet. Freyja lifted her hand slowly from the other woman's mouth. Freyja winked at the slave, trying to keep the woman relaxed.

She knelt by the woman's cot and began to saw the cord that bound her hands and feet, all the while keeping her ears on the breathing of the man sleeping on the other side of the tent.

Freyja, your heart rate spiked, what happened? Torne's thoughts interrupted her.

There are two people in the tent, it was not expected. One is a slave. She will have to fend for herself once she is out of the camp. The woman's bonds snapped under Freyja's knife. She pressed the hilt into the slave's hands and motioned for her to begin cutting the cord off her ankles. When Freyja was done, she slipped her mask back on.

As Freyja moved across the tent toward the military officer she could feel the slave's eyes following her. The slave still had her smaller knife so she pulled a second one from a sheath on her thigh. This one was larger, more appropriate for a quick kill.

She looked down at the man on the cot. His toes were sticking out from under the deerskin hide he was using as a blanket. The gypsies had been busy and had found out that this was the man who had sent Sholl across the border for prisoners. He had a lot to answer for. Normally killing a man in his sleep did not appeal to her, but silence was imperative in this case.

In one smooth motion she used her left hand to gently cup the man's cheek and push his head to the side and upward, exposing his neck. Because her touch was so light the man woke slowly, not sensing any danger. By the time his eyes raised to fix on hers, her knife was already half way through his neck. Freyja held his head down while his body jerked on the bed. He bled out quickly and quietly.

Her left hand came away from his head sticky and warm with blood. She used the blanket to wipe off what she could, and then cleaned her blade with the same cloth.

She returned to the slave, whose eyes were as wide as saucers, and leaned down to press her lips against the woman's ear, whispering softly, "If you are still here in the morning they will kill you when they find this man dead. They will have no one else to blame. Stay quiet and follow me out of the camp. Keep the knife. You are from this area?" She felt the woman nod. "Can you make it home once we are outside the camp?"

Again, a nod.

It is done. Am I clear?

There was a moment of silence while Torne double-checked the area outside the tent from where he sat. *Everything is quiet. The next wave of border guards will not find their dead for another two hours at the earliest.*

We are leaving to the south to make it easier for the woman with me to find her way.

Another small pause. *There is a string of horses directly south. You will have to swing wide if you don't want to spook them. I see only two hostlers with them, no more than children. They will not be hard to pass.*

She took the slave by the hand and pulled her to her feet before letting her go and trusting her to follow. *Haron?*

Here.

All is well?

She could feel him giggle. Most of the Valren were calm when they worked but Haron had a bit of an odd streak in him. *Waiting... If he is on schedule the target should be here within moments. And you?*

Target is down. About to make my way out. Heading more south, so I will not see you on the way. Happy hunting.

He slowly disengaged his thoughts from hers.

Torne, still clear?

All is quiet.

She slid out of the tent and moved outside, the slave following close behind her.

~

The slave left her side once they gained the cover of new growth forest south of the camp. Freyja assumed she would make it home safely, but whether the woman did was no longer her concern.

She could feel Haron moving north of her. She had traveled far enough south that Haron would probably beat her back to camp even while carrying his now prone target over his shoulder. At least it gave the slave a better chance of making it home.

Traveling down a mountainside was always easier than going up. The southern pass of the mountain was steeper than the western slope and there were two places where Freyja was forced to climb to reach her brothers. The ache in her ribs was returning as the adrenaline wore off and by the time she reached the first of the Valren, she was sweating from the mixture of pain and physical exertion. She hid it well, but both Torne and Brann noticed her strain.

Torne had taken the role of emissary while she had been in the camp and walked without his mask on. It was for the benefit of Brann alone. The brother's were used to communicating and living with each other from behind the shields of their masks, but outsiders always found it unnerving. They were not privy to the silent communication available to the Valren because of the orack metal. Even the gypsies, who were considered family by the Valren, had a hard time speaking to the warriors when they were masked. Though Brann never showed any unease at the situation, a merit in his favor, Torne had still kept his mask buckled to his shoulder whenever they spoke.The two of them had obviously been working toward an uneasy peace.

They had perhaps two hours before they would need to move their camp higher up the mountain's slope. Once the dead soldiers were found, the Oparel would most likely send scouts in a wide circumference. That meant the Valren had to move further away to ensure security.

If they were well up the mountainside, they could easily kill a scout before he could return to base in the off chance they were found. The gypsies had left discrete markers showing them the way to a small glacier-fed pond where they would spend the remainder of their stay on the east side of the mountain.

Haron and Freyja ate a hot meal together while the Valren began to group for the anticipated travel.

How they managed to heat a meal without a fire, which would surely be seen from the Oparel camp, was beyond Brann.

They began to move as soon as Freyja was done with her meal. Haron's captive was still unconscious and tossed over the shoulder of one of the Valren. He would get passed from brother to brother during the trip but he was small and would not weigh enough to truly tire them. The ponies wore their soft boots, ensuring silence, and followed the Valren without needing rope or tie.

Torne? She felt his presence immediately and knew his gaze was on her back. He was at the rear of the group, watching the others make their assent up the rock. *We will purge the information from our captive tonight. We can set our own plan once we know what they are up to and how soon they will move.*

We will need Brann out of the way. He will not approve of what we do.

She agreed with Torne. Brann would not approve of their method for extracting information. *I can keep him occupied for an hour. You should not need more time than that.*

No, we will not.

They found the pond without mishap. It was a small body of water that Brann could throw a small rock across without much effort.

But the water was fresh, cold and clear. Small alpine trees, no more than 10 feet tall, rimmed the pond and cascaded south down the rocky slope. The tree's roots clung to moist rock surfaces with determination. As long as they stayed toward the side of the pond abutting the face of the mountain, the Valren would be able to light small fires without being seen from the camp far below. The gypsies had done well to find this hideout.

Hyana spread grain out for the ponies but they would mostly be left to forage on their own. They were used to fending for themselves on rocky slopes and could find nourishment easier than the men at this height.

Three of the Valren dropped their gear and immediately left the camp, taking up scouting posts without needing to be told.

Brann saw to his own pony, running his hands along the shaggy beast's legs and picking up its hooves to check for any rocks that may be stuck there. When he straightened from his task, Freyja was at his pony's head, rubbing the inside of its ear with her fist, to the obvious delight of the animal.

"Just a moment's walk away there is an even smaller pond with warmer water. I'm heading over to clean up a little before resting. Will you join me?" Her hand slid to the pony's cheek and gave it a small rub.

"Of course." He motioned for her to lead the way and followed close by her side. This was the first time she had voluntarily asked for his company. It gave him a glimmer of hope that their private encounter back in Marrin had not scared her off. After knowing what she had been through in the last week, Brann seriously doubted there was too much that this small woman could not handle.

It took them only a moment to reach the small pond. Though the Valren were not far away, the area felt secluded and private due to the winding contour of the mountain.

Freyja was the first to test the water. The two of them sat side by side on a half submerged rock within jumping distance from the shoreline. She slipped off a soft-soled shoe to dip her toe in the clear pond.

Brann noticed her unease when he sat down next to her. She put on a good show, but he could feel the tension in her body when his shoulder brushed hers. He did not want to spook her after she had approached him to join her so he slid behind her, facing away from her so the two of them were back to back.

"Varonda and I, when we were little, used to always sit like this." He gently leaned back, careful of his weight, until their backs were touching, helping to support one another. He waited for her to pull away, but she took his weight, leaning back as well so that their shoulders were pressed tightly together.

She felt the immense heat radiating from his skin seep into her tired shoulder muscles and down to her stomach. She took a deep breath and let it out again, willing herself to relax. "Were you guarding each other's backs from evil monsters?"

He chuckled low. "Guarding each other from our tutors usually. We did anything we could think of to get out of our classes and cause mischief."

"The Marrin people really seem to love her. That kind of loyalty is hard to find."

"Like you with your brothers?" He turned his head to look over his shoulder at her. She was facing forward still, but her head tilted slightly, aware of his change of position.

She paused for a moment and then conceded. "Yes."

"It is a rare quality you have; the ability to rally people together. It seems that any one of your brothers would die for you without question."

She turned her head as well and they found themselves almost cheek to cheek. Had she been taller, they would have been. "They would."

He eyed the cut near her temple. It was healing well, but there was still an angry red ring around it that spoke of possible infection. "Are you in pain?"

She reached up and touched the wound lightly. "It's nothing, really."

"When I was little, my mother kissed my scrapes and bruises and they always felt better. May I?"

"May you what?"

"Try to make you feel better." He did not wait for her to reply, but turned his chest toward her, his hand moving up to cup her chin. His lips found her temple and lightly brushed over the sensitive skin. Her skin was warm and inviting but he did not linger against her as he wished to.

"How do you feel?" he asked close to her ear. Brann barely had to whisper for her to hear him. She felt goose bumps race up her body at the intimacy of him so close to her. It was like he was sharing his most secretive thoughts with her.

"Truthfully, My Lord, I am beginning to feel a little lightheaded." There was no sense in lying. Her skin was reacting to his touch like it was something to crave. There is no way he did not feel the rush of heat he had ignited.

He released his hold on her chin and settled his back against hers once more, offering his support. "It is strange to me, that I should have such an effect on you."

He took out the small piece of orack metal from his pocket and showed it to her. "Torne gave this to me when you went down to the Oparel camp. The whole time you were near them, no matter how close the enemy was, I never felt a moment of unease come from you."

He put the metal back in his pocket. "The only reason I could feel when you killed the officer was because your attention moved from within the tent to the noises coming from outside because there was no longer a threat to you."

"Does it bother you? That I do not feel remorse?"

Immediately he shook his head. "No, but you can imagine my surprise when I can feel your pulse race from my touch, yet killing a man in his sleep does not phase you. Am I that displeasing to you?"

She pulled her feet up, her knees to her chest, and rested her chin there. She spoke quietly. "Actually, it is the opposite with you."

She shifted against his back, obviously feeling uncomfortable. "When you are close I want you to touch me. It is something I have never felt before… It is strange to me."

Her voice became softer with every word, making Brann strain to catch what she said. "When we were in the salle back in Calin, it felt so right to be close to you."

"But you were nervous…" he prompted her when she faltered to a stop.

"Before we reached Calin, when we were traveling south from Andora, I realized something that disturbed me. Torne felt it, too. I think that is why you and he are not the best of friends."

She let out a breath. She was sure that if he had been looking at her she would not be able to speak like this to him. The fact that she could not see him was giving her a measure of comfort. "I realized that I wanted to feel you, and let you have that same freedom with me."

He closed his eyes. He could feel her muscles tightening with every word she spoke. This was harder for her than he had ever realized. "Is that such a bad thing?"

"I had thought, in the past, of finding someone I knew well enough to try and help me get over my fears."

He felt an instant stab of jealousy at the thought of another man touching her, his jaw flexed in agitation.

"But the Valren are like brothers to me, and there was never anyone else I would consider." It was obvious in the silence that ensued, that the thought "until now" was in her mind.

Once again he prompted her onward. "And you are still unsure of me?"

She continued slowly, "You said you were surprised at the lack of emotion you felt from me when I was in the Oparel camp. To be honest, I feel that way because I'm confident in my own abilities. I am a fairly good hand-to-hand fighter."

That was something he could attest to.

"And with a blade, in all honesty, I don't believe I know anyone who can best me, despite my size. In the time I have come to know you, I have realized that I had entertained the notion of, well…"

"Making love?"

"Yes… with someone I knew I could stop whenever I wanted to, if I needed to." She hesitated and he waited in silence. "I don't know if I could stop you without hurting you… And I have come to realize that I do not want to hurt you. Ever."

Brann's chest constricted. She sounded so forlorn.

His own voice sounded husky. "The only thing you would ever need to stop me is to say the word."

When she did not respond he looked over his shoulder at her, his breath tickling her hair. "Do you believe me?" He could hear her breathing quicken to match his own.

"I'm trying to believe you."

"Let me prove it to you." He slid to his knees and turned to face her. She kept her back to him and cast a nervous look over her shoulder.

Freyja felt his hands press gently against the small of her back. Her body shuddered in reaction. She didn't know if it was from fear or longing. Maybe both. Probably both.

His thumbs touched at her spine and his hands reached out across her waist. He slowly began to knead the knotted muscles at the center of her back, his strong thumbs running in small circles over her shirt. Both of them were silent except for their breathing.

Freyja's was coming shallow and quick, causing Brann to chuckle softly. "Breathe; no one here will harm you."

She slowly began to relax and he moved his hands higher on her back, letting his thumbs glide under her shoulder blades with loving care. His hands slid up to her neck and he felt her fighting the instinct to jerk away from him. She had done the same thing that night in the salle when he had touched her there. It was more telling than she would ever know. Had someone tried to strangle her before? He wondered if he would ever know the whole story about how she came to be a part of the Valren. He hoped so.

His large hand moved from around her neck and closed into a loose fist. He began softly running his knuckles over the base of her neck until he saw her begin to relax once again.

"Thank you for trusting me," he breathed softly against her hair. And he meant it. He knew this was not easy for her and the liberties she was allowing him were more than he would have expected. He could feel the blood rushing to his groin.

His hands opened and spread across her shoulders and he felt her wince in reaction. He immediately froze. The back of her neck flushed.

"I'm sorry. When I was taken by the Oparel they were always overzealous when helping me dismount my horse." He could picture the soldiers shoving her from the saddle and he fought back the urge to growl. "I had forgotten that I still have a bruise there."

He could not pass up the opportunity. "That's alright. I know how to make it feel better, remember?"

He pushed her shirt aside and she felt his lips, hot and firm, against her bare shoulder. Her breath caught in her throat. If she had told him to stop at that moment it would have killed him, he was so enflamed by her. He wanted nothing more than to feel himself press into her inviting flesh. Go slowly; go slowly… he repeated the litany to himself over and over again. "Talk to me, love, tell me what you are thinking. You're not afraid of me, are you?"

She leaned her head back to rest against his shoulder and raised her dark eyes to his bright ones. "I'm not afraid of you, Brann. I just don't know what to do; this is so new to me."

He held her gaze while his hands moved back to her waist and slid under her shirt, his fingertips running over her stomach in a light caress. "You can stop me whenever you want, love."

While he spoke, he gently pulled her back against him so she could feel the length of his chest. It took him a moment to realize that he had called her his love, twice. Though it should have bothered him, he felt nothing but pleasure at the realization.

When his hands moved to the sides of her breasts, he allowed his knuckles to run along her skin. Her gaze immediately fell from his and he could see her cheeks flush. Most of her weight was resting against his chest and he would have felt her move if she had tried to get up, but she did not.

He lowered his head until his lips were against his ear. "Gods, I have wanted to touch you like this for so long." The heartfelt confession warmed the nervous pit in her stomach but did little to ease her mind. Before she could make up her mind to tell him to stop she felt his hands cup her breasts and his thumbs lightly circle her areolas.

She sucked in a breath. She felt her nipples harden under his caress. Her mind may not know what it wanted, but her body did.

"Do you want me to stop?"

Brann's voice sounded neutral but she knew from the pounding of his heart that he wanted desperately for her to say no. She did not trust her voice, so she shook her head. His hands felt too good for her to want them to stop their exploration. For the first time since the Valren had found her all those years ago, an intimate touch did not remind her of her father and his friends' abuse.

Brann's body broke out in a light sweat from the strain of keeping himself in check. He was considered one of the most eligible men in Calin, someone with the Queen's own ear, and he had bedded his share of willing women. But he had never felt his body consumed with the need that was in him now, with Freyja. Her body, athletic and tight, would push a saint to lust. The fact that she had no sense of her own physical appeal only made him want her more. Her body was begging for release but she had no idea how to achieve it. He wanted to be the one to show her.

His hands left her breasts and she felt an unexpected sense of loss. His arms, being careful of her ribs, gently pulled her back tighter against his chest. This time she could feel the state of his arousal at the small of her back, and he knew it, holding her against him.

Little one, we have the information we need. Torne's thoughts met with hers quickly before retreating back to his own mind.

Brann felt her freeze in his arms. "Freyja, what's wrong?"

"Torne has information from the Oparel officer." She heard Brann let out a small moan.

"His timing leaves something to be desired." He wanted to keep holding her, she felt so right in his arms, but she was already beginning to untangle herself from his grasp.

"Brann, I'm sorry. I did not mean to…" She turned to face him and made to stand but Brann laid a restraining hand on her shoulder.

His other hand cupped her cheek; his thumb ran over her high cheekbone. "Give me one more thing to remember this night by before you run away."

Her brows furrowed in confusion, obviously not understanding what he meant. Then she understood, as Brann leaned forward and ran his lips over hers. Her tongue hesitantly slid along his lower lip, wanting to taste him.

Brann closed his eyes tightly and locked his hands at his side to keep from pulling her against him and taking over the kiss. He knew she needed to stay in control, but it took every inch of will power he possessed to let her have it.

When she pulled away from him her eyes were dark and she would not meet his gaze. He could see the heavy rise and fall of her breasts with each strained breath she took.

She stayed quiet while Brann got to his feet in front of her and helped her up. Once she was steady he let her go. Before she could leave the rock, he lightly touched her arm one more time. "Freyja, I hope you will not fear being alone with me again."

Her eyes met his before sliding away, but she seemed more embarrassed than scared. She answered very softly. "My only regret is that we did not have more time."

Then she stepped from the rock and returned to the Valren camp. It took Brann a few minutes before his body was calm enough for him to follow.

~

When Brann reached the Valren camp he was shocked to see the Oparel prisoner unbound and sitting on the ground. The man was swaying slightly from side to side. Freyja, Torne, Haron, and a man named Ramma were clustered together. They looked up at Brann when he entered the camp. They had obviously been waiting for him.

Brann kept an eye on Torne as he approached, trying to determine if the other man knew what went on between him and Freyja, but Torne's face was expressionless. The man did not need the orack mask in place to hide his thoughts; he was impossible to read. If Torne was upset about Brann's advances toward Freyja he would probably not know it until Torne had a knife to his neck.

Brann joined the group and cast a glance to the Oparel behind them. "You trust him unbound? And without a gag?"

The man named Ramma shrugged heavy shoulders, "He will not go anywhere. And will not talk." The four of them watched Brann carefully. They were waiting for his reaction. He knew, before he even moved to stand in front of the Oparel soldier, that he was not going to like what he saw.

Brann stood in front of the man sitting unbound on the ground. The man was still rocking slowly back and forth. Brann had seen caged birds make the same repetitive movement. The man's eyes were glazed over. He looked drugged. When Brann snapped his fingers in front of the Oparel's face there was no change in his movements, not even a blink.

Brann looked over the man to the Valren who had moved up behind him, his eyes caught Torne's. "What the hell did you do to this man?"

"We took the information we needed from him. It is unfortunate that we did not have more time, else we would have been gentler in our handling." The way Torne said it made Brann believe it was not unfortunate at all.

"Is he drugged?"

Torne and Ramma shook their heads no. Haron just stood there smiling, as he always did. Freyja made no move at all, just watched him and stayed quiet.

Ramma finally spoke after seeing his confusion. "The orack metal is good for sending information to our own men, and we learned a long time ago it is also good for getting information out of people."

"How is this done?" The thought of someone essentially being mind-raped was repulsive to him. "It cannot be voluntary."

Ramma crossed his arms over his chest. "Voluntary? Of course not. Fact is, the more you fight, the more it hurts."

"And this man was fighting you?" It was no wonder. Who would want someone they didn't know rattling around in their mind?

Heavy shoulders rolled in a shrug. "We could have done it without breaking him, I suppose, but what would be the point?"

Ramma was right. Even if the soldier's mind were sound after the Valren extracted the necessary information, they would be forced to kill him. They couldn't just let him run back to his camp, and he was a liability as a prisoner.

Brann knew Ramma was right, but the callous way they spoke about death bothered him. People should feel something when they are forced to kill another.

"And did you get the information you were looking for?"

They all nodded. Torne spoke. "The plan is to cross the mountain pass in one month's time. They have a unit of a thousand cavalry staked up in Marrin in a town called Cambar that they have been building for over a year. Since they have been moving men and horses three or four at a time, their small ships have gone undetected by your fleet.

He continued. "The army that moves through the Doranin Mountains is only a diversion to draw the bulk of the Marrin soldiers past the smaller Oparel party. In one month and two days they will make for Calin and try for the Queen." He paused. "It's a risky plan… but they know Marrin is weak in the number of able-bodied men left after the Bartorin war."

Freyja watched Brann's fist clench at his side and his eyes darken with anger.

"Brann," Freyja said, focusing his attention on her. "Brome is aware of the complications and is moving the bulk of the Valren to Cambar to take care of the threat there. Our job now is to stall these troops until the rest of the Valren can return to Della. With the commander dead they may try to pass over the mountain early so their troops do not have time to stew on the situation and get skittish."

"How do twelve people delay an entire army?"

Haron giggled, actually giggled, before he spoke. "We always have a plan. This one is a fun one." His eyes slid to the Oparel who was still swaying gently back and forth. "He won't feel a thing."

CHAPTER 6

The Oparel soldier, former prisoner and informant to the Valren, now hung, completely skinned, from a lonely tree that stood no more than a hundred feet from the southern edge of the Oparel camp. In hindsight, Brann guessed the man would have been glad he had lost his mind the night before.

To the Valren's credit, the man was killed quickly before they began the long process of skinning him. The Valren ponies had been restless all night because of the scent of blood in the air but they kept quiet despite rolling eyes and flared nostrils.

The Oparel had yet to send scouts up into the mountains, so the Valren had a perfect view of the activity below from their own camp. The scene looked like a beehive that had just been struck with a club. Tiny soldiers were flying all over camp. There were no formations. Messengers in bright robes sprinted from one tent to another. It was quite a display for the Valren, who had woken early to watch the activity.

By now the Oparel were aware of a few things: All of the scouts stationed on the south and west sides of the camp the night before were dead; the commanding officer of the army was dead; and there was a dead comrade hanging from a tree nearby. They had found the hanging man early in the morning, attracted to him by the voices of a murder of crows feasting on the suspended meat.

Brann watched Freyja assessing the chaos below. "Well, you have certainly got their attention," he said.

She gave him a half-hearted smile, her eyes never leaving the Oparel camp. She was waiting for something.

Brann followed her gaze to the brightly colored tents. "What are you watching for?"

"Water."

~

A handful of the brothers were constantly outside the Valren camp, scouting all sides of the mountain ridge, always vigilant. Brann and Freyja sat near each other, as they had for the last half hour, also watching the camp below.

He had tried three times to begin a conversation about their rendezvous the night before but every time he did one of the Valren would wander over within ear shot. The third time it happened Brann was fairly certain it was a deliberate ploy on Freyja's part to keep him from broaching the uncomfortable subject.

He was trying to work out a plan to get her alone so they could speak when, at his side, Freyja grinned and pointed to the field north of the camp where most of the livestock and food stores were kept. "There it is." The other four Valren with them all moved to sit close by, their unmasked faces turned to the land below.

Brann did not see it at first; he did not know what he was looking for. Freyja had said water, but what did she mean by that? Then he realized that the field below them was beginning to shine, reflecting the light of the sun into their eyes.

The water table in the field below was slowly rising; there looked to be a quarter inch of water permeating the surface of the field outside the camp. The cattle grazing to the north were churning the field into a giant pit of mud and Brann could see the water seeping slowly toward the stationary tents.

The cattle fields are soaked, Torne, the water is just beginning to reach the camp itself. Pull it back to a slow runoff to keep the field soggy. We don't want them to move quite yet, just be uncomfortable.

She lifted her gaze to Brann's face and smiled. His stomach did that curious flip that only she could make it do. "Only idiots base their camp on the lowest terrain in the area."

He grinned back at her, her energy infectious. "Where is the water coming from?"

"Torne and the others are diverting it from the Estone River. By tomorrow the Oparel will have to move the cattle a mile to the north to give them enough land to graze on. It should only take three or four of us to drive the cattle north toward the ocean once they move away from the main camp. We can scatter them across the range from there.

"The Oparel will never find enough food to keep their troops on full ration without their main source of meat," she explained. "Either that or the entire body of them will have to go wrangle." Her smile turned into a mischievous grin. "Either way, we gain more time, and they are unhappy."

"How are they diverting the river?" Brann had been wondering what the Valren were doing when they disappeared from the camp with a few of the ponies. They held their secrets close so he hadn't even tried to ask them, knowing he would be ignored or just waved off. The men were often gone too long to just be scounting an area, and they all seemed to return from the same direction when they reentered the camp, even if it was at different times.

"It's not the whole river they're altering; they just made a little offshoot to the side." She grinned. Seeing a plan put into action was always a pleasure for her. "There are tributaries into the river from up in the mountains. The gypsies gave us a lay of the land before we left Della, so we've know it was there. The ponies proved sturdy enough to pull down some of the larger boulders and it was easy enough to redirect the water downhill with those stones and a few smaller trees that were cut down. Obviously the Oparel were not thinking strategically when they built their camp. It really is in a terrible spot. Never choose the low ground." The last sentence was said almost to herself, as if she were quoting an old teacher.

Brann considered the Valren's tactics. When he was growing up in Marrin he learned to pay attention to his surroundings during a fight, but he never would have through of something on this scale. None of the Marrin men would. They hadn't been trained to. He had been taught an honorable way to fight. Head on. Face your enemy. These tactics should have disgusted him but the truth was he admired it. The Marrin army was severely outnumbered. These dirty tricks were exactly what were needed if they were to have a chance of a fair fight in the future. He wondered what else they had lined up for the men in the valley below. He almost pittied them. Almost.

The more time he spent with this group the more he realized he could learn from them. There was no laziness, no unnecessary loafing with them and there was never a moment in which they were not completely aware of their surroundings. Even when they knew they were not in immediate danger from an enemy, they lived and breathed tactics and fighting skills.

Brann took another long, hard look at the valley below him.

There were no physical attacks on the Oparel camp that night. After the loss of troops from the night before the officers were being more careful about where they stationed their scouts. Everyone was staying within sight and earshot of the main camp, which allowed the Valren to settle more completely into the cove that was hosting them.

~

The next morning there was a noticeable fatigue running through the Oparel camp. Apparently, finding a skinned body the morning before had an effect on some of the men's ability to sleep. There was already talk of descent being whispered across campfires.

As the Valren had anticipated, the Oparel drove their cattle north early in the morning. They traveled over a mile before finding enough unspoiled ground for the beasts to graze.

A small contingency of fifty men was left with the three thousand head of livestock while the rest traveled back to camp to begin the arduous process of moving the army's entire food supply from one side of the camp – the damp side - to the other. From the amount of wheat and flour bags Ramma counted going into newly erected tents in the south, and the ones that were tossed carelessly into the wood, it looked like an eighth of the Oparel food stores had been ruined.

The Valren, who had detoured the flow of the Estone River, returned to the main camp hours later. Each brother was holding a steaming mug of thick broth, as they stood shoulder-to-shoulder, eyes drifting restlessly over the enemy camp.

Freyja was the first to finish her meal. She bent to put the cup down and then straightened slowly, stretching her back and testing her ribs. Still sore, but not as bad as it could be. "Who is staying back?"

The Valren all knew what she meant. Even Brann had begun to pick up the nuances of the group and found that he could use the orack metal in his possession to follow their seemingly fragmented conversations. She was asking who would be staying back later that night when a group of them followed the cattle north.

"I will ride if need be, but my ribs could use a day's rest." Normally she would be the first to volunteer and the Valren knew it was a measure of her discomfort that she was passing. They all nodded their assent.

"I'll stay as well," said Ramma. He had the best night vision of the group and would come in handy scouting around the camp.

Brann should stay as well, little one. He is a good fighter... better than I thought, and quiet despite his size. He would fit well with us, but we will need to move quickly and he does not have experience with our ponies.

The Valren all sent agreement to her through the stone, though they were reluctant to do so. There were fifty men with the cattle, and only the twelve of them. Nine would be moving out to the north. They would need to be effective. But they were more concerned with her unease of staying at camp with only the three of them. They knew she wanted to avoid being alone with Brann, even if she wasn't going to say it aloud.

It grated her to ask, but she did anyway. "Brann, will you stay back with us as well? Three pairs of eyes will be enough in the camp, but it should not just be Ramma and me."

As expected, he agreed without complaint. "Whatever you wish."

The group broke off without further discussion. They had trained together most of their lives and knew what was expected of them. The ponies were tacked and waiting only minutes after the decision had been made to move the cattle that night.

One by one the Valren pressed a kiss to Freyja's cheek before they mounted up. Each said something softly to her.

Torne was last, his right as the Jroth, and kissed her cheek gently. He pulled her into a tight hug to hide his words against her hair. "If Brann lays a finger on you without your consent while we are gone, he will be the next one we skin and hang from a tree."

Freyja chuckled and gave his chest a small push. "No need to get snarly on me."

He backed away when she pushed him, giving her space, but he caught her chin in one of his large hands. "I am serious, Freyja."

Her eyes held his and she nodded. "I know."

He released her, letting his knuckles slide over her cheek before settling atop his mount his mount. The nine Valren moved off quietly, hooves wrapped to muffle sound. By the time they reached the bottom of the mountain it would be fully dark. They would remove the hoof coverings and make good time heading north to the cattle. If all went well, the fifty Oparel men guarding the livestock would be dead before the sun rose again.

~

Brann took his turn settling the three ponies that remained in the camp. They were restless and obviously wanting to join their brothers and sisters moving down the mountainside.

He kept a calming hand on his own borrowed pony's neck while he watched Ramma and Freyja. Ramma was pulling a tightly wrapped spool of stiff cloth from his saddlebag. He straightened, feeling Brann's eyes on him. "I ask that you take the first watch."

Brann nodded, picked up his weapons and buckled them against his side. The Valren had been taking two-hour watches since they arrived at the camp and he knew he would be doing the same.

Freyja surprised herself by joining Brann before he left the camp and brushing her fingers along the back of his hand in a small but intimate caress. Neither one spoke, but Brann felt her touch all the way to his toes. His groin tightened in response. It was going to be a long two hours.

Once Brann had gone, Freyja found a rock and sat. Her head came chest high on Ramma. At thirty-seven years of age Ramma was the oldest living Valren and the man that Freyja would be inclined to call father instead of brother. His was usually the voice of reason in a group filled with men who liked to be aggressors.

"Off with it," he said. He put the stiff cloth down on the rock beside her and helped her pull her shirt over her head. Her ribs and chest were bound so tightly that the movement was hard to accomplish on her own.

She dropped her shirt onto the ground beside her without a second thought and pulled her undershirt up so that it bunched around the bottom of her breasts. The treating of wounds was something that was always necessary in their group, and exposing her skin to Ramma raised no alarm in her head.

With deft movements, Ramma found the end of the wrap and began to unbind her bruised ribs. She helped when she could but knew from experience that the best thing she could do was to sit with her hands up and let him do the work.

When the cloth finally fell free she took a deep cleansing breath. Her ribs stung but it was worth it. Knowing how she hated to feel restricted, Ramma said, "Let's take care of your face before rebinding your ribs."

She smiled in thanks and put her hands down to her sides before turning her face to the moon so Ramma could see her better. He had a cool cloth in his hand and she could smell the medicine on it. He was quiet while he cleaned the wound above her eye. It had been healing well but was deep enough to warrant concern about infection. His face was close to hers as he cleaned the wound and she grinned up at him. "What would I do without you?"

He snorted. "You'd probably be six feet under by now." His eyes dropped to hers with a knowing look. "I will stay near to the camp during my watch if you wish."

She raised a brow at him. "Have you been talking to Torne?"

His gaze softened and he touseled her hair. "Lovely, I know you. I've known you since you were still tripping over your gangly legs and couldn't hold a dagger to save your life."

He became more serious as he continued. "You are not one to hesitate. You can be ruthless, and I have seen you do things that would have caused me to pause. But Torne is worried about how you act with Brann. The whole group can feel your reluctance to aggress with him around, even when he does overstep his bounds. It is unlike you."

Her lips pursed and she took the cloth from his hand, holding it to her own wound while he bent to retrieve the new wrap that would secure her ribs. "He has done nothing wrong."

Ramma's sharp eyes rested keenly on her own. "The orack metal told a different story last night."

She cursed under her breath. "I thought I had cut you all off."

"You did for the most part, but you know the link between you and Torne is stronger than with the others. You can break it when there is distance between you, like tonight, but not when he is just a short walk away. And not when you are being… distracted."

She put down the cloth and raised her arms again so he could begin the long process of wrapping her ribs. He started right below her breasts, holding the end piece in place until he made the first loop which would keep it tight. He reached around her to begin the second loop and Freyja caught sight of the laughter in his eyes.

"If I broke off contact with you, but not Torne, how do *you* know what I was feeling last night?"

Now the man rolled his eyes skyward and tightened the bracing about her ribs. "I near got a cramp in my neck watching the Jroth pace back and forth while I was digging in the Oparel soldier's mind. I lost count of his rounds when he passed in front of me seventy-three times. I knew he had no qualms with what we were doing; he has rifled through many unwilling minds himself, and so it had to be you. He covered himself quickly once you showed up, but he was itching to get his hands around someone's neck last night. Preferably Brann's."

Ramma made quick work of stitching the end of the cloth to secure it in place. "Now eat," he said, pushing a bundle of bread, cheese and meat into her hands. "You lost too much weight while the Oparel had you. You look half-starved."

He stood looming over her like a papa bear until she popped a piece of bread and cheese into her mouth. She finished the food in front of her before picking up her shirt and gingerly pulling it over her head. Her stomach was upset but it had nothing to do with the food. Ramma would take the second watch, which meant Brann would be back soon. And they would be alone.

CHAPTER 7

There had been little movement in the camp. Pageboys and slaves could be seen scurrying from tent to tent but the soldiers themselves were subdued. Brann kept a careful eye out from his vantage point, but the lack of activity allowed his mind to wander. And no matter how much he tried to fight it, it kept wandering to Freyja.

It had felt so right to have her in his arms, her back pressed to his chest. They fit perfectly together. He still did not understand how she had gotten under his skin so quickly. From the second he saw her on the beach he had wanted to bury his fingers in her hair and taste her. Being so close to her, yet having to keep his distance, was taking its toll.

Before he began to head back to camp, Brann thought of every fat old man he could to try and cool his loins. The plan seemed to work and his discipline was back under tight rein when he reached the Valren encampment.

The first thing he saw was Freyja's naked shoulders and back, the only thing covering her torso was stiff cloth wrapped around her ribs and chest. Heat flooded his body again. He could hear his own heart pick up to a pounding rhythm. He glimpsed her skin for only a moment before she pulled her shirt back over her red hair and settled it around her shoulders, but it was long enough. He gritted his teeth in frustration.

He was so focused on Freyja's back that he didn't notice Ramma until the man cleared his throat right by his side. "See something you like?" Before Brann could answer, Ramma continued, "Try to get her to eat before you both take your rest. She needs to put some weight back on if she is going to heal properly."

The Valren slipped on his ghastly mask and strolled out of the camp as silent as a shadow.

Brann checked on the ponies before he approached Freyja. She thought he was trying to give her enough time to get used to the idea of being alone with him, but in truth, he was giving himself time to cool off. He hadn't been so besotted since he was ten years old and met his first girl with green eyes.

He gave his pony a quick pat on the neck before picking up the food satchel Ramma had left behind. Her eyes were on him the whole time, but they never reached his face. Was she still embarrassed?

In a conscious effort to ease her worries, he took a seat on the ground in front of the rock she was perched on. It gave her the higher ground and she would not have to crane her neck to look up at him. Not that she was trying to watch his face.

He broke off a piece of bread and handed it to her. She took it and began to nibble on the crust, thankful to have something to do with her hands.

"I should probably get some sleep while I can," she said.

Brann forestalled her with a light hand on her foot. She froze immediately at his touch. "Will you stay and keep me company while I eat at least? Plus, you should share this with me. You look like you're starving."

She let out an unladylike snort. "You and Ramma both, you're acting like I can't take care of myself."

"I know you can take care of yourself, but I am worried about you." His touch on her foot became a caress as his hand slid up the back of her calf before letting her go.

She looked weary. "I'm surprised you are still with us."

"Why would I not be? I have more of a stake in this war than you do."

"I thought what you saw last night would push you away from us." She finished the piece of bread and rubbed her hands on her thighs to rid herself of the flour on her fingers.

"You would be surprised at what I have done for my country."

"You would be surprised at what I have done for my brothers," she shot back.

He paused, letting his gaze wander from her toes up to her eyes. "Are you trying to bait me?"

"I just think you should be warned, Brann." She waved her hand in front of herself in frustration while she spoke. "You call me 'lovely' and 'sweetheart,' but you don't know me. You have no idea what I've done in the past. If you did, you would not be quite as smitten as you seem to be."

"Smitten?" His teeth flashed in a roguish smile. "You think I am smitten?"

Her gaze shifted away from his, as she got more nervous. "Well… whatever you want to call it."

He reached up from where he sat and put his hand on her knee, palm up, asking silently for her hand. She hesitated, but complied, resting her fingertips lightly on his palm. He gently closed his hand around her smaller one. "There is a difference between being smitten and truly caring for someone."

"Yes, there is."

That got a laugh out of him. "I am not smitten." She looked like she wanted to argue with him, but she kept quiet. He let go of her hand, knowing it was making her uncomfortable. "Can we talk about last night?"

In the early morning light he could clearly see her flush. "We don't need to."

"I want to."

"How does it feel to want?"

Instead of getting mad at her retort, his eyes warmed. "You get fresh when you're unhappy, you know that?"

Her back stiffened. "We do not need to talk about it."

"Coward," he whispered up at her, knowing it would goad her.

And he got the desired response. Her eyes flashed angrily and she leaned in closer to him. "You're calling me a coward? Should we take bets like children to see who can sneak further into the Oparel camp without getting caught?"

He leaned in as well, until they were only inches apart from each other. "You may be brave in the battlefield, Freyja, but you are scared to death of touching me and feeling something that you do not understand."

He saw the hurt in her eyes before she looked away and he immediately regretted his words. "Freyja, sweetheart, prove me wrong. I know you want to."

When she didn't move he tried again, telling her the absolute truth. "I have tried so hard to leave you in peace, but I cannot. I need to be near you, I need to know you are safe. It was like hell sitting up here knowing you were down there alone."

She wanted to kiss him; he could see it in her eyes. Still she hesitated so he clasped his hands behind his back. "Kiss me. I swear to you I will not touch you. You will always be in control."

She leaned in until her lips were a scant inch from his, but she could not make herself close that last bit of distance. "Brann," his name on her lips caused a shiver to race down his spine. He clenched his hands tighter behind his back until his knuckles turned white. "I do not understand what you are feeling…"

"Yes you do. You feel the same way I do."

Did she? Was he feeling the same conflicting emotions that she was?

"I want to touch you more than anything, but I don't want to scare you. Please. Come to me instead."

It was the way he said please, his voice strained, that made her realize he was hurting just as much as she was. She did not want to be the cause of his pain.

Her tongue slipped out to wet her lips before she closed her eyes and pressed her lips to his. He was far enough below her that she had to brace her hands on his shoulders to keep from falling off the rock and into his chest. Her stomach clenched as the heat of his skin warmed her face.

He leaned forward, deepening the contact between them, but kept his hands clasped tightly behind his back.

She could feel the strain in his muscles where her hands rested on his shoulders. The strength there made her draw in a quick steadying breath. When her lips parted his tongue swept along them, tasting her, before he pulled back with a small growl. "Freyja, I need to touch you. May I touch you?"

His hands moved from behind his back to hover a hairsbreadth from her face, waiting. She felt herself nod before she truly registered what he had asked. His hands slid over her neck, pulling her harder against him. His tongue passed her lips, forcing her to give more of herself to him.

His hands were incredibly gentle on her face, suggesting strongly that she stay pressed to him, but not forcing her to do so. His left hand moved down her neck to her shoulder and back. He felt the ridge of a scar running along the length of her shoulder blade and he hastily broke off their kiss.

She was so surprised by his action she didn't protest when he stood up and moved behind her to see the scar with his own eyes. When he realized the size of the old wound, he saw red. "Who the hell did this to you?"

She blinked at him. Scars were such a common occurrence that it took her a moment to realize what had upset him. "They're only scars, Brann. They've healed."

"All of them?"

"Yes." She couldn't keep the anger from her voice. "I am well aware of my imperfections. I do not need you shoving them in my face."

He moved in front of her again, so that their eyes could meet. When he was standing he was a foot taller than she was where she sat on the rock. She had to look up at him. That made her even more irritated. He knew she had a violent past, but seeing the scars on her back had shaken him.

"I just wish I had been there," he said.

"Why?"

"So I could have killed him." He knew who had done it. It was an old scar, one she must have had since she was a child.

She reached up to touch her shoulder, finding the scar he had noticed, as if she needed to touch it to remember how she had gotten it. "I took care of that for you."

He closed his eyes and took a deep breath, reining in his emotions. "Every time I say I wish to help you in any way, you try to start a fight, or prove you can do everything alone. Why face something alone when I can be with you?

"Deep down, you want me as much as I want you." Brann said. "Let me take care of you tonight. Not because I pity you, or think you weak, but because I want to. I need to."

Her eyes had widened during his speech. When he reached for her she blurted out the first thing she could think of. "Ramma just bound my chest…"

His eyes softened and his lips turned up into a small grin, knowing she was in a near panic. "I can rebind it when I am done."

Her mouth turned dry. "Done with what?"

This time he did laugh, but it was soft. "With pleasuring you."

"I don't think you can."

He quirked a brow, looking affronted. "What did you say?"

She realized what she had said and covered her mouth, mortified. "That was not what I meant. I was talking about rewrapping my ribs."

His hand reached out to cup her chin, forcing her to look at him. "You believe me when I say I will not hurt you."

It was not a question, but she answered anyway. "Yes."

He bent over her, his lips brushing her cheek before pressing lightly against her ear. "We will go slowly. I promise."

When she felt his hand on the cloth binding her ribs she stopped him. She knew that with the cloth gone he would see far more scars on her body than he would be able to handle. "Leave it, please."

He hesitated, but agreed. His lips found hers once again, tenderly kissing her. He could feel her slowly relaxing against him. He waited until all her resistance melted before pulling back from her.

"Come with me." He took her hand and led her to his sleeping roll. His thick travel cloak was already spread out and he gently pushed her down onto it.

He knelt in front of her, eyes locked with hers, and untied her orack necklace. When she realized what he was doing she made to protest but he stopped her. "This should be between you and I, no one else. And I don't need a piece of metal to tell me what you want and feel. Your body will tell me…" He placed the necklace on the ground beside him.

His words made her shiver. "Brann, I don't want to give myself to you yet… I am not ready."

That 'yet' caused his blood to heat with anticipation – it meant that some day she would be ready. "There are other ways to give you pleasure."

Brann was true to his word. He went slowly with her.

She was weary at first, hyper vigilant to everything he did, every move his hands made. It took her a long time before her mind started honing in on the pleasure Brann was creating, instead of her worries. For the first time in years she dropped her guard, closed her eyes and focused inwards, on what she was feeling. Her reward was a rush of pleasure that had her arching against the hard rock at her back. She barely noticed when her own fingers fisted into his short hair and pulled him tighter against her.

Her last coherent thought was that she was glad Brann had taken off her orack necklace. This moment in time was for her and Brann alone.

Brann kept his eyes on her face while her body came down from its high. There was confusion in her eyes, but pleasure as well, and he saw no lingering fear. He could tell the moment her mind cleared of its sexual haze because her cheeks flushed to a bright pink that he could see even in the near darkness.

"I can't thank you enough for giving me this gift, Freyja." He bent his head and brushed his lips across the corner of her mouth.

She stared at his lips when she replied. "What gift?"

"Your trust."

That did get her to meet his gaze, and Brann saw her exhaustion as clear as day. He forestalled any further conversation by wrapping her in his cloak and telling her to wait for him.

He returned a few minutes later with a cloth and a small bowl of cold water, which he used to clean first Freyja then himself. By the time he repacked the bowl and joined her in the cocoon he made she was already sound asleep. He settled in behind her, one arm looped over her stomach while his fingers splayed over her soft skin.

He had no idea how she was going to react in the morning, or what he would do if she began to regret what they had done. He heard her sigh in her sleep and he tightened his arm around her waist. There was no way he was going to let her go.

~

Torne was still covered by the cloak of darkness when he hunkered down within earshot of the Oparel soldiers. The soldiers had settled in together, posting only two men on watch, both of which were found and dispatched with ease. The sounds of cattle were all around him, shuffling in the night, covering any noise that he or his brothers made.

Torne and Kuja had taken up the two most precarious positions for the attack. They were on the ground and near the Oparel. The rest of the Valren were still on horseback, leaning low over the strong necks of their mounts and unrecognizable from the thousands of cattle between which they moved. Once the sun came up that would change, but for now they would remain unnoticed, for a few more minutes at least.

Are we ready?

They were silent, even in his mind, but he could feel their assent. They were primed and ready. Torne could feel their anger at the hurt done to Freyja festering in them still. He slid his hand into the grip of his weapon, the favorite weapon of the Valren. It was familiar and cool to the touch. He knew the exact balance of the metal in his hands and the leather straps wound around the mental bar against his palm were worn and shapped to fit his hand perfectly from years of use. It was like an extentention of himself.

His hand closed around a small bar, fitted to his palm, and he strapped the four-bladed weapon to his hand with well-worn leather. All Valren carried such a weapon. The jagged blades could rip through skin, leaving behind a wound that looked like giant claw marks. It was the signature the Valren left behind on their victims, a calling card. The cold bar felt good in Torne's hand, like an old friend. When he was holding this weapon he didn't have to think about there the blades ended, or how his balance would need to shift when he attacked someone because of the weapon's extra weight – it was ingrained into him thanks to countless years of practice. His body knew what it meant when it gripped the metal and leather – it was an adrenaline rush like nothing else.He felt his pulse speed up in anticipation of what was to come.

Torne placed a calming hand on the gelded beast standing next to him so it remembered where he was. Its head was down, resting. When the bovine jumped, Torne wanted it to be away from his own smaller body.

Happy hunting, brothers.

South of him, on the other side of the Oparel, came a loud howl and a series of sharp barks. It sounded like a pack of wolves had erupted in the middle of the herd of cattle.

A second later, just as planned, all hell broke loose. The cattle spooked and began a headlong run away from the disturbance. The bull near Torne sidestepped once, felt Torne against him, then took off in the other direction, lowering its head and merging with the rest of the herd. Torne could hear the screams of the Oparel, some of whom, he hoped, were getting trampled by the large panicked beasts. They looked like giant shadowy boulders careening wildly all around him.

He ran straight for the camp. Dodging the cattle was like trying to swim up a waterfall, but he and Kuja hit their first two targets together without incident. Torne saw the enemy soldier's eyes widen in alarm as he jumped away from a raging bull and came face-to-face with Torne. Before the man could utter another cry Torne's bladed hand raked the man from shoulder to hip, disemboweling him in one smooth action. He saw another soldier drop to his left as Kuja mimicked the attack.

Torne barely dodged the horns of a panicked bull when he moved further into the camp, catching two more Oparel in the back as they turned to run from the charging two-ton animals. Both went down and Torne could hear them being trampled as he ran past to find his next target.

A third man spun around to face Torne and made a feeble swipe with his blade towards the Valren's neck. The blow was so weak that Torne did not try to stop it with his weapon; he simply raised an armored forearm and let the orack metal send a deadly shock through the blade and into the man's heart. The Oparel collapsed in a twitching heap.

It took only moments for the bulk of the herd to move through the Oparel camp. The obstruction of sight the cattle had caused began to thin out. Torne saw a group of men running alongside a cow to avoid being trampled and he tracked the night skyline to find one of his brothers. Reflections from Haron's mask identified him. *Haron, group of five north of you, twenty strides up.*

Torne saw Haron urge his mount ahead, fighting through the cattle to find its way to the enemies. The Haron spotted them with Torne's help and they were soon overrun. Haron dispatched three of the men before the other two could turn around and fight. When they did, Haron's pony reared up, its hooves connecting with the skulls in a resounding smack that could be heard over the din of the rampaging cattle.

Torne was outside of the rushing herd now, though he was still near the Oparel campground. He and Kuja stood with their chests heaving, counting the number of enemies who had fallen. Torne saw one man trying to crawl away despite what looked like two broken legs. He calmly walked toward the man while he checked in with the others. *Four down on my end. Looks like thirteen were trampled in the initial push. Haron, I saw you take out those other five.*

Nay, only three. My little beastie took care of the other two. Haron gave his pony a firm slap on the neck in thanks.

The other Valren checked in with their counts. There were still four or five stragglers hiding somewhere in the herd, but they would be found quickly by the mounted Valren.

Torne reached the man who was struggling on the ground. The enemy lay on his back, panting, staring up at the metal face of the Valren above him. Torne's mask caught the moonlight, giving it a ghost-like quality.

"Mercy… please." The soldier spoke in his native tongue.

Torne replied in the same language. "No."

A few seconds later Torne walked back to Kuja, blood stained the front of his armor. He looked up at the stars and then back to his brother. "Not a bad night to be outside, huh?"

The other man grinned behind his mask. "A very nice night…"

~

The sun was due to rise in under an hour's time. Torne regained his pony and the group soon split. Half of them herded the cattle with amazing efficiency further to the north. They would continue to do so until they reached the sea. The others turned their mounts south back to the mountains to rejoin Freyja, Ramma, and Brann.

Torne reached out to Freyja through the orack metal but could not find her. He immediately sought Ramma, his fist clenched at his side.

Torne. How did it go?

He ignored Ramma's question. *Where is Freyja?*

There was a short pause. *In the camp.*

Where are you?

On watch.

You left them alone?

Do you seriously think I would have left if Freyja did not want me to?

A resounding string of curses filled the air.

~

Freyja opened her eyes right as the sun began to roll over the horizon. She squinted, knuckled the sleep from her eyes, and let out a little groan.

A deep chuckle came from behind her and she froze. It took her a second before the events of the night before hit her full force. The feel of Brann's hand on her hip felt better than she could have ever imagined. But it also brought images to mind of her arching herself against his strong body. Gods, had she really done that?

She felt his breath tickle her ear as he whispered to her. "Freyja, there is no need to panic now."

She bristled and began to deny that she was panicking then came to the realization that the short shallow breaths she was taking were indeed the beginnings of full-blown panic. "I am not panicking," she muttered.

His hand squeezed her hip affectionately before he let her go. "Of course not." Apparently she needed time to adjust.

Brann detached himself from the warmth of her body and knelt beside her. "I'll get us some breakfast. Ramma should be back soon. Stay here and rest."

Freyja watched him go then put her hand to her neck unconsciously, looking for the comfort of her orack metal. She had forgotten that Brann had taken it off. How could she forget such a thing? The necklace was on the ground by her side and she quickly put it back on. The weight of the stone was reassuring. *Ramma? Torne?*

Good morning, Jaryth... Ramma's voice was neutral in her mind.

Freyja, by all that is holy… Torne's voice was not.

She cut him off. *Torne, tell me you are all alright.*

Of course we are alright. Are you?

Why wouldn't I be? She wrapped Brann's cloak around her and began to stand. She was sore where Brann had stretched her. She did her best to block any of her stray thoughts from Torne, but they had always shared a closer bond than any of the others. He knew what had happened.

His voice was clipped. *We'll talk about this when I get back.* Then she felt his consciousness leave her. Apparently he was just as uncomfortable knowing what she had done last night as she was.

It was Ramma whom she felt next. *I'll be back to camp in a moment, just making my last sweep.* He was giving her fair warning. She took it at face value and quickly dressed herself before wrapping Brann's cloak around her once again. His scent was oddly comforting and she was not yet willing to give it up.

Brann came up behind her and wrapped his arms around her shoulders, pressing a mug of broth into her hands.

"Ramma will be back soon." She did not know what else to say to him.

"I know." He took her shoulders and made her turn around to look at him, which she reluctantly did.

"You're not afraid to face me, are you?"

"I'm facing you right now."

"That's not what I meant." He found himself grinning. Gods, she was exasperating when she was flustered. "You have no regrets?"

Ramma stepped into view, catching her eye. Brann caught her chin and turned her attention back to him, waiting for her answer.

"No, Brann. No regrets."

He gave her chin a squeeze then let her go. Brann found another mug, filled it with broth, and passed it to Ramma. The man had his mask off, but Brann could do little to read his face. He must have been watching Ramma too closely because the man leaned in to whisper to him. "It's Torne you need to worry about, not me."

Ramma straightened and filled them both in on what he heard from Torne. "They should be back within the hour. The cattle are still moving north. They will be scattered along the coast. The Oparel will be short of food in a matter of days. We will have to see if they sit and try to regroup, or attack early."

Brann frowned. “We need them to delay, not attack early.”

Freyja blew over the top of her mug. “That’s why we need to go back in and remove more of their officers.”

“After the first two died they placed much more security in the camp. You won’t be able to sneak in like you did last time. Besides, the officers are never alone anymore.”

“Their priests are left alone, and the slaves have access to every tent in the compound,” she replied.

Ramma was already nodding when Brann crossed his arms over his chest. “You are going to kill the priests? Please tell me you are not.”

“You don’t believe in what they do. Why would it matter if they were priests? Take away their religion and they are just like any other soldier.”

“They are still holy men in their own right.”

She looked skeptical. “We’ll speak of this to the others when they return. If they agree, we will go in tomorrow at dusk.”

She knew whose side they would be on. So did Brann, and he hated it. She finished her breakfast and let Ramma take the cup from her. “I’m going to sleep until they arrive.”

Neither man argued. They could see how tired she was.

It took her longer than usual to fall asleep. Her mind was surprisingly calm, despite all that had happened between her and Brann. But she found herself missing his warmth at her back. It was over an hour later when she fell into a fitful sleep, curled into a ball.

~

Ramma was standing beside Freyja, using a small tool and what looked like ink to paint the mark of a slave onto Freyja's shoulder. It resembled a tattoo from afar but would never hold up under close scrutiny. Brann had argued about the plan with Torne when the man arrived back at camp, but he knew it was useless. The Valren would do what they wanted, and if he complained too much, they would just leave him out of any future plan.

For the second time that week, Brann had to watch Freyja sneak off alone into the Oparel camp.

Freyja snuck near one of the soldiers' latrine pits and smoothed her hands over her new attire of itchy and thick wool. The camp slaves did not have uniforms and they, for the most part, had been seen wearing the worn castoffs of soldiers. The clothes she now wore were from one of the smaller men the Valren had killed. The clothes were overly large, but she did not plan on wearing them for long.

She dumped water from her kidskin over her head then raked her fingers through her hair. She ruffled the red lengths until they were all dripping, some of them framing her face in the way she knew many men liked. If anyone took a good look at her they would assume she had been out at the river bathing.

She noted where the latrine pit was in relation to the rest of the camp then made her way between the tents, head bowed and eyes downcast. With so many people clustered together there was a steady flow of bustle moving in and out of the tents. She put on an air of submission, walking quietly and making sure not to look at any of the soldiers in their eyes. She followed the tents to where she knew the head priest was lodged.

She let her shirt slide off one of her shoulders to bare her tattoo. The shirt was so large that the front dipped down to expose a portion of creamy skin. Perfect for what she wished to accomplish. She kept her gaze down, hands folded in front of her, and stepped into the tent.

There were two men inside. One, as expected, was the head priest. The second was an ordinary soldier who was genuflecting in front of him, obviously performing some kind of devotion.

Both men looked up at the interruption. Freyja could feel their gazes turn hungry when their eyes raked over her exposed skin and wet hair. The water in her hair managed to work in two ways; it made her hair shine in the dim candlelight of the tent, alluring the men, and the cold water dripped onto her skin, which gave her a rash of goose bumps. To the men in front of her the goose bumps and tightened nipples seen through the fabric of her shirt were a temptation that set their mouths to drooling.

"We are done here." The priest spoke softly and waved the soldier to his feet. The man stood and walked out without a fuss, but Freyja could see the tightening of his pants from his spiked lust.

She kept her eyes down as would be expected of a slave, but watched the priest's feet as he came closer to her. The moment he reached for her she slid her blade from a sheath on her wrist, flipped it around in her palm, and smashed the pummel into the man's temple. She knew exactly where to hit. He dropped like a stone.

She left his side to tie the tent flap closed behind her and doused all but one of the candles in the tent. She hoped any passersby would assume the priest was sleeping and leave the tent alone.

It took her a few minutes to push and drag the heavy man into a limp seated position in front of his cot. Her ribs complained at the abuse and strain but she ignored them. She kicked the man's legs wide apart and knelt between them. She placed her palms on his temple then closed her eyes. The orack metal on her necklace grew warm as she pushed her consciousness into the priest's mind.

Her stomach tightened against the taint she felt coming from the priest. Her mind touched his and tried to recoil, but she forced the connection despite her own distaste. She easily broke through the barriers of his mind and dove headlong into his thoughts.

The man in front of her was not an evil man, but he was far from kind. Thoughts of lust and wealth were dominant overtones of his life as she filtered through it. She focused on the ideas of Marrin, Calin and the Marrin Queen. When she did so, the priest's thoughts shuffled themselves before her mind's eye then came into sharper focus. She took full control and sifted out all pertinent information, not caring if the rest of his mind would crumble from her meddling. He would be dead soon anyway.

She felt a bead of water from her hair trickle down her neck but did not take her hands from the priest's head. It took her less than five minutes to glean the information she needed. She heard the rumble of the roaming guards' steel-tipped boots as they made their rounds through the tents. She sat motionless until they passed.

Once the men were out of earshot she took her knife and slit the priest's throat, making sure to keep herself away from the spray of blood. It would not do to be caught leaving the camp with her sleeves stained blood red. She stood, stretched her protesting ribs, and then opened her mind to the whole of the Valren.

She expanded her awareness to them and they each took hold lightly, anchoring her so she would not have to expend more of her energy to keep the contact strong. She felt Torne lend his strength to help her reach the far away brothers in Andora.

My brothers, there is a spy in Calin. She took the mental picture she found in the priest's thoughts and pushed it to them. The picture was weak, but they would be able to use it.

Parth replied first. *That is Laren, the Queen's own advisor.*

Haron's laughing thoughts came next. *The Queen is going to be so mad.* Haron could find humor in anything.

She addressed the men at Calin next. *The Queen will not believe you if you go to her directly. It would be the word of strangers against her trusted friend. Do not confront him until I get back to the capital with Brann. I wasn't able to determine from the priest how this man was connected to Oparel. There may be more like him that we have yet to find.*

Priorities?

Keep the Queen safe. Then we will exterminate the rest of the Oparel in the city. Laren will get twitchy once he realizes the troops he is expecting from the mountains are not coming. Make sure he does not get to the Queen. Have the gypsies start sniffing around as well.

Understood.

She broke contact and rubbed her hands on her shirt to warm them. She took one more look at the priest then untied the tent flap. Her eyes were downcast as she walked the worn path to the latrine pit. Once there she picked up her kidskin from where she left it and began the long jog back to the Valren camp.

Torne, the army is going to be on the move in two days. We'll pull everyone back to Della. Brann and I will head south to Calin from there. You will lead the stand in the north.

~

Brann watched the Valren prepare the ponies for the ride. They would move back to Della to pick up their horses then Freyja and Brann would head to Calin on the larger, faster animals. The rest of the Valren would stay in Della to help with the oncoming battle. The Marrin troops were going to be severely outnumbered and would need their help.

Ramma came up beside Brann and gave him a friendly nod. Brann shook his head in agitation. "She needs some rest before she can travel across country without hurting herself further. Or are you all too busy to notice she is still favoring her ribs?"

The older man was thoughtful for a moment before replying, picking his words carefully. "She is more capable than you give her credit for. If she cannot do something, she will tell you. She's slept on her horse more than once. I am sure that is what she is planning again."

Ramma gave him a light slap on the shoulder. "She does not need someone to give her permission to do things, Brann. She needs an equal partner. If you haven't noticed, she leads. The rest of us try to keep up."

Brann gathered his things and packed them alongside Freyja's. He was up on his pony and ready by the time she arrived at camp. She swung up onto her own mount without a word to the other Valren. Torne handed her a tightly packed ration of food that would be easy to eat with one hand. She thanked him with a nod and the group left, headed back to Della.

~

True to Ramma's prediction, Freyja slept on her horse. There were rings on all of the saddles that allowed the Valren to strap themselves in if need be. In truth they had been put on so that any horse could carry equipment, or a dead body, as the need arose. But the Valren had discovered years before that the rings were also good for catching some sleep while riding. Freyja gave a silent command to her pony to stay with the others while she strapped her legs in. Tying herself tightly to the saddle with strips of leather, she made a cocoon out of her cloak and promptly fell asleep.

Some of the Valren nudged their mounts ahead of hers until her pony was in the middle of the group, the most protected position. They knew from years of experience that she would not be coddled in any way while she was awake. As Jaryth she always expected to be under the heaviest amount of threat but while she was asleep, the Valren could watch over her.

~

Della came into sight when the group rounded the side of a lesser mountain crest and the ground began to level off. The ponies, who caught the scent of their herd, picked up their pace and made short work of the rest of the trip. Their little legs were surprisingly quick despite the heavy men they carried.

The Valren had their masks in place before they reentered the soldiers' camp. Even Freyja had slipped her mask back on. They were in the public eye once more, and appearances counted for a great deal. Brann felt his heart constrict every time he saw her mask. The beauty and sadness reflected there were impossible to ignore.

They joined the other Valren first. There were more brothers there now than when Brann had left days ago. Each metallic face, some beautiful, some grotesque, kept the other Marrin soldiers at bay. The Valren wanted to be left alone, and they were.

Even though Brann knew Freyja and the others had been communicating during the long ride over the mountains, he was still surprised at the efficiency of the group as a whole. They had food and bedding prepared for the travelers, and others were on hand to take ponies when they arrived. Being able to debrief her men while still in the saddle and miles away saved her a good amount of time as well. If not for Brann's need to inform Ghent of the next stages of the plan, the two of them could have been off on the next leg of their trip in minutes.

Instead, Torne and Freyja joined him to meet with Ghent. He could feel them, always on guard, at his back. They were surrounded by his people yet they were still not relaxed. He doubted there was much that went unnoticed when the Valren were around. The Marrin soldiers hailed him when he walked by, but they kept their distance. The Valren were not like their own men at arms, and were obviously feared.

Ghent, unlike the other soldiers, met him with a firm embrace and a polite bow of his head to the two Valren behind him. Freyja's voice was clear behind her mask. "How have your defenses been improved since we left? Are you ready for an attack?"

Ghent nodded crisply. "The men have all been working alongside your own up on the ridge. The only way the Oparel can get out of the mountains to Della is through a specific run, the same way you came. We've completed all the plans Lintha drew up for us. Many tons of rock and slag are perched along the ridge. They will come tumbling down with little persuasion. If Lintha's calculations are correct, it should easily plug the ridge and slow the army."

"They will still make it through eventually." Brann's eyes were dark. He was uneasy about leaving his men, even though he knew he was needed with the Queen.

The older soldier nodded and crossed his arms. "They'll make it through alright. But it will take some days to dig their way out. The Valren are a canny lot, Brann. Lintha has plans to let a group of the men through before triggering the slide. Cut a bunch of men off from the others. This way we can take them out in a chunk while we outnumber them. Some will be crushed by the rockslide, and the others we will deal with when the time comes. None of your men are squeamish, Captain. They know what they need to do."

"Yes. I just wish there were more of them."

Torne spoke up from behind him. "You have the Valren as well. The Oparel soldiers will be cold and hungry by the time they arrive. They have no meat left and most of their food stores have been ruined. It is forcing them to attack before they are truly prepared. Morale is worth its weight in gold in a battle, and they are running low."

Brann and Ghent spent only a few more minutes together. Brann was satisfied that his men were in good hands. He was impatient to get back in the saddle and closer to his Queen.

Freyja must have sent word ahead because their two horses, Brax and Breyog, were saddled and ready for them when they arrived. Freyja said her goodbyes in her thoughts to her brothers and felt their warmth and strength rush back to her.

She turned Breyog south and let him stretch his head. The horses were kept to a trot until they were warm, then the two travelers were galloping south toward Calin.

~

It would take a few days to reach Calin on horseback, even with the ground-eating strides of their two mounts. Brann tried desperately to keep his thoughts on his Queen and his soldiers back in Della, but more often than not he found them straying to the woman riding beside him.

She rode with her mask off. They were following the most direct path to the capital city, which was not the most traveled road from Della. Breyog was a born runner with a smooth rolling gait but a body could only take so much. Only a week before, Freyja had been trussed up and beaten at the hands of the Oparel. If Brann was tired, he knew she was exhausted.

They stopped before sunset on the first day. Brann knew the area well and soon had them unpacked by a stream with enough of a clearing to make a small fire and lay out some blankets. It was early to stop, considering how urgent their mission was, but Freyja did not complain. She, too, knew she needed the rest.

Brann finished washing in the stream and walked back into camp to sit down by the fire. They ate in comfortable silence, but he could feel Freyja's stress rising as the night grew darker and colder.

His eyes caught hers across the fire. "There is no need for either of us to keep watch tonight. We are well off the usual path and our horses will warn us of any intruders."

She nodded and dropped her gaze to the flames, her chin resting on her knees with her arms wrapped around her legs, lost in thought.

"Freyja?"

"Hmm?"

"Will you share a bed with me tonight? For warmth?"

Her face flushed. "I have extra blankets…"

"For comfort then."

She was silent, trying to gauge his intent.

"Didn't it feel right to you? The two of us together that night?" he prodded.

Her eyes glittered warmly when she remembered what it felt like to wake up in his arms. "Brann, I don't think my body can take another experience like that tonight."

Gods, she sounded shy. "Will you be able to sleep, with me by you?"

She let out a soft sigh that cut straight to his heart. "I think… that I would sleep better with you than without."

He slid down onto his back and lifted the corner of his blanket in invitation, his head resting on his cloak. She took the invitation and stepped quietly around the fire to kneel by his side. She slipped in beside him but stayed on her side with her back to him, not wanting him to see the anxiety in her face. It also took some pressure off her bruised ribs. He shifted his weight behind her, laying his arm out so she could use it as a makeshift pillow.

They stayed like that in silence until Brann realized she was too tense to fall asleep. It was amazing how new all this was to her, and he was grateful that he was the one she finally trusted after all this time.

He moved the hand she was not laying on and rested it lightly on her back then began to stroke her skin softly, trying to sooth her. "You cannot rest if you are tied up in knots, love." The fingers at her back pressed harder, massaging the corded muscles there.

"Maybe I should sleep somewhere else," she said quietly. Her slow exhale of breath ran over the skin on his forearm, sending chills down his spine and blood pooling at his groin.

"What if I make a promise to you? Will that help you to sleep?"

"What promise?" came the soft reply.

Unable to help himself, he pressed a kiss to her temple. "I promise I won't touch you tonight, nor any other until we reach Calin. You need sleep, Freyja."

She rubbed her cheek against his skin without thinking. The warmth he was giving off felt so good. "You want me to sleep?"

"Yes."

"That is not what your body is telling me." She could feel his erection at her back, thick and hard.

He closed his eyes and willed his body to relax. It didn't work. "My body and mind are not always on the same page. Rest." His fingers combed through her hair, spilling the silky red strands along his chest. "Please. You are safe with me."

She didn't agree with him, but she didn't disagree either, and simply let the silence take over once again.

Brann continued the slow strokes through her hair and along her back, soothing her like he would a small kitten. He felt her sigh once more and knew the moment she gave up fighting. Her muscles loosened and she tucked herself tighter against him for warmth. They fit together perfectly. He watched the rise and fall of her ribs as her breathing slowed and she fell asleep. He knew his own dreams would be long in coming. His body was hot and tense with wanting.

When he finally did sleep he dreamt of red hair, dark eyes, and the smell of the ocean.

~

Two days after Freyja left Della, Lintha stood at the top of the precipice looking down into the ravine below. His own cona was spread out along the ridgeline, waiting for his signal. From where he stood he could also see Ghent and a seething mass of Marrin soldiers on the plains behind him, still forming ranks. They were all afoot. The horses would be needed during the next wave of defense if the landslide failed.

The first of Oparel troops were directly below him now. Despite the cramped and uneven ground within the ravine the soldiers were still formed into their own tight units of one hundred men. It made the counting much easier for Lintha. He would let one thousand troops through before he triggered the landslide. Maybe even a hundred more would be crushed by the rocks and, with the massive amount of slag and debris that would rain down on the men; it would take them days to dig through the pass to attack Della with the rest of the army. With luck they would just turn around.

The Oparel below were moving quicker now. They could see the Marrin soldiers when they left the mountain pass, and adrenaline was getting the better of them. Ghent and his men would take the brunt of the attack. All of the Valren stationed at Della were tucked away with their ponies along the bottom of the mountain. They would be unnoticed by the Oparel until it was too late. By that point the enemy would be flanked on both sides.

Ghent gripped his sword tighter in his hand as he remembered Lintha's parting words. "I'll meet you in the middle." If Lintha's plan worked, the Oparel would be outnumbered and outflanked.

Time to start the rain. Lintha's thoughts spread to the men in his cona easily after years of working side by side with them. His men pushed as one. The rocks they moved were not overly large. It was what they disturbed on the way down that would wreak havoc on the Oparel.

The first of the Valren rocks landed with a thunderous crack on a larger boulder. Days before, the Valren had dug the ground out from under it and thus, it started to roll, looking deceptively slow. It picked up speed quickly. All along the precipice, this action was repeated in unison. Loose rock and slag went tumbling down onto the soldiers, creating a chain reaction that would crush anyone below. Lintha heard the Oparel soldiers shout when they realized what was happening. Then he saw them panic.

The men in the middle pushed the men in front and behind them, knocking them over in their haste to escape. Lintha had seen it before. Once one man was knocked to the ground others would go with him, slowing down more and more men. They were getting in their own way.

It took a full five minutes before the dust settled enough for Lintha to see the results of his handiwork. Men were still screaming; he was sure some were trapped alive under the boulders.

The noise of a thousand foot soldiers running into Della masked the sound of the crashing boulders from the men in the lead. They did not know most of their army was no longer behind them. Only a few soldiers in the back turned and saw the devastation. Their eyes went wide and they yelled to their comrades. But it was too late. The bulk of the Valren, mounted on their ponies, came up behind them and dispatched the stragglers before they knew what was coming.

Arrows. Now that the dust had cleared, Lintha could see the men below him. Like fish in a barrel. Each of his cona had one hundred arrows. By the time they were done their arms would be protesting madly against the abuse. But they had time to rest later. The enemy had nowhere to go but back, and the bulk of the army was keeping the front pressed against the rockslide. The boulders blocking the path were now piled over twenty feet high.

Lintha picked his first target. He pulled his bowstring back to his cheek and sighted down the arrow shaft. His arrow took the target in the neck, instantly felling the man. The rest of the cona followed suit, each picking an unlucky victim.

The screams below started all over again and panic resumed. Men were sacrificing their own friends in order to escape the trap. Lintha picked up a second arrow, sighted, and let fly. Above the screams of the men below came the soothing twang of the bowstrings as they were loosed. This was familiar, and it was welcome. It was like target practice back home in Andora. Besides, his brothers all knew what the Oparel had done to Freyja. They were indifferent to the suffering of the men trapped below.

~

A half hour later, Lintha let loose his final arrow. His brothers were not far behind. They all stood and made their way down the west side of the mountain to their ponies, shaking life back into their tired arms as they went. Even with the heavy leather forearm guards that they wore while shooting, they would each have dark bruises soon.

The Marrin soldiers were winning the battle in the valley, as they should be since they outnumbered the enemy by more than two to one. But still, Lintha promised Ghent they would meet in the middle, so he added himself and his cona to the mix.

Another hour passed before the battle was over. Few Valren were hurt, none seriously. The death count for the Marrin soldiers would take longer to determine. The Oparel had been decimated. Lintha and Ghent stood in the middle of the field.

The Valren, masks shinning even as blood dripped from them, formed a line and took on the gruesome task of finishing off the soldiers who still suffered. Most of the Oparel looked like they would beg to live, until they saw the masks on the men looming above them. Then they closed their eyes and prayed.

Lintha's strong hand clasped Ghent's shoulder. The Marrin man was like a tree trunk, his chest so large that it was hard for him to cross his arms. "It almost wasn't fair once you cut off the rest of the army. We outnumbered them and had the advantage of knowing the lay of the land."

Lintha spoke through his mask. "If you find yourself in a fair fight you need to hire a new tactician, because the one you have is obviously not doing his job. It's not about being fair it's about winning.

"Besides, war is not the time for your moral compass to begin spinning," said Lintha. "The rockslide will buy us some much needed time. The Valren will be picking off Oparel soldiers as they try to clear the rubble. The army may be forced to try and find another way through the mountains. We will have to wait and see what they do."

Lintha nudged the head of a dead soldier with his toe. "Make sure the horses are ready for the next battle. We'll do what we can to care for your wounded men."

~

The following day, Freyja and Brann met up with a contingency of fifty Valren who were returning to Della from their trek south. Brome was in charge. He moved his horse up beside Breyog and clasped Freyja's elbow in his strong hand. "Jaryth."

"It is good to see you, Brome." Her eyes ran over the other men as well and they all nodded back to her. She knew them all by name. She opened her mind to them through the orack metal and felt their mood. They were all happy to be traveling together, and glad to have seen some fighting. "I see that your task went well."

Brome knuckled his forehead in thanks. Before he became a brother in the Valren he had been a country farmhand. Some habits were hard to lose. Two sensitive eyes were etched into his mask. The rest of the metal was designed to look like he had covered his face with a plaid. The plaid was in the pattern of his own family colors. Each color was depicted in the metal by varying the amounts of crosshatching in an area so the blue of the orack metal took on different qualities in the light. The intricate design made the plaid-like portion look bundled and folded over to look like a heavy cloth being used to stave off the cold. She knew that Ramma had created that mask. Brome was one of the first men Ramma had brought to the Valren once he himself had earned his mask. Freyja had always admired his skill. She had personally never brought a single warrior to the Valren for training so she had never created a mask for another.

"Everything went as planned, Jaryth. We met the Oparel a few miles south of Canbar. They never made it near the palace or the Queen."

She could feel Brann relax behind her. He knew that this was the group they had sent out days ago to head off the direct attack against Varonda.

"Tried to get some information out of them," Brome continued, "but the last two alive killed themselves when they realized we were trying to take them for questioning."

"You've still done well."

Brome's wide shoulders lifted in a shrug. He had the build of a blacksmith. "We're all happy to get on to Della and meet with the others. It's been a long time since we had a chance to fight together. This is good for us."

They said their hasty goodbyes before parting. Brome and his men moved quickly north to Della while Freyja and Brann continued south to the capital.

CHAPTER 8

Three days later, near midnight, Breyog and Brax took their riders into Calin. Breyog pinned his ears back when a hustler tried to take his reins. The man hastily backed away and stood by Brax instead.

They both ended up taking care of their own horses; Freyja from preference and necessity, and Brann because he did not want to leave without Freyja by his side. After a few days of being alone with her, he was beginning to realize it would be a challenge for him to be without her. His need to protect her was stronger than he could have imagined. He now knew how the Valren felt – she was a treasure.

Freyja walked into the stall where Breyog would rest. The large horse followed her in like a besotted puppy, his nose an inch from her shoulder the whole time; they both curried down their mounts. There was no need to rush. The Queen would already be in bed, so they would not have a chance to speak with her before morning.

The stable door opened just as they finished settling the horses. Brann saw two Valren step into the torchlight. He did not know them by their masks, but Freyja obviously did. "Here's trouble."

The two Valren were introduced as Nolan and Bastien. Compared to the rest of the Valren Brann had so far seen, these two were small in stature. They were obviously strong but were both of average height and would not stand out in a crowd. They were forgettable. These were exactly the kind of men he liked to have as spies and assassins. If they were dressed in civilian clothing they could walk through a crowd and no one would give them a second glance. Even their masks were nondescript. Beautifully worked, but with no extra flare or decoration. They simply bore faces, unblinking, that stared back at you.

Between the four of them it was easy to carry the supplies into the palace from the stable. The Valren knew where Freyja's suite was to be, so Brann and Freyja followed them through the marble halls. Judging by how nonchalantly they led her to her room, Brann guessed they had no idea his own sleeping quarters were right next to hers.

Bastien opened the door for Freyja and let her walk into the room first before the three men followed behind.

Nolan took a chair and crossed one ankle over the other. He and Bastien watched Brann expectantly. The message was clear. They wanted to speak to Freyja alone.

Brann couldn't help but wonder if Torne had put them up to this. Fine, he would let them talk. He reached a hand towards Freyja, palm up. She took it. Nolan and Bastien looked from Brann's face to Freyja's and back again.

"If you need anything, I am only next door." He felt Nolan's and Bastien's eyes on his back as he left.

~

Nolan and Bastien took their masks off and stood, wrapped their arms around her and gave her a tight hug. She hadn't realized how much her brothers had worried about her when she had been caught by the Oparel. She hadn't thought about it until now. She surprised herself by tightening her own arms around them, squeezing back, before letting go.

The two men settled into the chairs while Freyja seated herself on the floor, as was her preference, crossing her legs in front of her. "As cona leaders you both have been kept abreast of the dealings in the north?"

Bastien nodded. "Yes. And we have much to report of our own."

Nolan rested his chin on his hand and let Bastien talk. "As you requested, one of our men is with the Queen at all times. She is never alone with her advisors. The crotchety Bartorin man, Laren, has been getting more and more anxious since you left us. He's still waiting for the Oparel contingency to come crashing into Calin and assassinate the Queen."

Bastien snorted. "Little chance of that since Brome got his hands on them."

Nolan cracked his knuckles and looked to Freyja. "The Queen will never believe that Laren is on the side of the enemy."

"She'll believe Brann."

"Torne told us he had a way with women."

She lifted a brow. "Are you implying something?"

They shook their heads.

"We'll speak with the Queen in the morning. You both will be in attendance. Now, what have you learned about Laren?"

"Brandon has been suspicious of Laren since the Queen took over Bartorin." Nolan glanced at Bastien, who nodded in agreement.

"Brandon? The Queen's other advisor?" Freyja raised a brow. "How did you get him to confide in you?"

Bastien wiggled his fingers in the air. "He's of gypsy stock. Or, he was when he was younger, though he lives a more settled life now that he has a place in the palace. Still has a piece of orack though." Bastien laughed then. "He's got it on a ring, sitting proud as can be on the leftover nub of one of his missing fingers.

He has quite a bit of pride about that. It was he who first started spreading the knowledge north that your man Brann was looking for the Valren. He told one gypsy in the city and off it spread like wildfire, just as he knew it would. Good man, he is."

"What did he have to say about Laren?"

Nolan spoke up this time. "He says Laren and the Mad King were scheming something with the Oparel long before Marrin absorbed the land in the north. It's my bet that Bartorin and Oparel armies were to invade Marrin together, but King Harton beat them to it and invaded Bartorin before they could make any solid plans. For all we know Laren is from Oparel, though he has a Bartorin accent."

Knowing Brandon was suspicious of Laren, and pulling the older man's image from the priest's mind back in the city of Garnal, Freyja had no doubt of his guilt. What she was not sure of was Varonda. There was little love, or even friendship, between the two women. Freyja thought the Queen would take Brann's word if he told her Laren was a traitor but she wasn't completely sure. She was going to have to find another way to get Laren to reveal himself.

~

Brann set down the tray of food he collected from the kitchens below. The stoves were cool but there had been bread and fruit aplenty. While Freyja and her brothers spoke he spent his time bathing and collecting his own turbulent thoughts. Varonda was not going to like what she heard come morning.

The marble walls between his own suite and Freyja's were thick enough that he could not hear a conversation, but he hoped the two brothers were gone by now.

Brann picked up the tray of food and wrapped softly on her outer door. She opened it quietly with one hand at her waist. He knew she had a weapon there, though he couldn't see it, ready to use if needed. When she saw him she smiled and dropped her hand. "It's hard to sleep indoors after being out in the wild for so long, isn't it?"

In truth he was finding it hard to sleep indoors because he knew her bedroom was only a few feet from his own. But that would not have been a polite response. "I do miss the stars."

He walked past her and set the food down between two chairs. "Torne told me he wanted you to eat more, and we haven't had much aside from troop rations in a while. Will you eat with me? Or would you prefer I let you rest?"

He straightened and let his eyes run over her body, assessing her mood. She looked tired, but who wouldn't be after all she had been through? He doubted she got more than four hours sleep a night in the last three weeks and she still kept a good pace while they traveled. He couldn't help but admire her.

Her red hair was loose and spilled over her shoulders in unruly waves. She had changed from her dark uniform to what looked like doeskin pants and an oversized man's shirt that he assumed was either Nolan's or Bastien's. He wished it were one of his.

"I was getting really tired of eating the same bland cakes every day. This is a treat. Thank you, Brann. I would love it if you joined me." She ran a hand through her hair and shook it back over her shoulder before sitting in one of the chairs and tucking her feet up under her.

Brann took the other seat and they ate. They sat quietly for a few minutes until Freyja said, "Can I talk to you about tomorrow?"

"Of course." He had been expecting it, and wanted to know what she had planned.

"Technically, since Marrin provided the Valren with Zaven and Lian before we were sent north, the Valren are working for the Queen. I am more than happy to brief her about what happened in the mountains and near Della, but I'm not sure she would believe me if she heard about her advisor from my lips. She and I got off to a bad start."

Freyja still disliked the woman, but the Marrin people seemed to have affection for her. "I can have him detained before we meet with the Queen, but I am not sure she would believe even me in this case," said Brann.

"She may not need to, actually." Freyja found some nuts buried under a few slices of bread and ate them. "If I bring up Brome's cona and how we found the assassination team heading for Calin, Laren may just try to kill her himself. He'll know he is a dead man as soon as he hears about the fate of the others. He won't have anything to lose."

Brann shook his head. "But Laren is an old man. He can barely walk without his cane. You think he would try to attack the Queen himself? With us present?"

She grinned, her eyes sparkling. "Actually, he walks very well. We've been following him. No one in Calin aside from the gypsies and yourself know what any of my brother's faces look like. Nolan suspected the man was putting up a bit of a farce so he trailed him to a tavern and started a little brawl between himself and a few of the other brothers. They made sure Laren got caught in the middle of the fray. Not only does the man not need his cane, he knows how to defend himself. He's been putting on an old man show for years and had no trouble slipping out and around anything coming his way."

Angered flowed through him immediately. It didn't even cross his mind that Freyja would be wrong. He knew her information was always correct. "So we let him take a chance at the Queen?"

"One of my brothers will be beside her at all times. They can handle themselves, or anyone who gets in their way."

He leaned back, his blue eyes holding hers. "I don't doubt it for a second." He paused, framing his question carefully. "Do you realize the power the Valren hold?"

She was silent a moment before answering. "Yes."

"People would give up towers of gold to have you on their side."

She shrugged. "We don't need gold."

"Well, tomorrow, when you are speaking with Varonda, remember that I thank you for all you have done, even if she will not."

Heat crept into her cheeks. "I will."

He stood. She watched him from her seat when he moved in front of her. "Promise me you'll try to sleep tonight."

His voice fell like warm rain over her skin and she nodded.

He bent down and framed her face with his two warm and calloused hands. She looked at him warily but didn't pull back. He brushed his lips over hers lightly then waited, holding her mouth only a half-inch from his.

She surprised him by leaning forward and shyly kissing him back. She even let out a happy little sigh when he gently bit her bottom lip.

"Freyja?" He still held her face lightly with his hands. "Get some rest. I want to see you tomorrow night, without your brothers hounding you."

"I don't know if that is a good idea," she hedged.

"You trusted me before, don't change that now." He gave her chin a squeeze before letting her go. "I'll meet you in the morning before we see Varonda. I'll get you some real food."

~

He was true to his word. When the morning came she was treated to a full array of breakfast choices. Bastien and Nolan had eaten earlier and waited patiently with their masks in place. Even the servants had never seen one of the Valren without his mask on. Brann noticed that the servants often muttered prayers under their breath when a Valren brushed near them. No one was sure of the brothers, or whether they were even human, and that was exactly how they wanted it.

Brann met with Freyja and the other two Valren then escorted them to the throne room where the Queen waited.

Varonda was in a sour mood, as was Freyja. It was a volatile mix. She had been told of Brann's arrival the night before and it grated on her that he had not seen her immediately. She expected he had his reasons, his judgment was never flawed. But when she saw Brann walk in close beside Freyja she couldn't help but think his reason for staying away last night came complete with a head of red hair.

It was remarkably similar to the first time the two women met. Gareth was standing behind the Queen, and her advisors, Laren included, stood slightly to the side. Freyja and Brann walked in together with two other Valren in tow. A third brother, wearing a mask Brann did not recognize, was standing a half step behind Gareth and the Queen. Apparently no love was lost between the Valren and Gareth. The man behind Gareth was in a perfect position to not only protect the Queen, but also take out the burly man at arms if need be. Gareth looked uncomfortable.

The Queen did not look happy either. "I assume you have a good reason for not making yourself known last night when you arrived? Considering the ramifications of the actions I assume are going on in the north, I would have thought you would need to see me promptly."

This was a side of the Queen Brann did not often see. He blinked slowly and bowed to her, giving him time to gather a proper reply. Varonda really was an even-tempered woman, but seeing Freyja seemed to bring out the worst in her. "My Queen, there were some matters that needed to be discussed in private before I could bring them to your personal attention. I regret having caused any distress."

"We are at war, Brann. There can be no secrets here if our country is going to survive the next few months. Now, I don't care what you and this woman talked about, or did last night," Brann saw the masked man behind her shift his weight slightly, prepping for an attack. He was obviously taking offense to the Queen's implication. "I need to know what is going on in the north, and what I can do to protect my people."

Freyja made a small hand motion and the masked brother reluctantly settled back. *Shorith, leave her for now. Be wary of Laren.*

"Your Majesty," Freyja spoke up. "A large army had settled on the east side of the Doranin Mountains. We were able to gain some information about their plans after speaking with a few of the officers, and we…"

"Speaking with them?" Varonda rose from her throne.

"Yes, we were able to…"

"To what? Walk up and say hello?"

"Well, perhaps I misspoke. Let me try again," Brann groaned inwardly as Freyja's voice dripped with false sincerity. This was not going well. He heard Freyja move on with her explanation before he could stop her.

"After risking our lives to pull a few strategic individuals from the middle of an enemy camp, we proceeded to torture them. We broke them down until they would have sworn to us that the sun was purple if that is what we wanted to hear. Don't worry, though, your own men didn't have a hand in it. The Valren did it all themselves on your behalf. Does that make you feel better?"

Varonda wasn't the only one with a mean streak. The Queen wanted to have the moral high ground? Fine. The three advisors in the room looked shocked.

"Would you like to know more, or is that enough for one day?" asked Freyja.

Varonda flushed with anger or embarrassment, Brann could not tell which, but he guessed it was a bit of both due to the Queen's reddening face and downcast eyes. He doubted anyone had ever spoken to Varonda in this way before, especially not in her own palace.

"And I will have you know," it was usually hard to wind Freyja up, but she had had enough of the woman standing in front of her, "that you would not be in the mess you are in if you were smart enough to recognize your own enemies when they smile and lie to your face."

Brann heard a gasp of outrage come from Varonda, but he had shifted his attention to Laren. Freyja was upset, but she was using her anger to prod the advisor into action. Though Brann was sure that was not the only excuse. He would have to remember to try and keep the two women apart.

Freyja saw that Laren was still not ready to attack. Gareth was between him and the Queen. Freyja took a threatening step toward Varonda that made Gareth move forward as well to protect his Queen. "The last man we got a hold of was a sniveling priest who had a lot to say about your own personal court."

Varonda's eyes widened and she looked to the two Bartorin advisors, obviously thinking them the culprits. Laren saw his chance, while Gareth's attention was still on the smaller woman in front of him, he lunged at the Queen.

Shorith gave the Queen a firm shove, knocking her away from Laren, just as the man raised a blade from the folds of his clothes. Brann caught the Queen before she fell.

Shorith ducked Laren's blow easily and a knife appeared in his own hand. Almost hugging the man, he slid his knife under the ribs of the advisor. When Laren doubled over in pain, Shorith grabbed the back of his head and brought his own knee up to connect with the man's nose. Blood began pouring instantly, staining the marble floor.

Gareth and Brandon stood in mute shock as the scene unfolded before their eyes. The Queen was shaken and had a death grip on Brann's arm.

Shorith let Laren's body drop to the floor unceremoniously. The knife under his ribs would have killed him soon, but Shorith's knee pushing broken bone up into the man's brain had done the job. He landed on the ground with a dull thud.

Shorith removed his knife and bowed slightly to his Jaryth. *Is there anything else I can do for you, sister?*

We will be going into the city later today to speak with the gypsies. You are free to do what you will until we return with news.

He made a second bow then simply walked out, seemingly oblivious to the havoc he left behind.

Gareth stuttered, "You were trying to bait him that whole time! He could have killed the Queen!"

Her dark eyes moved from Gareth to Varonda and back again. "She looks fine. You're welcome."

Gareth was turning a bright shade of red. "The Queen is not someone you use as bait!"

"Gareth, the Valren have been working together for longer then you've been alive. We are not a nascent group of wanderers." She gave the dead man a small shove with her boot then turned and stalked out the way Shorith had left. Nolan and Bastien followed on her heels.

As she passed Brann, he heard her muttering under her breath, "He's still an idiot…"

Brann let out a deep sigh. He hoped Freyja would be calmer by the time he saw her that night.

~

She was not. Her meeting with the gypsies had gone well. But the family she saved when she traded herself to Sholl for them had showered her with attention, hugs, and tried to give her gifts as soon as the formal meeting ended. Freyja hated the attention. She had just been doing what was right in her mind. Anyone would have done the same. At least, any of the Valren. She didn't believe she deserved all of the praise. By the time she left the gypsy camp she was on edge. It made her even more upset to admit that it was not only the gypsies that had wound her up, but the thought of seeing Brann later in the night as well.

Brann knocked on her door. It opened, and was almost shut in his face a second later. A quick hand shot out and caught the door before she could close it.

"Freyja?" He tried to pick a safe topic as he continued, "The Queen is very grateful for what you did today. May I come in?"

She stood back from the door, every line on her body drawn with reluctance.

He eyed her clenched fists. "Freyja, can we just relax and pretend we're actually friends again?" He moved across the room and leaned against the window frame, casting his gaze to the buildings below. He spied the salle and grinned. "I have such fond memories of that building."

Curious, she went over to him and leaned across his outstretched legs to see what building he was looking at. When she spotted the workout arena they had sparred in she turned a deep shade of red.

Brann found it endearing and couldn't help pointing it out. "You're not embarrassed of what we did, are you?"

"I'm glad that what happened between us did happen, but," she shrugged and avoided his gaze, "it's not a subject I've ever talked about."

He took her hand and brought it to his lips, kissing it lightly. "Not even with Torne?" He tried to keep the jealousy out of his voice.

That got a laugh out of her. "Oh Gods no. If Torne heard about what we have done straight from my own mouth he would have strangled you back in the mountains."

Brann shrugged his large shoulders. "He cares for you. I don't blame him. If you cannot talk with him, will you talk with me?"

"About Torne?" She was being intentionally obtuse.

"About us."

She rubbed her hands together as if they were cold. It was a nervous action. "If you have questions, I will answer whatever I can."

Brann laughed low. "I wasn't intending to make this an inquisition. I just want to know where you stand."

Her mind was running in circles. "I enjoy spending time with you."

"So glad to hear it. What else?"

Was he being patronizing? She crossed her arms and lifted her eyes to his face. "What answer are you looking for? What are you expecting to hear?"

"I am expecting to hear you try and dodge my questions," he grinned down at her, but held up his hands to show he meant no harm. "But I would like to hear your thoughts on us. Being together."

"We have been together, Brann."

"I mean for more than just physical pleasure, and more than just one night." His voice dropped low as he thought about their time together. "There is so much more that I want to show you. I think Torne would tolerate me if he knew we were committed to each other."

She raised a brow. "But we are not committed."

"We can be."

Gods, she had been right to be nervous all day. Her heart was pounding faster with every breath she took. "I've never considered being in a relationship like the one you are looking for."

"Maybe you should."

He could see her formulating all kinds of arguments in her head so he decided to persuade her with something he knew she enjoyed. He cupped her cheek with his hand and ran his thumb over her mouth. That got her immediate attention.

His hand was extremely warm against her face. The calluses on his palm reminded her of all the rest of her brothers. It was something every warrior had. It was familiar, just as Brann knew it would be.

"Freyja, it is killing me that I have had a small part of your trust, but not all of it."

Her eyes shifted from his face and her reply was so low he had to strain to hear it. "What do I need to do?" She was being brave.

Heat licked across his skin in anticipation. "For starters, I need to know that you are alright. You've been hurting for over a week. You said that you are better, but let me see for myself that you're okay."

She moved herself closer to the window and turned her cheek to the sky so the sun would highlight the cut healing above her eye. His hand skimmed over her skin, barely touching the wound. It was healing cleanly, but would leave a scar. He lowered his lips to the bruise and pressed a reverent kiss to her temple.

She felt her breath hitch in her throat. "Are we playing that game again, where your kisses heal all wounds?"

His grin made her stomach clench. "I do believe we are."

"Well then we can stop right now because you've seen the worst of them."

"I want to see your ribcage, love." He shook his head when she started to protest. "I have watched you wince with every stride your horse took on our trip down to Calin, and every time your pony slipped up in the mountains." He took her shoulder and gently moved her to the bed so she could sit. Then he tapped her arms lightly. "Up. You owe me this reassurance."

She did owe him this, she thought to herself, after all they had been through. And deep down, somewhere she had buried long ago, she knew she wanted it as well. She just had to let it happen. That was the hard part.

She trained her eyes on his chest, thinking it would help her nerve to have something solid to concentrate on. But as she raised her arms for him she couldn't help but notice how well-formed his body was. Her eyes started drifting lower before she could stop them, and she had to pull her attention back to his chest.

Brann grasped the bottom of her shirt and slid it over her head in one smooth motion. He didn't even jar her ribs. He'd had more than one friend who came home from a battle with broken ribs. He knew what he was doing.

Her ribs were still wrapped, shielding his view of her stomach and breasts. He wanted to focus his attention on her bruised ribs but another portion of her body, slightly higher up than the ribs, kept coming to mind instead. When he had her laid out under him up in the mountains she had not allowed him to undo her chest bindings. Thoughts of what she looked like naked had been running through his dreams for days. It was driving him to distraction.

He took out his small hunting knife and carefully slid the tip between her skin and the binding. She didn't utter a protest. She was not one to be squeamish about sharp knives. With a deft flick of his wrist he cut the first few inches off the bottom of the material. His breath hissed out when he saw her ribs. They were still covered in dark bruises. The rush of adrenaline he felt had nothing to do with lust, and everything do to with anger.

"It's really not that bad." She covered the bruises with her hands so he would not have to look at them. They were obviously bothering him.

He grasped her hands and pulled them away from her body. Hot eyes raked over her skin. "Not bad? Any worse and you would have died. I can't believe you have been traveling with this."

She snorted. "I was worse off than this when Torne found me in Tauber."

"Never again. Do you hear me, Freyja?" He caught her chin and kept her eyes on his. "Do you hear me?" His voice came out rough with emotion.

She was about to tell him not to make a promise he could not keep when he locked his mouth with hers. Unlike their previous kisses, this one was not gentle. It was possessive and dominant, like he was trying to mark her to keep other men away. Her first instinct was to pull away from him but she couldn't help but notice how incredibly gentle his hands were on her, even though they were restraining her.

She hadn't realized her fingers were curled around his thick forearm. Even as she let him go her fingers lingered against his skin. Rebellious little digits. When did they get a mind of their own?

"I am going to protect you whether you like it or not, Freyja. If you try and sacrifice yourself for your brothers again, your enemies will have to get through me first. And your brothers can go six feet under if they don't like it."

Freyja studied the hard plains of his face. His strong jaw was covered by day old growth that she was dying to touch. "I have people to protect me, Brann. My brothers have always protected me. I may have scars, but I'm still alive. If I have to sacrifice smooth skin to keep the rest of my family whole then that's what I am going to do."

He nodded, knowing she would never abandon her family in such a way. "You sacrifice for them, and I will do the same for you. Whether you allow me to love you tonight, or any other night for that matter, I am staying with you."

He willed her to see the truth in his eyes. That he was already in love with her.

Something moved in her, and when she stared back into his blue eyes he saw her acceptance. It was like a switch went off in her mind. "Before you avow your life to mine, you should see all of what you are so willing to fight for, shouldn't you?" She couldn't believe those words came out of her mouth.

Brann did not wait for a second invitation. He slid his hand under the cloth binding her chest, between her breasts, using it to protect her skin from his knife when he cut the cloth loose.

Her heart picked up its tempo. She kept talking to try and mask her nervousness. "Brann, if my brothers accept you into their ranks, they will be able to teach you so many things. With your bulk, and our techniques, you will be one of our best fighters."

She felt the binding snap free and she looked away quickly, not sure what to do.

Brann froze, stunned by the perfection of her body which was obvious despite the bruises on her skin. Her breasts were small and high, her nipples a rosy pink against her flushed skin. His hands gently cupped the weight of them as he leaned in to run his lips over hers. "You are beautiful."

She felt his hands leave her chest to cup the necklace she wore. He held it away from her skin and raised a brow in question. She silently thanked him for giving her this moment to collect herself. Her head was spinning from his touch already. "It's alright. I cut my thoughts off from the rest of them. Even Torne. It is easier now that he is so far away from us."

He let the necklace drop back in place. He was trying to give her time to get used to him being so close to her, but he noticed her hands were still trembling.

He kept his underclothes on when he joined her on the bed.

Freyja was used to seeing large men because she lived with the Valren, but never had she felt such a rush of heat and anticipation as when her eyes ran over Brann's chest.

She pressed her cheek to his. He felt her eyelashes flutter across his skin when she closed them. Gods, she was perfect. So confident in everything but this. He touched her. Her soft moan and exhalation of breath twisted his stomach into a knot and he felt an urge to protect her that was stronger than anything he had felt before. No one was ever going to see her vulnerable like this again. No one except him. She was all for him.

His arm went around her and he helped her lay back down against the bed. He looked down into her eyes and read the uncertainty there. Despite her obvious pleasure, she was not comfortable with what he was doing to her. He pressed his chest against hers, the orack metal between them, and opened his mind to hers. His thoughts were instantly flooded with her happiness and pleasure, but he didn't need the metal to tell him that she was shaking with her need, he could feel it. He looked deeper, as far as he could with the little training he had, then he found her problem. She was under him, just like she had been when she was younger and being held down.

He immediately rolled onto his side and removed all his weight from her. He took his time to draw her confidence out again. His hands roamed over her body, attentive to every inch of her. It was not until much later that he felt the hesitation leave her hands when she touched him in return.

When they finally came together Brann was on his back. His hands were on her hips to steady her but he gave her complete control, knowing it would be easier for her. Watching her face, looking for any sign of distress, he picked up a slow and deep rhythm that was all his own. In moments he had her writhing above him, her hands fisted in the sheets by his head.

Though he wasn't trying to communicate with her through the orack metal he felt her emotions running wild every time it brushed across his chest.

Brann bit the base of her neck gently then whispered up into her ear. "You just need to let go, love. Let go and trust me not to lose you. Trust me to keep you safe."

It was one of the most difficult things she had ever done. She forced her mind and body to relax and she let herself go. Brann held her tightly while he continued to move in her, accepting her weight against his body. She stifled a cry against the side of his neck when the orgasm hit her like a tidal wave.

~

It took him a minute to realize his own hand was shaking. Even still, he placed it at the base of her neck to stroke her flushed skin and sooth her trembling body.

Neither one of them spoke. There was no need. Freyja came back to reality as Brann gently eased himself out of her. Even though he was no longer erect, the thickness of him sent a shiver racing up her spine. He was reluctant to leave her body, but knew he should give her sore muscles a rest.

They lay together in comfortable silence, the smell of their sex surrounding them, until Brann felt Freyja's mind slip off toward sleep. He eased himself from under her and silently padded across the room to the small washing bowl. With tender care he washed her, then himself, before rejoining her in bed.

As soon as he got under the covers she pressed her naked body against his, warming his skin. She tried to stay awake, fighting against her dreams as long as she could. But in truth she was fast asleep before Brann could even settle himself.

Her breathing was deep and even. Brann listened to it for hours before he, too, let sleep take him.

~

Tripan stood beside Lintha, looking down into the plugged crevasse that had once been a pass through the mountains. Even though the weather was cool and the winds still, the stench from the dead bodies was beginning to waft up to their vantage point.

Tripan covered his lips and nose with a cloth, but Lintha just stuck his hands in his pockets and continued to survey the bodies. "Glad it's not too hot, then we would really have ourselves a nasty case. Makes me kind of hungry." Lintha was not a mean man, but he did like to tease.

Tripan shot the Valren an indignant look before taking a few steps back from the cliff's ledge. After only a few days with each other the two had found an easy friendship. "You are disgusting, Lintha."

Lintha grinned and rubbed his jaw, his gaze focusing further down the pass. "Looks like they've fallen back to the east side of the mountains. If that's the case, then we've gained more time to prepare for the next attack. We may need to bring the fight over to them."

The two men walked back to the Marrin camp side-by-side. Lintha's mask, which he slid over his face before returning, was now a welcome sight in the camp. They were a motley crew. Ghent met the two near the first row of tents surrounding the city proper and the three of them made their way to Ghent's private map room.

Once they were alone Lintha flipped off his mask and took a long pull of the mulled ale placed in front of him. Lintha was one of the stronger talents with the orack metal within the Valren, though he could not rival Freyja's ability. He kept up an easy conversation with the two men in front of him while reaching out to his Jaryth.

Her response was slow and slightly groggy. She had been sleeping, he thought. He could only imagine how tired she must be, having physically been through more in the last month than any of her brothers. He sent his apology to her. *Freyja, forgive me for waking you. I should have waited longer.*

He felt their bond tighten as she came fully awake. She kicked off the web of sleep and added her own mental strength to his. *Never apologize to me, Lintha.*

He smiled as he lifted the mug of ale to his lips. Ghent and Tripan were talking about something, while he let his thoughts travel. Dishes. They were talking about the dishes the soldiers use. That was a conversation he could miss.

The Oparel have retreated back to the east. Scouts are moving into place to keep an eye on the main horde. But it does not look like they will muster a second attack anytime soon.

Then we will bring the war over to their side, and we will fight our own way. Freyja sighed and she felt Brann's arm tighten around her waist. His fingers began a slow caress on her lower stomach that made heat pool between her legs despite the tenderness there. She kept all thoughts of Brann firmly shut away from her brother. *How is Tripan?*

He is well. In fact he is sitting across from me. Do you have a message for him?

Only that I am glad he is feeling better, and sorry I did not see him before leaving Della.

Lintha relayed the message to his companion.

Tripan looked stunned for a moment before he remembered the stone. "You are speaking with her?"

"Yes."

Ghent's face became guarded. Brann had warned him about the orack metal and its uses, but it gave him the chills to think such a thing was being used right by his side.

"Thank the Gods she made it safely."

He is glad you made it to Calin. She was still a little lethargic in his head so he cut all small talk and got down to the point. *What are your orders?*

The Oparel are running desperately short of food after their supplies were flooded. If they are staying near the mountains then they will have to send riders out to hunt and forage while whatever supplies they are expecting from their King reach them. Just make sure our scouts pick off as many hunting groups as they can without putting themselves at too much risk. The more we kill now the less we will have to deal with later.

Yes, Jaryth.

Once the enemy is completely flushed from Calin the rest of our brothers will join you in the north. When we are all together again we will begin our own infiltration into the enemy camp, but we will be more successful by going straight after the King. If you cut off the head of the army the rest of the soldiers will be useless. I expect our business in Calin to take no more than a week's time. Can you keep steady until then?

Of course.

Freyja looked across her room to the open window and saw the sun peaking over the sill. She couldn't believe how long she had slept. *Good. Stay in touch.*

Be well, little one. Lintha broke the contact between them then leaned back in his chair. "The rest of the Valren will be joining up with us soon. Some of us will travel into Oparel and do some damage closer to home while the rest of us continue where we are."

Ghent raised a bushy brow. "You plan to march straight into the Oparel capital?"

He chuckled. "A small team of two or three Valren can get almost anywhere. All we need is one opportunity to get at the King. Without him, and a few other key players, the whole country will turn on itself. They will be too busy fighting a civil war to bother with us."

He sounded so matter-of-fact about it that Ghent almost believed it would be that easy.

CHAPTER 9

Freyja stirred in Brann's arms. He loosened his hold on her, knowing she hated anything that reminded her of being trapped. She woke with her cheek resting on his bicep, her back pressed tightly to his chest. The warmth coming from him was amazing. She felt like she was wrapped in a cocoon. She didn't even feel the morning wind that came through the open window.

She knew Brann was awake. His breathing was deep and even, but she still knew. She took a breath, mentally pulled her wits together, and then rolled over in his arms to face him.

He saved her from having to come up with something to say by tenderly kissing her. His hands swept down her body possessively. When he lifted his head he was the first to speak. "Good morning, love."

For some insane reason her eyes started to tear up and her chest tightened. She told herself it was her ribs hurting after such a long night. Too bad it is always so hard to fool yourself. For a second she almost believed that lie. "Good morning," she replied.

"Tell me you have no regrets." He kissed her forehead and held her tightly to him, as if he was afraid to look at her until he knew her answer.

In response he felt her arms tighten around his waist until he thought his ribs would crack. "You gave something back to me last night that I thought I had lost forever."

They dressed in silence. Freyja had decided to keep her ribs unbound since she did not plan on doing anything strenuous. Brann could not keep his eyes off her body when she slipped from the bed to pad across the room, hunting for her clothes.

He felt badly about staring until he noticed she was having trouble keeping her eyes from him as well. He sat on the end of the bed and flexed his muscles in a dramatic stretch. He knew it was childish. But the look on Freyja's face when he did it was worth it. He was never going to get enough of her.

They were eating a light breakfast in the palace kitchens when Bastien and Nolan joined them. Their masks were tucked under their cloaks, hidden but easily within reach if they were needed. They both had small packs slung over their shoulders.

She had told Brann that she would be spending the day with her brothers, but he was still reluctant to say goodbye. Even if she would be with two of the best killers in the country he did not want to let her out of his sight. He was tempted to give her a kiss goodbye but had the distinct feeling that he would have a knife in his back before he could get a chance to explain himself to her brothers.

Feeling robbed of that kiss put him in a foul mood. He went off to the salle to loosen his muscles. His one condolence was the the orack piece he was carrying in his pocket.

~

There were very few individuals in Calin who had seen Freyja's face, aside from the Queen and Brann. But there were some servants that would be able to recognize her if they saw her, so Bastien and Nolan were forced to keep a distance from her as they meandered down the busy main street.

For this kind of work both of the brothers were dressed in clothes locally bought in Calin. Their masks, a sign of their true loyalty, were tucked in their packs. Today, all three of them — Freyja included — were posing as citizens of Marrin.

Nolan kicked at a loose coddle stone and won himself a glare when it hit the shoe of a man selling hot meats in the street. He dropped his eyes and scuttled away, playing his roll of a normal man who wanted to stay out of trouble.

Bastien stepped out of an alley and went shoulder to shoulder with Nolan before giving him a shove. Bastien liked it when Nolan had to play the shy average man. It meant he couldn't retaliate. Nolan shot him a look that promised good-natured retribution in the future before shuffling off down the street. Freyja's red hair was easy to spot through the crowds. They could follow her without trouble.

A little girl with golden ringlets dashed out from a doorway and threw her arms around Freyja. "Auntie Clora!" If Brann had been there he would have remembered the little girl as the one who gave him his own special necklace back in the small town of Sall.

Freyja hugged Lorna tight. The child always had a different name for Freyja when they found each other. The child knew never to use Freyja's real name in public. Clora was actually one of Lorna's old dogs. The reference made Freyja roll her eyes. The two grasped hands and Freyja let the child lead her down the street, chatting away as if they really were auntie and niece.

Lorna pulled Freyja into a well-lit inn. The first floor had been turned into a tavern. It was obviously a local favorite, as there were many city men throughout. The clientele seemed to be of the wealthier ilk.

Lorna moved through the crowd like she owned the place, keeping a tight hold of Freyja's hand as if she were afraid to lose her.

Freyja grinned and embraced the child's father when he stood up from a table to greet them. "Sister, dear!" He hugged her tightly and saw Nolan and Bastien over her shoulder, moving into the tavern.

Most dangerous men had an air about them. Something that warned others to stay away. All Valren gave off that menace if they chose to. It was as natural as breathing for them. What gave Palonel the shivers was that the two brothers who just walked in looked like normal men, on a normal day, doing what they normally did. If he did not already know what they were capable of he could walk right by them and never know them for the dangerous men they were.

Bastien elbowed his way rudely to the bar and sat down. Nolan had already tucked himself into an unobtrusive corner where he could watch everyone, looking meek and put out.

Palonel sat across from Freyja. Their table was made for two and was small enough that they could speak quietly without having to lean in to hear. Lorna sat on her father's knee and scooted up close to him, proud that she had helped.

"Thank you for keeping an ear to the ground for us, Palonel. And you too, Lorna." She winked at the child, who beamed up at her.

"There is nothing that the Horani gypsies will not do for you. We owe you a thousand times over. The Oparel are as much a threat to us as anyone. Of course we would help you in whatever you needed."

He leaned forward, dropping his voice lower as he spoke over his daughter's head. "There are three men sitting together, if you follow the line over my left shoulder."

Freyja lifted her gaze and saw the men in question. She nodded. They looked anxious. Nolan and Bastien followed the line of her sight and also made note of the men sitting together. Nolan stood up and left the tavern as quietly as he had come. He would be waiting to follow the men when they left. He now knew who his targets were.

Palonel continued. "They meet here then leave the city through the north gate. Have been doing so for weeks. We don't dare follow them once they're out of the city proper, but they are the ones you need. There's no doubt in it."

That was all Freyja needed to hear. She put on the smile of a sister entertaining her niece and spent the next half hour playing games with Lorna and teaching her slight of hand tricks. The girl picked them up in no time. It was a positive side effect of her father teaching her to pick pockets at an early age.

Finally, the three men sitting across the room stood and left.

Nolan, she sent through the orack metal. The brother would follow them like a shadow. Two minutes later Bastien finished his beer, let out a loud belch, and sauntered out the door. Freyja saw him filch a full bottle of potent liquor from the bar on his way out.

Freyja was the last to leave. She stood, said goodbye to her two supposed relatives, and left the tavern. She linked deeply with Nolan through the stone. He opened himself to her, allowing her any information she needed. She was the only member of the Valren with this much control over the stones, and she used it to her advantage.

She dug deep, sifting through his memories until she could see where he had been. A cobbler's sign, blue on a brown background. Then an herb shop. She felt Nolan grumble as he walked over uneven stones. His father had been a stone layer and the son had always hated shoddy workmanship.

Freyja saw a kicked stone roll down the street through Nolan's eyes. One of the city guard stations was in front of him. She knew exactly where he was.

She took off at a brisk walk, hands in her pockets, toward the north gate.

~

Nolan followed the men out of the city limits. They surprised him by doubling back south, toward the sea. He saw the dock they were headed to and the ocean-faring ship harbored there.

They have a ship. They were probably waiting for Laren to join them before making off for good with news of the Queen's death.

Bastien swore and changed direction, running now through the city and onto the docks. He took a swig of liquor from his stolen bottle without breaking stride.

Freyja cursed as well and cast her mental net wide to her brothers. *Our targets are on the docks, trying to leave on a ship. There will be a whole crew on board that will need to be taken care of. Mask up, any of you who are close enough, and join us immediately. Track onto me.*

She felt their instant response, a surge of adrenaline through the usual calm of their minds. Then she felt Nolan's growl of approval when their collective thoughts were joined with Brann's through his own stone. He had felt her call and he was answering like one of her brothers.

She was outside the city walls within minutes, with a clear view of the docks below. Nolan and Bastien, masks hiding their faces, were sprinting after the three men who were scrambling up a rope ladder to get onto the ship's deck.

She swore to herself anew when she saw the ship up close. It was large and would need at least a crew of twenty to sail, which meant there were more men on board. At least something of this size would take a few minutes to launch, which would give her and her brothers time to catch up. *You better start hauling, my brothers, or you'll miss the fun.*

Nolan slowed down so that Bastien could catch up to him. No matter how good a fighter he was, he was not stupid enough to try and board a ship alone. Luckily, Nolan had other plans. Freyja could hear Bastien bellowing from where she was running – something about wasting good alcohol – while he stripped off his shirt.

Nolan ripped his brother's shirt into strips, dowsing each with liquor from the half-filled bottle before tying the strips into tight knots. The brothers took out their pieces of orack and hit them together over the wet scraps. Blue sparks shot from the stones, igniting the fabric. Nolan picked up the flaming knots with his leather gloves and hurled them into the sails of the ship.

A tiny spark caught. Freyja could hear a collective inhalation of breath from the ship's crew. It looked like the fire would go out in the sea breeze before it spread. But Nolan dashed all hopes of that when he threw the entire bottle of liquor onto the wood plank holding the main sail in place. The bottle exploded. The alcohol caught fire and spread like hundreds of tiny arrows licking up the sail.

That had done it.

Freyja stopped next to her two brothers. The three of them could hear the ship's crew yelling at the slaves below deck to put out their oars and push the ship back. But they wouldn't, even under threat of death. The slaves knew the ship was afire and they were safer in the harbor than out at sea if the ship was going to sink. Without sail, and without willing manpower, the ship's crew could not escape by sea.

"Good thinking, Nolan. I knew there was a reason we kept you around." Freyja nudged him with a smile.

He bowed back to her with a grin. "Jaryth."

It took the crew only a minute to rally. The crew men began to pour over the sides of the ship. Freyja risked a glance behind her and saw a handful of her brothers running from the city limits to join the fray. It would take them another two minutes to reach her. She pulled out the short daggers she had hidden in her boots. *Anyone have an extra blade?*

Nolan and Bastien were in the same position. They had not carried any long-edged weapons because they would have been impossible to hide in the city.

Brann cleared the city gates and his heart nearly faltered. He saw the three of them standing weaponless before the Oparel and he started praying aloud as he ran.

The first man to land on the dock in front of the three Valren went down with a dagger embedded in his neck. He had a short sword strapped to his side that Nolan dove for.

We've got you. Freyja and Bastien took up on either side of Nolan to cover him while he untangled the dead man's blade.

A sword hammered down onto Freyja's crossed daggers, aiming for Nolan's exposed neck, and her ribs screamed a protest at the jarring weight. She stepped inside the man's attack and pulled her blade across his stomach. The man's scream was enough to distract his friends, giving Nolan the precious second he needed to get back on his feet.

Just then the second flight of Valren reached the docks. The command *Down!* rang in their minds and the three in front dropped to their knees. Freyja heard a whistle of wind in her ear when a thrown blade whipped by her head before landing in the chest of an enemy. The thrown daggers took down the first run of the Oparel, but there were more to replace them.

She took the dead man's short sword in one hand and kept her dagger to parry with in the other. Without hesitation she stepped up to her next opponent.

Brann hit the docks and saw two of the Valren in front of him throw knives right over the top of Freyja and her two companions. He saw that Freyja had a blade and gave his thanks to the Gods above. With luck she could defend herself until her brothers got to her side.

But she did not have defense in mind. She went right for her enemy, despite his greater size. Brann had forgotten how quick she was. Her hands moved with blurring speed as the left parried a blade away from her body and the right thrust her sword into an enemy's ribs. The man went down and Brann saw her kick the body off her blade when it looked like it was going to get stuck. Then she twirled to meet yet another opponent.

Two men came at her together. If she had her own blade she might have been quick enough to take them both on, but the short sword in her hand was bulkier than what she was used to. She focused her attention on the man closest to her, knocking his blade aside with a sweeping parry. She saw the other man lunge for her, prepared herself to take the hit, when Brann cut between her and the offending blade.

His large bulk blocked his counterattack from her sight, but the enemy screamed and fell to his knees. The man she had parried also went down. Freyja flicked her gaze up and saw Shorith's mask next to her. *Timely as always, my brother.*

It would be a shame to let you hog the fun, little one. We did come all this way...

The fight was over in minutes. Eleven Valren and Brann stood shoulder to shoulder, their large bodies breathing heavily. The Valren masks were spattered with blood, but none of them bothered to wipe it off. They just let it drip onto the ground in front of them, or onto their chests, as it would. Freyja, not having the protection of her mask, made use of her sleeve to wipe away the grime.

Most of the Oparel had died on the docks, though two were alive and trussed up like game hens. A few had tried to swim for freedom but had been quickly picked off by Valren arrows. Brann's men would be arriving shortly to search the ship for any stragglers trying to hide among the slaves.

Freyja looked over her brothers. They all seemed fit. A few minor cuts, but nothing serious. Aside from their deep breathing, they all looked relaxed, and their presence through the orack metal was one of contentment. Fighting together was a pleasure for them.

She smiled to them all, and knew they smiled back from behind their masks.

All of them but Brann. He was not happy. In fact, he looked irate. She quirked a brow in his direction. He was counting to ten in his head. All the brothers could hear him through the stone. Freyja cleared her throat. "Counting does not really help if you're feeling stressed. It's a bit of an old wives' tale."

The counting stopped. Freyja smiled. Brann took her wrist firmly in his grasp and tugged her along with him back toward the palace. The Valren tensed, but a quick flick of her wrist told them to stay away.

Nolan bent over the dock and splashed his mask with a handful of salt water. "She has no idea why he's mad, does she?"

"Nope. She never has understood when any of us worry about her." Shorith was leaning against a post. "But he'll be sure she figures it out quickly."

If there were even a sliver of suggestion that Brann would hurt their Jaryth in anger, the Valren would not have let them leave together. But none of them had failed to notice Brann's reaction to seeing Freyja facing danger head on. He may want to throttle her, but he would never hurt her.

The Valren left the docks. The commotion had caused a crowd to gather a safe distance from where the fighting had broken out. The crowd saw the Valren coming, masks still stained with blood, and scattered.

~

Brann didn't talk the entire walk back. He didn't dare open his mouth because he knew he would yell at her if he did. He was praying that the long walk to the palace would give him enough time to cool down.

He stopped only to demand bath water be brought to his room. A moment later he pushed open the door to his quarters and gave Freyja a small shove inside. The door slammed shut behind them. Freyja spun around to find Brann leaning against the door, arms crossed tightly over his thick chest.

"What the hell were you thinking?" He took the orack metal from out of his pocketand crossed the space between them in two strides. He pulled her necklace over her head and tossed both ornaments aside. He did not want her brothers butting in on this conversation.

"We couldn't just let them leave." She tracked him with her dark eyes as he moved across the room to grab a washbowl and a clean cloth.

He sat her down on the bed and caught her face in his hands. The cloth was cold on her face, but it felt wonderful. His fingers were gentle as he rubbed the blood and sweat from her cheeks, but his words bit into her skin. "If you ever do something like that again…" His hand stopped moving and he just stared at her. "You didn't even have a weapon!"

She thought it was better not to mention that she, in fact, had two knives on her. "You're upset that I helped stop the Oparel from leaving?"

His fists clenched at his sides, unintentionally wringing water from the cloth he held poised near her face. "I am irate because you put your life in danger without a single thought to your own safety!"

"I was thinking about my safety. So was Nolan. Didn't you see him dive for the enemy's sword when the man died? He knew we would be safer if one of us had a longer blade. He is always thinking about safety."

"Tell me you are joking."

"What?"

"Don't you understand? I saw you standing in front of the enemy and…" He shivered, "Gods, I could barely breathe for fear you would be hurt."

"You were worried about me?"

"Is that such a difficult concept to grasp?" He finished cleaning her face then put the cloth down.

"Actually it is," she replied. "My brothers care about me, Brann, but they don't worry about me being in a fight. I'm not trying to upset you. I'm not really used to anyone worrying about me. My brothers see me as a partner, not a liability."

"You think they don't worry about you?"

"They taught me to fight so I could be at their sides."

"That doesn't make you indestructible."

"I never said I was. But I trust them to keep me alive in a fight, and they trust me to do the same for them."

His voice hardened with his reply. "None of us are infallible, and it only takes one mistake to die."

She grinned. "And you keep saying that I am the one with trust issues."

A loud knock on the door interrupted them. "Come in," he answered.

Servants carried in a deep tub, followed by steaming buckets of water.

Brann shut the door behind the last servant and clicked the lock into place. Freyja's stomach did a funny little flip at the sound of the lock moving into place. "I am not going to sit here and watch you bathe."

"You're right you're not."

She looked confused until he stood her up and pushed her towards the tub. Her arms crossed under her breasts. "I am also not going to bathe while you sit and watch me."

His eyes locked with hers, drawing her complete attention. "Right again." He grasped the hem of his shirt and pulled it over his head. His chest muscles rippled under his tan skin. "You're going to bathe, and I am going to help you."

Her whole body flushed hotter. "I don't need help."

His hands went to her waist, preventing her from moving away while he crowded her body with his. She had to crane her neck up to see him. "I need to see for myself that you're still in one piece."

He pulled her shirt over her head, not waiting for her answer. He just continued talking. "I saw you out on the docks, then you disappeared behind a group of Oparel and I thought I would never see you alive again. I still don't know if I completely believe you're here."

He tossed her shirt behind him and ran his hands gently down her ribs. He felt the muscles of her stomach, flat and tight. Gods, he wanted to be inside of her again.

She shivered under his hands. His eyes warmed and he pulled her against him, letting her feel the hard length of him against her. "Don't be scared."

Her hair tickled his nipples when she shook her head. "I'm not scared. That was a… good shiver."

He kissed the top of her head and replied softly. "The water is going to get cold."

She cast him a sidelong glance then she slid out of the rest of her clothes. She didn't dare look at him while she did it. Good thing, because the degree of devotion and love she would have seen in his face would have scared her, even if his large body no longer did.

Brann kept back, giving her space while she stepped into the tub. The water was still hot. It felt wonderful against her skin when she sank into it. She let out a deep sigh of contentment while she settled her back against the side of the tub. It was hard to concentrate when the heat was seeping into her skin, drawing out all of her body's aches and pains. She hadn't had a chance for a hot bath like this since she and Brann left Andora together.

Brann waited until she settled in then moved behind her. His hands rested on her shoulders, thumbs caressing and massaging the muscles there. Freyja didn't dare open her eyes - it would remind her of the view he must be enjoying at that very moment. The bath water was steamy, but not nearly enough to provide honest decorum. Her breasts were on obvious display.

She heard him reach around, then the smell of lavender fell around her. He scooped up handfuls of water and let it trickle over her head. Then he used the lavender soap to lather her auburn hair. His fingers massaged her scalp and she sighed out a, "Thank you."

He worked the soap from her hair with infinite care. Each lock was lovingly stroked and rinsed clean. She felt like he was worshiping her. His ministrations and the heat of the water had completely diffused her.

He helped her stand in the tub so that he could dry her body with a soft cloth. Her eyes tracked his arm muscles with every stroke they made. Her breathing sped up as the cloth skimmed over her breasts. The material came to a stop at the small of her back with one of Brann's arms wrapped around her waist. He purred into her ear, "I want you, now."

The heat in his voice made her shiver. "My goodness! We finally agree on something today."

He smirked and nipped her neck in retaliation. "You can be fresh, you know that?"

"You keep telling me that, but no one else has ever mentioned it to me before. It must be you."

Without warning he scooped her up out of the tub. He stifled her laughter with a kiss that soon had them both gasping for air.

He fell backwards onto the bed with her on top of him. Somehow he had managed to maneuver her legs so that she was straddling his waist.

Cold water drops fell from her hair onto his chest and tightened his nipples. "Good Gods, that is freezing."

She responded by giving her head a shake so that more drops rained down on him.

He leaned up, grabbed her around the waist and flipped her over on her back. Her eyes were dancing with mirth. "That's what you get for calling me fresh."

Brann was being careful not to put any weight on her, he was always conscious of her ribs. With infinite care he spread her red hair out around her head so she would not have to lie on it while it was wet. "I was only telling the truth. You are fresh." He leaned down and brushed his lips over hers. "You're also lovely. And brave."

She colored. "I'm not always brave…"

"I've never seen you run from anything."

"I was scared of you." It hurt her pride to admit that. He slid his arm around her back and pulled her up against his thick chest.

"I will never give you reason to be afraid of me."

She buried her face against his neck; he smelled like leather, horses, and spice. It was a heady mix that seemed to flip a switch in her mind, exciting her.

He gently laid her down so he could see her face. She had bitten her lower lip out of nervousness and the sensitive skin turned bright pink – begging to be licked. He bent his head to her. She closed her eyes just before his tongue made contact with her lips. His hand stroked up her stomach and circled her bellybutton while his tongue mimicked the action in her mouth.

She gazed up at him from where she lay. Her eyes never left his face, even when she felt his hand move between her thighs.

"You're going to be fine." He realized how nervous she really was – saw right through her brave front.

"Thanks to you…" There it was. Her acceptance. She was committed to follow through with whatever he had planned.

They spent the night talking and exploring each other's bodies. He learned things about her that she had never told another soul. He came to realize that at some point in the last few days she truly had learned to trust him. She had said as much before, but this was proof. It was humbling.

Hours later, they finally came together, and Brann realized it felt like coming home. This was where he belonged. By her side, always next to her. Surrounding her.

Suddenly she came, her back bowed, pressing her breasts against his chest. Brann bit her neck and growled low in his throat. He followed her into oblivion.

~

Brann collapsed next to Freyja, not sure if he could concentrate enough to keep holding himself up on his arms. He pulled Freyja tightly to his side. She was still shaking from her release, which pleased him. She rested her head on his shoulder. Her eyes ran down the length of his sculpted body.

He kissed her on the forehead. "How do you feel?"

"I love you."

He blinked slowly.

Two spots of red rose on her high cheekbones.

Brann could not respond. He did not know what to say, and his throat felt strangely tight. She had never said those words to him before, and he had never expected to hear them.

He kissed her gently and let her roll over onto her side. He pressed his chest to her back and curled his larger body around hers. They fell asleep, entwined together.

~

Freyja woke feeling sore, warm, and completely loved. It was a wonderful combination.

Brann was already awake. He felt her stir and lifted his arm from around her. She responded by flipping over and burying her body closer to his. For the first time since she was a child, Freyja was comfortable being with a man who was not one of her brothers. They stayed silent, enjoying the feel of one another.

Her necklace was wrapped in the blankets by her knees. She reached down and ran her fingers over the stone. *Torne?* Finding him across the country would have been a challenge for the other Valren. But it was an easy exercise for her.

He responded immediately. *Good morning, Jaryth. I heard that you had some fun last night.*

Torne felt her mind color with embarrassment. Despite his initial unwillingness to accept Brann, he had to smile. *I meant fighting the Oparel. Nothing more.*

So you already know what I am going to tell you?

A small pause. *Nolan implied that your feelings toward Brann were... warmer... than he expected.*

I wish to invite him into the brotherhood. He earned his place yesterday on the docks.

He earned his place as soon as you realized you loved him, and doubly so when he fought alongside us. There is a great deal he will need to learn, but he already has a knack for using the orack metal.

Torne and Freyja were both silent for a few minutes, taking pleasure in their shared thoughts, letting their minds wander. Freyja picked up an image of Haron packing his gear. *You are readying to leave for the Oparel capital?*

We will leave within the next few days.

Do you think I will be able to reach you through the orack metalwhen you reach the capital? We have never before been that far apart.

He paused to consider. *There is very little you cannot do with the metal's powers. We'll have to find out what your range is while we travel.*

So you accept him? She moved the subject back to Brann. Torne easily followed her train of thought.

I do. That was a surprise.

She cast her mental net wide, catching as many of her brothers as she could. *Valren.* Their attention was instantaneous. *Yesterday an outsider fought among us, by our side.* They all knew whom she meant. *I will give him the choice to become one of us, a brother, if you would allow.*

She was flooded with immediate acceptance. Word of the man from Marrin had spread like wild fire among them. Speculation on Freyja's feelings toward the man had spread just as quickly.

Eyes closed, she released her thoughts from those of her brothers.

Brann felt Freyja rub her cheek against his chest. He tilted her chin up and ran his lips over hers. "You look so serious."

"Torne and Haron will be heading into Oparel soon. We were just wondering how far our reach with the orack metal is, and if we will be able to keep in touch with each other."

He rubbed her back lightly, his fingers found tension in her muscles and soothed it away. "They are both amazing fighters. If anyone can pull this off, it is the two of them. To tell you the truth, Haron disturbs me. I don't think his mind is completely right."

"He is… special," she replied. She put her hands on his chest and pushed herself away from him until she could see into his eyes. "I need to see them before they leave."

He frowned. "The city is going to be in an uproar today once word spreads about the fight on the docks. Plus, the fire on the ship put up a smoke signal that could be seen for miles. The surrounding towns are going to be uneasy. I need to stay here until things calm down."

"I'm not asking you to come with me. I know you need to stay. And not only for your Queen. Tripan is being escorted to Calin. I wish you to introduce him to Varonda."

"Wait here for a few days, and then we will go together."

"No. Torne and Haron are leaving soon and I would miss them."

His fingers felt like magic against her back. They never stopped their slow and soothing circles. "You push yourself too hard, Freyja. No one should ride with the rib injuries you have."

She laughed. "You rode me pretty hard last night and didn't hear me complain."

His head jerked back. "Did I hurt you?"

"Of course not." She put a calming hand on his stomach. "Brann, will you meet me in Andora? Once things settle down here, and Tripan has arrived. Will you come find me?"

"You don't wish to come back here?"

"There are things I need to take care of in the north," she hedged, "before anything more happens on the eastern border."

He sighed. "The coups in the mountains will not keep them away for long." His bright eyes never left her face.

"No. But Torne and Haron will do what they can. Marrin could not be in better hands."

He took her hands in his. "I've seen you every day for so long, it will be strange not to have you by my side. Plus, every time you leave my sight you get into trouble. I don't like the idea of you leaving."

But as much as he wanted to protest further, he knew she would not be dissuaded. She had to do what was best for the Valren. He didn't like it, but he would have done the same.

Chapter 10

Breyog jigged his bridle and let out a piercing whinny. They were close to Andora and he had just picked up the smell of his herd.

Most of the Valren were now in the east, preparing for war. It left Andora strangely empty. Children in training were there alongside a few of her brothers. But even the gypsies had only a small contingency left in the town. It had been hard for her to say goodbye to Torne and Haron. The trip from Della to Andora had been a lonely one.

Parth and Realla met her less than a mile outside of town. She dismounted and the three of them walked home together. Lian and Zaven, the two initiates from Marrin, were both doing well. The men were pleased with the children's training. At the rate they were progressing they would be ready to fight with their older brothers in only a few years.

"You're heading up to the node then?" Realla had a hand on Breyog's glossy neck.

"I know it's strange to initiate someone who has not grown up within the brotherhood," she started to explain.

Parth's tone was soothing. "You do not need to explain yourself. Even Torne has seen the worth of this man."

The brothers all seemed to agree. She had felt no uncertainty from them through her stone. They would accept him. She could only hope Brann would do the same.

Quick reports came in from the gypsies while she ate at the inn. The country seemed to have been holding its breath, waiting for the outcome of the conflict in the mountains, so things had been quiet in the west.

Her brothers left her alone, knowing she liked solitude. They sent their greetings to her through the orack metal, but gave her space to unwind. She turned Breyog out with the rest of the Valren mounts then started the long climb up the southern face of the Sumaritan Mountain.

She followed the worn path that wound up the mountainside. Hundreds of her brothers had walked there before, making their own way to the node. After an hour of climbing she came to a warning sign, etched into the ground before her.

The orack node was protected by her brothers to ensure no one outside of the Valren ever entered. She palmed her piece of orack and sent her thoughts in front of her. She connected with three beings. One was Tharrow, a brother, who sent a welcome back to her. The other two minds she touched were not human.

They were Tharrow's pets, which guarded the node day and night. They spoke to Freyja through colors and sounds but were still more than able to make themselves understood. They ingested small amounts of orack metal as part of their natural diet, which allowed the Valren to communicate with them.

Tharrow mused that the large cats used the metal like some birds do, to help break down other food in the stomach. Aside from Tharrow, the cats had few friends, and very little was known about them. The cats were relaxed, which was good. Freyja never wanted to be on their wrong side.

She climbed the last few natural stone steps and waited for the two animals to greet her. Once they recognized her they would let her into the node without hesitation.

The two beasts resembled the tigers she had seen locked up in traveling circus acts when she was younger. They were slightly larger than the captive cats she remembered, and were dappled all over with blacks and greys. They were naturally nocturnal and had no trouble disappearing into the dark of night. Their bright green eyes were the same size as Breyog's and looked oversized even on their massive heads.

One of the beasts pressed his giant nose into her palm and she scratched its ears in reply. Tharrow called to them through his stone and they bounded off the path and out of sight.

She used a piece of orack metal to light some candles that had been thoughtfully left in a bundle for her. The node ran right under the surface of the mountain and she walked less than thirty feet into the cave before she hit the vein. Tharrow was there, and already had a clean mask in his hands. He gave it to her and smiled. "You should have everything you need. I'll bring food when you get hungry."

"Thank you, Tharrow." The man was an enigma, even to the Valren. He much preferred the company of his cats to that of any of the brothers. So he was left to guard the node.

She looked down at the mask in her hand and ran her fingertips over the smooth metal. It would be Brann's mask – if he accepted it.

She sat down at the wooden workbench build into the side of the cavern wall and lit more candles. Then she began to work.

~

Two months passed before Brann was able to leave Calin and head north to Andora. Tripan, with a small contingency of Marrin soldiers, had made it back to the capital.

After what felt like years to Brann, he was finally confident that the Oparel would make no move to cross the Doranin Mountains until after winter. Which meant he was free to leave Calin. He had tried to contact Freyja through the orack metal but he could not yet span the distance between Andora and Calin.

Two children met him outside Andora. They were wrapped head to toe in warm clothes to fight back the late autumn chill but Brann still recognized them.

Zaven and Lian grinned up at him when he reined Brax to a halt. They both looked like they had grown a few inches since they left Calin. Zaven especially was flourishing now that he was getting regular meals. The boy was starting to put on muscle. Brann doubted any of the dock boys would bother him now.

They told him where Freyja was before he could even ask. Apparently he had been expected. With the network of spies the Valren had, it did not surprise him.

He found her sitting in the sand by the ocean, throwing small stones into the cold clear water. She looked up as soon as she heard him.

Brann's chest constricted. She was so beautiful. Never again could he go that long without her. He knew at that moment that he would do whatever he needed to keep her by his side.

She stood up and brushed the dirt off her clothes. She had spent weeks practicing what she was going to say to him. But now that he was in front of her she couldn't remember a thing. The butterflies that had been dormant for the last two months took flight in her stomach once again.

Brann didn't give her time to become self-conscious. He jumped off Brax and wrapped her in his strong arms before she could stammer out a proper hello. It felt so good. Gods, she had missed this. Missed him.

His hand cupped her cheek and his thumb ran over her temple where she used to have an angry cut. It was healed now, with only a tiny scar as a reminder of her ordeal. He let out a shaky breath and bent his head to kiss her. His adrenaline kicked into overdrive the second his lips found hers.

Now that they were this close Brann could feel her through his orack metal. She felt like she was on fire, but she was trying to keep her head clear. She wanted to talk to him. Reluctantly he broke their kiss and took a small step back. His hands stayed on her though, not willing to let her go completely. "What is it? What do you need to tell me?"

She stared at him but her mind was in a fog. She could not find the right words. Finally she gave up and picked up a small bag that she had been sitting next to. She held it against her chest, her eyes searching his, then opened the bag and pulled out a mask.

She flipped it over in her hands so that he could see the design, then held her breath and waited. He knew what she was asking him.

He took the mask from her and noticed that her fingers were shaking. She was terrified of his rejection. He didn't need the orack to tell him that.

The mask was paper-thin and weighed no more than one of his gloves. He stared at the design, not knowing what to say.

The face that stared back at him from the metal looked just like his own. Each line and shadow had been carefully notched to create his likeness in incredible detail. The hair looked as if it were being tussled by a strong wind – it covered much of the rendered forehead.

He looked down to Freyja, utterly amazed. It was almost a twin to her own mask.

"You made this?"

She stared at his chest, then his boots, anywhere but his face. "You were all I could think about…"

"I thought only Valren could have a piece of this armor?"

Her eyes shot up to his, then away. He took her chin in his hand and forced her gaze up to his face.

"I had hoped… that you would consider joining us."

He was dumfounded. Hundreds of scenarios had gone through his mind in the last two months, but he had not expected this.

"You already fight so well, and your mastery of the metal is astonishing considering you've had no real training. I believe that it would be beneficial to Marrin if we had a stronger tie between us. If you joined the brotherhood it could only strengthen both of our causes."

"Don't you dare tell me to join the Valren to help Marrin."

Her dark eyes widened.

"My wish to join the Valren has nothing to do with Marrin and everything to do with you. Do not think for one second that my feelings for you come from anywhere by my heart."

She took a deep breath. "Then you will consider joining us?"

"I've already made up my mind. I don't need time to consider."

She could hardly believe it. "What about Varonda?"

"We have until the spring to get me up to speed and able to fight with your brothers." It was a challenge if she had ever heard one.

She bit her bottom lip to keep from laughing. "You're truly going to join us?"

"Will I be able to fight beside you?" He moved in closer to her, crowding her body with his.

She grinned. "If you can keep up with me."

Freyja's heart soared. Brann's kiss melted away any remaining doubt she had of his commitment to her. She opened her mind through the orack metal and told her brothers the news. Their happiness and warmth brought tears to her eyes.

Whatever happened during the upcoming war, they would face it together. She was not alon

~

Torne and Haron sat back to back and started off into the night. The gypsies said it would take three weeks to make it to the Oparel capital once they reached the other side of the mountain range. That meant they should be at the city in only a few more days, and it gave them most of the winter to get close to the Oparel King.

They had felt Freyja's joy days ago, and Torne knew Brann had found her and accepted his mask.

If they were successful in killing the Oparel King, it could stop the enemy army in its tracks. They could not afford to fail.

2011 TLT Releases

The Seventh Blessing by Melissa Buell

Dartboard by JD Gordon

Reaching Riverdale by Geeta Schrayter

Demons Are Jackasses by SM Blooding

Concealed by Sang Kromah

Little Red Wolf by Paul Schumacher

BAY STATE EQUINE RESCUE

KERRY'S CHARITY

The Bay State Equine Rescue was founded in 2002 with a mission to preserve equine integrity through care that provides physical, mental and emotional health. Our focus is the rescue and rehabilitation of equines void of human advocate, abused, neglected, or abandoned. Our goal is to raise public awareness of equine neglect through regional youth education, legislation, horsemanship education, animal care awareness, and community service opportunities. We are working toward a standard of excellence to create a model which, when duplicated, will unite rescues nationwide to abolish mistreatment and disrespect of horses in this country.

For more information go to:

www.BayStateEquineRescue.org

CPSIA information can be obtained at www.ICGtesting.com
Printed in the USA
BVOW041706191011

274059BV00001B/2/P

9 780984 401383